"I could swear I heard you say we could get married. Isn't that ridiculous?"

"I don't think it sounds ridiculous at all," Brady replied. "Given what you've just told me, it sounds downright necessary."

For the briefest of seconds, Haven allowed herself to indulge in the fantasy of what it would be like to be Brady Ross's wife in the fullest sense of the word…to wake up beside him every morning, to feel his possession at night. Desire roared through her veins like a flash fire, obliterating all rational thought and making her weak at the knees.

"You're kidding," she said, her voice deep and husky.

His gaze didn't waver. "I don't kid, Haven. From where I'm sitting, it looks like the only sensible solution."

D0956656

Dear Reader,

Summer's in full sizzle, and so are the romances in this month's Intimate Moments selections, starting with *Badge of Honor*, the latest in Justine Davis's TRINITY STREET WEST miniseries. For everyone who's been waiting for Chief Miguel de los Reyes to finally fall in love, I have good news. The wait is over! Hurry out to buy this one—but don't drive so fast you get stopped for speeding. Unless, of course, you're pulled over by an officer like Miguel!

Suzanne Brockmann is continuing her TALL, DARK AND DANGEROUS miniseries—featuring irresistible navy SEALs as heroes—with *Everyday, Average Jones*. Of course, there's nothing everyday about this guy. I only wish there were, because then I might meet a man like him myself. Margaret Watson takes us to CAMERON, UTAH, for a new miniseries, beginning with *Rodeo Man*. The title alone should draw you to this one. And we round out the month with new books by Marcia Evanick, who offers the very moving *A Father's Promise*, and two books bearing some of our new thematic flashes. Ingrid Weaver's *Engaging Sam* is a MEN IN BLUE title, and brand-new author Shelley Cooper's *Major Dad* is a CONVENIENTLY WED book.

Enjoy all six—then come back next month, because we've got some of the best romance around *every* month, right here in Silhouette Intimate Moments.

Yours,

Leslie J. Wainger
Executive Senior Editor

Please address questions and book requests to:
Silhouette Reader Service
U.S.: 3010 Walden Ave., P.O. Box 1325, Buffalo, NY 14269
Canadian: P.O. Box 609, Fort Erie, Ont. L2A 5X3

MAJOR DAD

SHELLEY COOPER

Silhouette®
INTIMATE™ MOMENTS®
Published by Silhouette Books
America's Publisher of Contemporary Romance

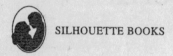

SILHOUETTE BOOKS

ISBN 0-373-07876-5

MAJOR DAD

SHELLEY COOPER

first experienced the power of words when she was in the eighth grade and wrote a paragraph about the circus for a class assignment. Her teacher returned it with an *A* and seven pluses scrawled across the top of the paper, along with a note thanking her for rekindling so vividly some cherished childhood memories. Since Shelley had never been to the circus, and had relied solely on her imagination to compose the paragraph, the teacher's remarks were a revelation. Since then, Shelley has relied on her imagination to help her sell dozens of short stories and to write her first novel, *Major Dad,* a 1997 Romance Writers of America Golden Heart finalist in Best Long Contemporary, which she hopes will be as moving to her readers as her circus paragraph was to that long-ago English teacher.

To Ann Sherwood, for her unerring vision

To Joy Hopkins, Colleen Kulikowski
and Donna Valentino,
for their friendship, support and laughter

And to my husband, Pat, for never doubting

My love to you all

Chapter 1

Brady Ross knew three things with certainty.

Number one: If he had to, he could live without sex.

Number two: Beneath their smiling faces, 99.9 percent of all men—and women—cared only about the pursuit of their own happiness, and woe be it to anyone foolhardy enough to stand in their way.

And number three: He wasn't cut out to be a father.

The first he'd learned during the three years, seven months and seven days he'd been held captive in a South American jungle prison. A captivity that had ended a mere three weeks earlier.

Funny, the things a man thought about when he was confined to a cell barely three feet wide and seven feet long and he had nothing but time to think. Brady had spent endless hours recalling the things he missed most: the warmth of a fire on a cold winter night, the energizing jolt of black coffee first thing in the morning, the smell of fresh air after a summer rain. When it came down to it, sex paled in comparison with the ultimate pleasure: freedom.

His childhood had taught him innumerable lessons on the true nature of humanity. Abandoned by his father before birth and by his mother when he was three, Brady had been kicked around from one foster home to the next until he was thirteen years old. Except for the five, too-short years he'd spent as the adopted son of a unique and caring man, he had rarely witnessed the overflowing of the milk of human kindness. Nothing he'd experienced as an adult had changed his conviction that his fellow man was basically a selfish, uncaring, amoral creature.

As for his merits as a father, instinct, rather than experience, was his guide. Being a father entailed many things, chief among them the ability to care. An ability Brady had lost long ago.

"Emotionally challenged" was how the last woman he had been involved with before his capture put it. Others had said more or less the same thing. "You don't share your feelings." "I never know what you're thinking." "Your heart stopped beating long ago, but your brain hasn't figured it out yet."

A favorite pastime of his captors had been the tormenting of those unfortunate souls who had been unable to hide their emotions. Brady had gotten so adept at suppressing all feeling it took a conscious act of will for him to summon up a smile. He supposed that made him even more emotionally challenged now.

No, he wasn't cut out to be a father.

And all the excuses in the world wouldn't change the fact that he *was* a father, something he'd been unaware of until two weeks ago. Which was why he found himself on a sunny May morning rooted to the sidewalk in front of the Melinda Dolan Center for Children. Somewhere inside the ordinary, square, red brick building he had a daughter. A daughter who would soon turn three. All he had to do was make himself go inside.

The timing couldn't have been worse. Not only did he have to readjust to a world that seemed to have changed radically—

and not for the better—during his absence, but he also had to find a purpose for the rest of his life. He wasn't sure he could handle the complications that parenthood would add to the mix.

Still, badly as he was tempted, he couldn't turn his back and walk away. This was his reality, and he would have to deal with it. The concept of duty and honor might be laughable to most, but to Brady it meant everything. He'd spent years devoting duty and honor to his country; he couldn't shirk his duty to his child. No matter what, he couldn't abandon his daughter the way his parents had abandoned him.

Squaring his shoulders, and mentally squaring his resolve, Brady took the first step down the concrete path leading to the glassed front doors.

"Ready or not," he murmured, "here I come."

With a sigh, Haven Adams collapsed into her chair, tilted her head back and closed her eyes. The stillness of her office washed over her, soothing tense muscles and frayed nerves.

"Five minutes," she murmured. "Just give me five minutes, and I'll be able to handle—"

A sharp rapping on the door interrupted her.

"Anything," she finished, suppressing a groan. What now? She hoped it wasn't Chad, one of the more challenging children in her care. Twice already in the past hour she'd been called into his classroom, and her patience with him was wearing dangerously thin. Of course, compared with the other fires she'd already put out that morning, handling Chad would be a snap, patience or no patience.

Sounding louder, the rapping was repeated. Haven drew a deep, bracing breath. While she adored her work and wouldn't dream of doing anything else, there were days when it didn't pay to get out of bed. Today was proving to be one of them.

Smoothing a hand over hair that was far more disobedient than even Chad, she plastered a polite smile on her face. "Come in."

The door opened, and she saw a tall, lean man who appeared to be in his early thirties. He had pale-blond hair that hung to his shoulders, framing hard, chiseled, Nordic features. Gray eyes the color of molten steel made a quick survey of her small, cluttered office before coming to rest on her. The utter lack of emotion in their depths should have chilled her to the bone. Instead, she felt a gathering warmth in the pit of her stomach.

"May I help you?" she asked, remembering her manners and scrambling to her feet.

"I'm looking for Haven Adams."

He didn't offer an answering smile, and she felt her own slip a fraction. "You've found her."

When he crossed to her desk, she saw that he walked with a slight limp, and that, despite the broadness of his chest and the muscles she could glimpse in his forearms, he was far too thin, almost gaunt. His skin was also paler than the unusually harsh winter they'd recently left behind them would warrant. Still, there was an aura of power about him that would not be ignored.

"My name is Brady Ross," he announced, as if the appellation should mean something to her, but it evoked no sense of recognition.

She barely came up to his shoulders and had to tilt her head back to see him better. There was something about his face that made it more than the sum of its parts. He had, she realized, the kind of face that would be fascinating to stare at while he slept. She couldn't help wondering when the last time was that anyone had done that.

Suddenly, she wanted him sitting down. If he was sitting down, she wouldn't feel at such a disadvantage. She'd be able to think more clearly.

"Please," she offered, indicating the chair in front of her desk, "have a seat, Mr. Ross."

"I'm here about my daughter," he said when they were both comfortable.

Haven prided herself on knowing each of the two hundred children in her charge by name. But when she scanned her memory, she came up blank as to a little girl with the surname of Ross. Of course, in these days of interchangeable families, that meant nothing.

"I'm sorry. Perhaps if you told me your daughter's name, I could be of more assistance."

"Dolan. Anna Dolan." He paused for the space of a heartbeat, then added calmly, "I believe she's your ward."

It was obvious he'd expected his announcement to throw her off balance. It probably would have, too, had she not been through this scene before. Far too many times.

Not another one, was her first thought. On its heels came disappointment. For some reason, she'd expected better from him.

Leaning back in her chair, Haven folded her arms across her middle. Of all the crises she'd faced that morning, this one would by far be the easiest to handle.

"You're late," she said.

His eyes flickered briefly, betraying his surprise. "Excuse me?"

"Your counterparts were here weeks ago."

One pale-blond eyebrow lifted. "My counterparts?"

Oh, he was good. He was very good. Just the right amount of polite inquiry mixed with a tinge of confusion. Haven gave him full marks for knowing how to stall. He was definitely a cut above all the rest. Not only did he look like a Viking warrior come to life, he stood apart from the crowd because he didn't wear his greed like a cheap cologne, the way the others had.

"That's right," she said. "All of Anna's *other* fathers. They were lined up around the corner after the article in the *Post-Gazette.*"

She'd known she was in trouble the minute she saw it. Spotlighting the steel industry, the article had focused on three of the families who had helped to make steel Pittsburgh's number-one product. Featured prominently were the Dolans.

The reporter had been thorough, writing that except for a great-aunt, Anna was the sole living heir. While the Dolan fortune was not what it had been before steel's decline in the early eighties, Anna was still a very wealthy little girl. The article had gone on to list Haven's name as guardian, mentioned the day care center and revealed that the identity of Anna's father was unknown.

Those last tidbits were what had given Haven nightmares. Through her friendship with Anna's mother, she had learned there were people in this world who would do most anything to acquire money they didn't deserve. She'd stood by Melinda through more than one nasty encounter. After the article, she'd braced herself for the worst, concerning Melinda's daughter.

And gotten it. The center had been flooded with fake fathers the day the article came out. Over the succeeding week, the flood had receded to a steady stream. After two weeks, the stream had slowed to a trickle. After three, it had dried up altogether.

As annoying and disheartening as the appearance of these frauds had been, they'd proved amazingly easy to discredit. A few basic questions, along with a request for a DNA test, were all it had taken to send them running for the door.

Now, when she'd thought she'd seen the last of them, this man was here.

His gaze unblinking, Brady Ross settled back in his chair. One long, lean, jean-clad leg lifted indolently to cross over the other. He seemed in no hurry to leave, nor did he seem the least bit daunted that she'd found him out so easily. If anything, he seemed amused.

"You'll have to enlighten me," he said. "I'm afraid I didn't read that particular article."

She didn't believe him. "It would have been hard to miss, seeing as it was a full-page color spread. Quite informative, too. It said that Anna's father never had been identified, then spelled out in elaborate detail the size of her inheritance.''

"I see. And that's why you think I'm here?"

"Isn't it?'' she challenged.

His air of amusement evaporated. "I'm not a child, Ms. Adams. Your schoolteacher act doesn't intimidate me.''

No, he wasn't a child, she conceded. He was all male. Disturbingly so. It annoyed her that she was unable to ignore the tug of attraction she felt for him. Also galling was the way he was treating her as if she were in the wrong, when he was the one trying to get his hands on a little girl's inheritance.

"Are you saying you're not here because of the money?''

"I'm here because Anna Dolan is my daughter. Period.''

"Do you have any proof to substantiate your claim?'' she asked coldly.

He reached into his shirt pocket and withdrew a folded piece of paper. After unfolding it, he leaned forward and placed it on her desk.

"I have this.''

It was a photocopy of a letter, Haven saw. She was unable to suppress a gasp when she recognized the familiar handwriting scrawled across the page.

Hands unsteady, she lifted the paper, then fumbled for the reading glasses she kept on her desk. When they were squarely on her nose, Haven quickly scanned the words written by Anna's mother:

Dear Brady,

I'm not sure you'll remember me, but perhaps the date, August 13, will have some significance for you. I know it does for me. I'm the woman you met that night. I'm writing to tell you that you're going to be a father. I'm not doing this to ask for your support, but because I feel you have the right to know. If you wish to be a part of your child's life, please contact me. If not, I will understand.

Yours truly,
Melinda Dolan

Haven was trembling when she finished reading, and her heart beat so loudly she was certain he could hear it. Her first instinct was to order him to leave, but that wouldn't solve anything.

She glanced around the room where she'd spent so many pleasurable hours since opening the Melinda Dolan Center for Children two years ago. Her framed diploma and certifications hung on one wall, along with a corkboard covered by dozens of crayoned pictures. Built-in bookcases filled with child care books covered another wall. A clutter of paperwork that she never seemed able to conquer littered her desk. Nothing had changed.

But how could that be, she wondered, when her entire world had turned upside down?

"Are you ready to concede that I'm Anna's father?" she heard him ask.

She dropped both her glasses and the paper onto her desk. Right now, the only thing she'd concede to him was that the sky was blue.

"I will, of course, want to see the original," she said.

He nodded. "In the proper company."

Meaning legal counsel, so she couldn't tear it up.

She'd never thought this could happen. Whenever she'd questioned Melinda about this very eventuality, her best friend had dismissed it as inconsequential.

"Anna's father wants nothing to do with her," Melinda had always said in a voice of absolute conviction. "He won't be bothering you."

Haven never had discovered his name. Melinda hadn't listed it on the birth certificate, and she'd made it quite clear to anyone with the temerity to ask that the identity of Anna's father was not a subject open for discussion. Out of respect for her friend, Haven hadn't pried.

Now she wished she had.

Why hadn't Melinda told her about the letter?

Because it was a clever forgery, she decided. Yes, that had to be it. Melinda had never told her about the letter because she never wrote it.

"I'll have to insist on a DNA test," she said, thankful her voice didn't betray her inner agitation.

"Of course. The sooner we get this matter cleared up, the sooner I get to know my daughter."

Icy fingers of fear squeezed around Haven's heart. He was too calm, too assured. Every other so-called father had left on a run at the mention of DNA testing. But not this man. Either he had nerves of steel or he sincerely believed he was Anna's father.

Dear heaven, could this really be happening? Could she lose Anna? No. She refused to believe it. Anna was Melinda's gift to her, the fulfillment of a prayer she'd thought would never be answered.

She fought to control her rising panic. She had to stay calm. For Anna's sake.

Something still bothered her, something that wasn't quite right. She latched onto it like a drowning person grabbing at a life preserver.

"According to the date on this letter, Melinda was around two months pregnant when she wrote it. That was…" She did a quick calculation. "Over three and a half years ago, Mr. Ross. You weren't here for Melinda while she was carrying your child. You weren't here for her when she was sick and dying. You certainly weren't here when Anna was born. Where were you?"

His eyes flashed with an emotion she could describe only as pain—deep, searing, gut-wrenching pain. A second later, he'd schooled his face back into its impassive mask, leaving her to wonder if her imagination had been playing tricks on her.

It had to be her imagination, she told herself. Looking at him now, she found it hard to believe that he ever smiled, or that a sense of humor lurked somewhere beneath his ultra-serious exterior. An emotion as deeply felt as the pain she'd thought she'd glimpsed seemed utterly foreign to him.

"I don't believe that's relevant," he said.

Obviously, whatever the excuse he had for his absence, it wasn't a compelling one. Telling her the truth would do little to curry her favor. Not that he seemed to be going out of his way to get on her good side.

"I think a judge might find it extremely relevant," she retorted. "You say you want to get to know your daughter. If you're so anxious, why'd it take you so long to put in an appearance?"

He spoke with obvious reluctance. "For what it's worth, I didn't receive the letter until two weeks ago."

"You mean it took the post office that long to deliver it to you?" She didn't bother to hide her disbelief.

"No, they delivered it on time."

"But you just said you didn't receive it until two weeks ago."

"I didn't. I…moved shortly before it was sent. It just now caught up with me."

Unlike his claim to paternity, his words had the feel of a lie, of something conjured up on the spur of the moment. When had it ever taken the post office three and a half years to track a person down, even if a Change of Address form wasn't on file? Obviously, he didn't want to tell her where he'd been. Why?

She examined his face, once more noting its pallor. "Were you in prison, Mr. Ross?"

Again, she was surprised by the flash of emotion in his eyes. This time, she saw not only pain, but also admiration. The pain was directed inward, but she could swear the admiration was for her.

"If it eases your mind at all, Ms. Adams, I wasn't in prison. At least, not the kind of prison you mean. Not that it would change anything if I was a convicted felon. You see, I *am* Anna's father."

Haven's knees started trembling so badly she was glad the desk hid them from Brady Ross's overobservant gaze. What were his rights where Anna was concerned? She was simply the little girl's guardian. If he could prove he was Anna's father, surely his rights would supersede her own.

Anna. The daughter of her best friend, the precious little girl whom she loved more than life itself, was in a room on the floor above them. Did this man mean to pluck her from everything she found safe and familiar and take her away with him? Haven couldn't allow that to happen.

What did he really want? She had to find out. If it was money—and logic told her that was what it had to be—maybe something could be worked out. She'd get what he wanted if she had to beg, borrow or steal. Much as she loved the day care center and the work she did there, she'd sell it in a minute if she had to.

"How much?" she asked.

"Excuse me?"

"How much to make you go away and never come back?"

The tightening of his mouth was the only outward sign that her words had affected him. "Are you trying to bribe me?"

His voice was dangerously soft, and Haven felt a chill race up her spine. Brady Ross would make a formidable opponent. She'd be wise to keep her wits about her.

"All I'm saying is, if it's money you want, you might be able to get it. Without the nuisance of having to care for a small child."

His eyes narrowed. "Do you find it a nuisance to care for my daughter?"

"Of course not," she denied hotly. "Taking care of Anna is a joy."

Dismayed, she bit her lip. Already she'd revealed too much. If he discovered how desperate she was to keep Anna, he might name a price far beyond anything she'd be able to pay.

"Then why should I find it a nuisance?" he countered.

"Are you saying you don't want the money I'm offering?"

"I'm saying there's not enough money on the planet to make me abandon my daughter."

She refused to look away from his penetrating gaze. "Every man has his price, Mr. Ross."

"Do you?"

She was silent.

"You'd do anything to keep her, wouldn't you?" he said.

To deny it now would be pointless. Haven lifted her chin. "Yes."

"Good." He nodded in satisfaction. "The report was right, then."

Confusion made her blink. "The report?"

"I had a private investigator do a background check on you."

She went cold. "You had me investigated?"

"I had to know about the character of the person in charge of my daughter's welfare."

He made it sound so reasonable. What had he found out? she wondered. What secrets had been laid bare, what judgments had he formed? And why should she care?

She cared because the thought that he could examine her private life without her knowledge made her feel naked and vulnerable. Not a comfortable feeling under the best of circumstances, but exceedingly disturbing where Brady Ross was concerned. She cared because, despite everything, she was attracted to the man. He could destroy her life, steal her dreams, and still she was attracted. What a fool she was.

"I see," she said slowly.

"Aren't you curious to know what else the report said?"

She summoned up her pride and lied. "Not particularly."

"I thought it might interest you to know that I've decided not to remove Anna from your care. At least for now."

Surprise momentarily robbed her of breath. "You're not going to take Anna away from me?"

"I don't believe in removing children from stable homes, Ms. Adams. Unless, that is, circumstances warrant it. I will, of course, expect to set up a schedule of visitation."

"Of course," she echoed, more puzzled than relieved. Just who was Brady Ross, and why didn't he want custody of his daughter? If, indeed, Anna truly was his daughter.

"May I see her, please? From a distance?" His lips curved sardonically. "I promise I won't snatch her and run."

She opened her mouth in automatic refusal, but no words emerged. Despite the cynical curve of his mouth, there was something in his voice, faint but unmistakable; a quality of yearning that touched her heart. She supposed it wouldn't hurt to have him look at Anna. From a distance, as he'd said. Besides, if he really was the little girl's father, she didn't want to antagonize him unnecessarily. Somehow, they would have to find a way to work things out. Together.

Haven rose on legs that weren't quite steady. "Follow me."

He should have told her why the letter had taken so long to catch up to him, Brady thought as he followed Haven Adams out of her office. Especially since the truth about his absence might have served to allay her understandable suspicion of him. His reluctance to reveal anything personal about himself was an ingrained habit. But that wasn't the reason he'd stayed silent. To speak of what he had endured would be breaking a vow.

For three years, seven months and seven days, his life had been a living hell. Upon his release, he'd recounted every detail of that hell to his superiors during countless hours of debriefing. The pain of that recounting had been almost more than he could bear. He'd felt as if he were living it all over again. When he stepped off the plane returning him to Pittsburgh soil, he'd promised himself to put the entire experience behind him. Thoughts of his time in captivity were forbidden. He would speak of it to no one, unless required by law.

Besides, it truly didn't matter whether or not Haven Adams felt sympathetically toward him. The law was on his side, and she knew it. He wouldn't be on his way to see his daughter otherwise.

Her hips swayed as she walked, and his gaze appreciatively followed the motion. Among her other womanly attributes, she had a terrific pair of legs.

She was nothing as he'd imagined. After reading the detective's report, he'd expected to find a shy, retiring woman who was a cross between a librarian and a nun. Instead, he'd tangled with a petite tigress, a voluptuously rounded female with red curls that gleamed like fire and bottomless blue eyes so dark they appeared black. Back when he had cared about such things, he'd always been a sucker for red hair and blue eyes.

Her appeal went beyond the way she looked, though. She'd kept her cool, had met his gaze directly and unflinchingly, and that impressed him. It also made him wonder what it would take to make her lose that steely control she maintained over her emotions. Was she as full of fire and passion as her wild mane of hair and lush, kissable lips seemed to imply? Too bad her being his child's guardian made that one question he could not pursue.

As they passed gaily decorated rooms full of laughing, playing children, Brady couldn't help drawing a contrast to the spare, utilitarian office he'd just left. Who was Haven Adams? he found himself wondering. Her name implied safety, a refuge from the havoc of everyday life. That certainly seemed to be what she provided in this open, cheerful and inviting place.

According to the report, she had been twenty-five when she'd quit a well-paying job as a chemist to nurse Melinda Dolan during her final battle with the cancer that had claimed her life when Anna was only seven days old. Had it been solely for the money, or had Haven done it out of devotion to her friend? Had he been a betting man, Brady would have chosen the money.

Still, he mused, following her up a staircase and out into another brightly lit hallway, if her motivation had been money, why had she used the bulk of her own bequest to open this center? As an investment, it wasn't the smartest choice she could have made. It would never make her rich; she'd be lucky if she broke even.

The center was located in one of Pittsburgh's most economically depressed neighborhoods, and its clientele consisted mainly of the children of single mothers who struggled at minimum-wage jobs just to make ends meet. The tuition Haven Adams received from them barely matched her expenses, and she had to rely on donations to make up the shortfall. On top of that, each child received a hot meal at lunch—and sometimes breakfast—every day. No, running this center was not the act of an avaricious woman.

She stopped abruptly outside the doorway of a room, jolting his thoughts to a halt, along with his body. Inside, ten toddlers sat listening while a woman read them a story.

"Which one is Anna?" he whispered.

"Near the middle. The one in the blue pants and red shirt."

She's so little, was his first thought. Even though she was almost three, he hadn't expected her to be so tiny. Or to have such a serious face as she listened intently to the story being read to her. He most definitely hadn't expected to feel the urge to put his arms around her and hold her close, to shield her from the harsh realities of the world they lived in.

"She doesn't look like me," he murmured.

"She's the picture of her mother," Haven replied softly.

He tried to recall Melinda Dolan's face, but the image that formed in his brain was ill-focused and fuzzy around the edges. What remained vividly imprinted on his memory was the pain and disillusion he'd been feeling the night his child was conceived. Melinda Dolan had also been in pain. Together, for a few brief, sweet hours, they'd been able to comfort each another.

Turning his attention back to his daughter, he asked, "What happened to her arm?"

He felt, rather than saw, Haven's grimace.

"She's always trying to keep up with the older kids, to do what they do. She hates being left behind. Anyway, she made it to the top of the jungle gym before we could get to her, and fell and broke her wrist. The cast should come off in a week or so."

"A pistol, is she?" he asked.

"A human dynamo," she replied, and he heard the pride in her voice.

He was standing so close he could smell her skin. During his years of confinement, he'd spent a lot of time in complete darkness. To compensate, his other senses had grown sharper. Particularly acute was his sense of smell. From Haven Adams he caught the aromas of strawberry shampoo, perfume-scented soap and baby formula. His senses swam with her, until he didn't know what he wanted to do more: reach out and tangle his fingers in the soft curls of her hair or pull her into his arms and kiss her breathless.

"I've seen enough," he said abruptly, turning on his heel. Relying on the sense of direction his military training had made second nature, he headed for the building's main entrance.

"When will I hear from you again, Mr. Ross?" she asked when she caught up with him.

He looked at her out of the corner of one eye. "My name is Brady, Haven. Since we're going to be seeing a lot of each other, it only makes sense to drop the formalities, don't you agree? You'll be seeing me first thing tomorrow morning. That's when we have an appointment to have the blood work done for the DNA testing. I wrote the address and time on the back of the letter I showed you."

"*We* have an appointment?"

She sounded dazed, and he felt a sudden burst of sympathy for her. This had taken her by as much surprise as Melinda's letter had taken him. She would need a while to adjust.

"The appointment is for Anna and me, but I thought you'd like to come along."

In truth, he'd known she would insist. Until he had positive proof, there was no way she'd leave him alone with the little girl. "After all, they can't tell if I'm her father without taking a sample of her blood, too, now can they?"

A host of emotions coursed through Haven as she watched Brady Ross stride down the path to the compact car he'd parked at the curb. Disbelief, confusion, desperation—she felt them all, in varying degrees of intensity. But by far, the primary emotion making her heart pound was fear.

When his car disappeared from view, a sense of urgency propelled her up the steps two at a time in a headlong rush for her office. Her breath coming in quick gasps, she began rummaging through the papers on top of her desk.

"Where is it, where is it?" she muttered.

Her gaze fell on the photocopy of Melinda's letter, and she sank down hard in her chair. Was it only minutes ago that she'd stared down Brady Ross, certain she could dispose of his claim as easily as snapping her fingers? She'd been so sure he was a fraud. Now she didn't know what to think.

One of two things could happen, she decided. Either he had played out the charade while he was here, and she'd never hear from him again. Or he really was Anna's father, in which case she'd hear from him all too soon. Tomorrow morning, in fact.

She had the dull feeling it would be the latter, because she couldn't forget the look in his eyes when he'd gazed at Anna. It was the look of tenderness mixed with awe and wonder that most first-time fathers wore when they saw their newborns and realized they'd played a part in the miracle of creation.

Many things were still unclear, but of one thing she was

absolutely convinced. Brady Ross was not playacting. He truly believed he was Anna's father. The letter from Melinda supported his claim. Like it or not, she had to face reality. When the results from the DNA tests were returned several weeks from now, it was highly probable that Brady would have positive proof of his paternity. From now on in, her every action had to be with Anna's welfare uppermost in her mind.

Where had he really been for the past three years and nine months since Anna's conception? Had he really only learned of her existence two weeks ago? And why didn't he want full custody? Full custody was the only way, given the terms of Anna's inheritance, that he'd be able to get his hands on a sizable chunk of money.

Haven let out a ragged sigh. She'd drive herself crazy searching for answers. The important thing was that he'd said he didn't believe in removing a child from a stable home, unless circumstances warranted it. But what circumstances would warrant it for him? What would happen when he disagreed with her child-rearing methods? What would happen if he just plain didn't like the brand of toothpaste she bought for Anna?

Despite his reassurance, the threat of losing the little girl still hung like a noose around her neck. It would continue to tighten so long as Brady Ross was around.

Haven glimpsed the object of her search under a sheaf of papers and pounced. Opening the Yellow Pages, she riffled through the book until she came to the listing for detective agencies. It was time to fight fire with fire, to find out exactly who and what Brady Ross was. It was time to use whatever she found in whatever manner necessary to keep Anna.

Picking up the telephone receiver, Haven dialed a number and listened to the subsequent ringing. If he thought she would give up Anna without a fight, he had another think coming. No one was going to take Anna away from her. No one. Not while she still had breath left in her body.

Chapter 2

"'And from that day forward,'" Haven read, "'Evangeline never again talked to strangers. The end.'"

If only life were like a fairy tale, she found herself wishing as she closed the book in her hands and dropped a kiss onto the forehead of the little girl snuggled to her side. Then she could pray for a gallant white knight to save Anna from the menacing stranger, the way he had Evangeline.

"Again, Binny!" Anna begged. "Again!"

Laughing, her worries temporarily banished by the young girl's enthusiasm, Haven reached out a hand to ruffle soft brown curls. "I've already read it to you three times tonight. Besides, it's getting late. Time to go to sleep."

"Please, Binny? Puh-leeee-ze?"

Green eyes uncannily like Melinda's beseeched her, and sad fingers squeezed Haven's heart. It was at times like these she felt most keenly the loss of her best friend.

They were only six years old when they met in boarding school, and theirs was a bond that had remained unbroken until Melinda's death nineteen years later. Together, they had forged the family neither had ever had. Melinda, because her parents were dead, and her guardians cared only for the money they received from her trust fund. Haven, because her parents were too immersed in their scientific research to pay much attention to their only child. Melinda's death had left a gaping hole in Haven's heart that even Anna couldn't fill.

"All right," she said, giving in. "I'll read it just once more." She opened the book. "'Once upon a time, in a land far, far away, there lived a little girl named Evangeline....'"

Ten minutes later, Anna was asleep, and the only sound in the room was the pattering of rain on the roof. After extricating herself from the arms wrapped around her, Haven walked to the door. One hand on the light switch, she glanced around the room she'd so painstakingly decorated.

Sheep frolicked around the mint green walls on a border that had been installed at Anna's eye level. White-and-gold French provincial furniture hugged the walls, the focal piece the beautiful canopy bed where the child now lay sleeping. Stuffed animals of all shapes and sizes cavorted in the antique cradle that had been Melinda's when she was a baby.

How different it was from the room Haven had occupied as a child. This was a room for dreams and fantasies, for laughter and shared secrets. A room to come to for shelter and comfort. A room to foster security and the knowledge of being loved.

And now that security was being threatened by a tall man with uncanny gray eyes and unknown motives.

"Good night, precious," she murmured. "Sweet dreams."

A lump closed her throat as she flicked off the light. She knew that her own dreams would be far less peaceful.

"Anna sleeping?" Josephine Clark asked when Haven wandered into the kitchen.

"Like a log."

Josephine had been Haven's nanny. Because her parents had never been home, it was to Josephine that Haven had run with cuts and bruises. Josephine's strong brown arms had cradled her when she'd had a nightmare. Josephine's long, slender fingers had wiped her brow when her body raged with fever. Until she was six years old and bundled off to boarding school, Josephine—a mere eighteen herself when she'd come to care for Haven—had been the one constant in her life.

They'd kept in touch over the years. Josephine had never married, and after Melinda died, she had insisted on coming to help. What had started out as a temporary arrangement had quickly become permanent. During the day, Josephine ran the kitchen at the day care center. At night, she helped Haven with Anna and the housework. Haven didn't know how she would have managed without the woman's assistance. Or her friendship.

Haven picked up a tea towel and began drying the wet dishes stacked in the drain. Although the kitchen had come equipped with a perfectly functioning dishwasher, Josephine insisted on washing the dishes by hand, saying that no man-made machine could clean them to her satisfaction.

"You going to tell me what's eating you, child, or are you just going to stand there and stew?"

Lost in thought, Haven started at Josephine's words. "What makes you think something's bothering me?" she hedged.

"You just put a pile of plates in the refrigerator."

Haven opened the refrigerator door and grimaced. "Guess I did."

"Care to tell me why?"

Haven wanted nothing more than to dump her problems onto Josephine's broad, capable shoulders. But it wouldn't be fair. The woman had shouldered too much for her already these past few years.

She didn't delude herself; she'd have to tell Josephine about Brady Ross eventually. Especially when he started visiting with Anna. Because if his claim was true and he really was Anna's father, even if the law would permit her to do so, she couldn't deny the child the right to know him. She couldn't deny Anna the fulfillment of the dream that had haunted her own childhood and had lasted well into her adult years.

Though she'd had twenty-eight years to accept it, it still hurt to know that her parents hadn't wanted her, had in fact found the contents of a petri dish more fascinating than they'd ever found her. How many nights had she cried herself to sleep, aching for their touch, for just a word of love and encouragement from them? If Brady Ross could keep Anna from experiencing a similar loss, she wouldn't deny him.

Yes, Josephine would have to know. But not now. For now, Haven would keep her own counsel. This was one problem she would handle on her own.

"Haven?" Josephine prompted.

She moved her shoulders in what she hoped was a nonchalant shrug. "I just have a lot on my mind, is all."

"Want to talk about it?"

"Not now, thanks. Don't worry, I'll be okay." She carefully placed a handful of knives in the silverware drawer and hung up the tea towel. "I think I'll put on a pot of coffee. Want some?"

Fifteen minutes later, the dishes were done, and Haven and Josephine sat across from each other in the breakfast nook.

"Haven," Josephine said.

"Hmm?"

"You just put ten teaspoons of sugar in your coffee."

Haven took a sip of the cloyingly sweet liquid and made a face. "Ugh. Seems to be my night for absentminded behavior."

"I've never seen you act this way." The older woman peered at her closely. "It's not a man, is it?" The note of hope was unmistakable in her voice.

In vivid detail, Haven saw Brady's face. The words popped out of her mouth before she could bite them back. "Yes, it's a man."

Josephine looked thrilled. "Who is he, child? How'd you meet him? What's he do?" She held up a hand. "No, don't answer. You'll tell me in your own good time. I'm just happy you're finally having a life of your own."

"I already have a life of my own."

Josephine's snort was worth a thousand words.

"What's that supposed to mean?"

"It means that, between Anna and the center, the only thing you've curled up in bed with lately is a book. When was the last time you had a date, child?"

Feeling restless, Haven rose and dumped her coffee into the sink. "I don't see you out on the town every weekend."

Josephine tilted her head, her brown eyes bright with curiosity. "What *do* you think I do on the nights I spend away from here?"

After pouring herself a fresh cup, one into which she stirred only one teaspoon of sugar, Haven crossed her ankles and leaned against the counter. "Visit your parents. That's where you always say you're going."

The older woman rolled her eyes. "Child, you really are an innocent. I visit my parents for a couple of hours, but the rest of the night I spend in the arms of a warm, tender, caring man."

"Josie," Haven said with a delighted smile, "you wicked woman you. Who is he? Why didn't you tell me about him before?"

"His name's Jackson. And I never said anything because I didn't want to flaunt my happiness in your face. Not with you working so hard and sacrificing so much. But now, child, I'm starting to wonder."

Haven knew she shouldn't ask, but she did anyway. "Wonder what?"

"Whether you're using Anna and the center as an excuse to hide from the world."

"Well, you can stop worrying. I'm not."

"Good. Then there's no reason for you to be sitting home alone at night. If this man asks you out, go for it."

The phone rang, and Josephine answered it. A minute later, she was deep into an animated conversation with one of her bridge partners.

Grateful for the distraction, Haven rinsed her cup and saucer out in the sink. After waving good-night, she wandered upstairs to her bedroom.

Was Josephine right? she wondered as she washed her face. Was she using Anna and the center to hide from the world? She'd never thought so before. Since Melinda's death, she really had been too busy for a relationship. Still, before Josephine had brought it to her attention a few minutes ago, she hadn't realized how long it had been since she'd had a date. Or how many excuses she'd made whenever she'd been asked.

She hadn't realized how much she missed being enfolded in a pair of strong arms and simply held close.

Josephine's words echoed in her ears: *If he asks you out, go for it.*

Inevitably, Haven's thoughts turned to Brady Ross and their coming meeting. Incredible as it seemed, she found herself looking forward to it with an eagerness that had nothing to do with her desire to have the matter of his paternity settled.

She shook her head at her own foolishness. It figured she'd be drawn to the one man who had the power to do her the most harm. Josephine would be thrilled to death if she knew.

Other than the occasional passing car and barking dog, the only sounds to mar the silence of the night were the rain, the slap of his footfalls against the wet pavement and the rush of his breath as Brady negotiated one of the hills that were a Pittsburgh trademark. The lungfuls of freshly washed air that he pulled greedily through his nostrils carried the scents of spring buds.

He'd started running as a child, when speed and agility had meant survival. What had begun as necessity had soon turned into a lifelong passion. In high school and college he'd been the star runner on the track team. When he hadn't been jogging in place in his cell or doing calisthenics to maintain his muscle tone, one of the ways he'd relieved the boredom of his captivity was to relive in his mind every footfall and every breath of every race he'd run. It had kept him sane.

Of course, with his limp, he wouldn't be running in any more races. But he could still run for the sheer joy of it, slow and awkward though he might be. For that small pleasure, he was heartily grateful.

The rain didn't bother him. On the contrary, he relished the clean feel of it on his face and shoulders. The blackness of the night didn't bother him, either. During his captivity he'd spent so much time in darkness that it had become, if not a friend, no longer an enemy to be feared.

What did bother him, had in fact propelled him from the warmth of his bed in the middle of the night, were not nightmares of his time as a prisoner but the faces of Anna Dolan and Haven Adams. They seemed to be indelibly etched in his brain. Memories of his captivity, when he couldn't stop them from bulldozing their way into his consciousness, didn't begin to disturb him the way thoughts of the two new women in his life did.

His years as an army major had taught him to plan, down to the smallest detail, every operation he undertook. That was precisely what he had done before he'd approached Haven Adams. Everything had been mapped out carefully, from the initial contact, to the scheduling of the blood tests, the verification of his paternity and eventual visits with his daughter. He'd taken into consideration every obstacle, every contingency. Or so he'd thought.

As he'd discovered that morning, planning for parenthood was not the same as planning a clandestine operation. He'd thought—mistakenly—that he would just do his duty, and that would be that.

One look at both Haven Adams and his daughter had rid him of that delusion. He'd found it impossible to remain neutral toward either one. That he had any feelings at all came as a revelation. The only other person who had ever provoked such a strong response from him on first meeting had been

Charles Ross, his adoptive father. As disillusioned and mistrusting as he'd been at the time, Brady hadn't been able to ignore the man's innate goodness and honesty, any more than he could brush aside the pull he felt toward Haven and Anna.

His attraction to Haven wasn't the problem. He'd been attracted to many women over the years. What bothered him was that his attraction to her shouldn't have made any difference to him, one way or the other.

But it did. His formidable self-control seemed to take a hike in her presence. He took some solace in the knowledge that his feelings for her were purely physical, and thus would fade over time.

As for his daughter, his feelings toward her defied definition. They were elemental in nature and totally uncontrollable. That was what terrified him.

Never promise more than you can deliver was the first rule of guerrilla warfare. What if Anna wanted more from him than he could give? What if he failed her the way his biological father had failed him?

Anna didn't need him. Financially, Melinda had seen to it that she would never want. And, from all reports, Haven was more than adequately meeting her emotional needs. He could leave now, ensuring that he would never hurt or disappoint her, the way he had every other woman in his life.

Always deliver what you promise was the second rule. Years ago, he'd made a promise to himself that he would never abandon a child of his own. Besides, there was one thing he could give his daughter that Melinda, with all her money, and Haven, with all her affection, couldn't. He could give her answers.

Growing up, he'd had so many questions that had gone unanswered. Most of them were still unanswered, and the not knowing had left an emptiness inside him that had seemed to grow larger with every passing year. The one thing he wanted above all else was for his daughter to grow up with as few unanswered questions as possible. He wanted her to grow up whole. He owed her that much, at least. He would simply have to make sure that his shortcomings didn't get in the way.

At the crest of the hill he paused, gasping for breath. The cramp in his side reminded him of his weakness. Despite the hours he'd devoted to keeping in as good a shape as a three-by-seven-foot cell would allow, he still had a long way to go to regain his former level of fitness.

A soft mewing sound caught his attention. Ahead of him, under a pool of light cast by a streetlight, he saw what looked like a discarded duffel bag. As he approached, the sides of the bag moved.

"What have we here?" he murmured, grasping the zipper and pulling. Inside he found three gray kittens, soaking wet and shivering. By their size, Brady guessed they had just been weaned from their mother.

He swore. Though he'd been disenchanted with the human race since the age of three, he could still be surprised by those who would deliberately harm the weak and defenseless. He supposed he should be grateful that whatever coward had dumped the kittens on the side of the road hadn't dropped them into the river.

After zipping the bag shut, he carefully arranged it in his arms and jogged toward home. Briefly, he considered taking the animals to a shelter, then discarded the idea. He would not be responsible for any animal being in a cage. After he was sure they were healthy, he'd place an ad in the paper and give them to a good home.

Thirty minutes later, he entered the furnished efficiency he'd rented upon his return to Pittsburgh. It was nothing much, but then, he didn't need much.

Ignoring his own sodden state, Brady carefully placed the bag on the kitchen table before hurrying to the bathroom and grabbing a handful of towels from the closet. He rubbed each kitten until its fur was dry and it purred in contentment, then he went to the refrigerator for some milk.

While he watched them eagerly lap at the bowl, he found himself wondering if his daughter liked cats.

Haven didn't sleep well. After tossing and turning for most of the night, she at last succumbed to exhaustion toward dawn. When her alarm went off, she groaned and wearily climbed into her jogging clothes. She groaned again when she returned from her run and looked in the mirror to find dark circles beneath her eyes.

After listening to the weather report, which promised plenty of sunshine and temperatures in the upper seventies, Haven did something she rarely did: agonized over what to wear. She finally settled on a sleeveless yellow linen sheath dress with a bright-pink hip-hugger belt and matching yellow sandals.

Makeup helped disguise the evidence of her sleepless night, but, as usual, her hair refused to cooperate. Curls rioted around her head in every direction but the one she wanted them to go, and she finally tossed up her hands in defeat. Who was she trying to impress anyway? Certainly not Brady Ross.

Liar, her inner voice chided. Haven ignored it and went to wake Anna.

For once, the weather forecast was on target. As Haven marched up the curved sidewalk leading to the laboratory's main entrance two hours later, Anna's small hand clutched in hers, the sun gently bathed her bare shoulders with warmth. Dogwoods in full bloom lined the path, along with tulips and azalea bushes, their bright colors dazzling to the eye. Birds sang in the trees, and the air smelled fresh and clean.

It was the kind of May morning Haven loved. This morning, however, she was too keyed up to enjoy the wonders of nature.

"Pwetty flowers, Binny!" Anna cried, tugging her hand free and running to investigate.

"Careful," Haven cautioned automatically. She crouched beside the little girl, who was reaching a pudgy hand toward a bright-red tulip. "Be gentle."

"Beautiful, aren't they?" a deep voice asked.

Haven's heart skipped a beat, then thudded fiercely as she shaded her eyes and looked what seemed a long way up into Brady Ross's face. The beauties of nature might have escaped her notice, but there was no way she could ignore how magnificent he looked in a pair of faded jeans and matching denim shirt, his long blond hair gleaming in the sunlight. And if he looked this good in a pair of worn jeans, she hated to think how devastating he'd be in black tie and tails.

She stood up quickly, smoothing the wrinkles from her linen dress. Somehow, the man always managed to make her feel at a disadvantage.

"Who's minding the store?" he asked.

"The store?" she murmured, still too disconcerted to think clearly. "Oh, you mean the center. My assistant."

She still felt guilty about leaving Violet in the lurch on such short notice. Violet hated to be left in charge and usually needed a couple of days' advance warning to prepare herself for the responsibility. Haven felt even more guilt for lying to Josephine. She'd told the woman she was taking Anna to the pediatrician for a checkup. On the drive to the lab, she'd explained to the little girl that a doctor was going to check her blood.

Wearing a sailor dress the same color blue as the small cast on her right arm, and with matching blue ribbons in her brown hair, Anna abandoned the tulip and approached Brady with open curiosity.

"Hi. I'm Anna."

Haven resolved to have a stern talk with the child. Forty thousand readings of *Evangeline and the Stranger* and still the little girl approached Brady without hesitation. Not that Haven really blamed her. The man was as handsome as sin. Maybe the discussion should center on the dangers of good-looking men, instead. And Haven would be wise to listen to her own advice.

She waited for Brady to introduce himself and was surprised when he said nothing. Turning to him, she saw a curious thing.

His throat worked, and there was an odd light in his eyes as he stared at Anna. If she didn't know better, she'd say he was terrified.

Understanding dawned, and with it, an unexpected compassion. He was meeting the little girl he believed to be his daughter for the first time, and he didn't know what to do. He didn't know what to say or how to act.

"This is Mr. Ross, Anna," she said. "He's having his blood checked, too. I think he's a little scared about it."

His gray eyes filling with warmth, Brady shot her a look of gratitude. At that moment, he looked not only heart-meltingly handsome, but also far too human.

Haven didn't want him to look human. If he looked human, she might forget herself and start acting like a woman in the throes of a powerful physical attraction. She might be tempted to flirt with him—if her old skills hadn't dried up from lack of use—and see what happened. And that would be dangerous. For her and for Anna.

"Are you ascared?" Anna asked.

Brady knelt so that he and Anna were at eye level. "A little."

"I'm not ascared."

"You're very brave. I wish I were as brave as you."

The little girl's chest puffed out with pride. "Binny holds my hand when I'm ascared. Want to hold my hand?"

"Thank you, Anna," he said solemnly. "I'd like that very much."

A mixture of emotions swirled through Haven as she watched the two of them together. Anna had taken a step toward the man who, in all likelihood, would prove to be her father. That meant she'd taken a step away from Haven.

Unsettled by that troubling thought, Haven led Anna through the laboratory's front doors.

The testing went smoothly. Anna didn't let out so much as a peep when the needle pricked her skin. Murmuring soft words of encouragement, the little girl held Brady's hand while his blood was drawn. Afterward, she praised him for his bravery.

He still seemed a little dazed by the whole thing when they emerged from the lab into the sunlight an hour later.

"I think you two deserve a treat," Haven found herself saying. "There's a fast-food place across the street."

"Does it have a playland?" Anna asked.

"Sure does."

"Yay!" the little girl yelled. She skipped ahead of them down the street, then dutifully stopped to wait when she reached the corner.

"She's something, isn't she?" Brady said. He seemed to have recovered his composure.

Another pang squeezed Haven's heart at the fatherly pride in his voice. Whether he knew it or not, he was rapidly falling under Anna's spell. Would there come a time when, despite his promise, he would decide he couldn't live without her? What would Haven do then? The thought was unbearable.

"Yes," she agreed quietly, "she is."

A few minutes later she was seated in a booth directly across from Brady, her hands wrapped around the steaming cup of coffee he'd insisted on buying. Ten feet away, Anna played happily in a tent filled with brightly colored balls, her orange juice and cheese Danish untouched.

"For someone who's not quite three, she seems pretty mature," Brady commented.

Haven nodded, her gaze on the little girl. "That's because she's always been around older children. She took her first step and spoke her first word at nine months. Josephine's fond of saying that she hasn't stopped running off at the legs or the mouth since."

Brady chuckled, and Haven's gaze flew to his face. "You do know how," she said in wonder.

"How to what?"

"Laugh."

"You seem surprised."

"I am. I got the impression yesterday that it's been a long time since you laughed."

He seemed to think it over. "It has been."

"So you always take life seriously?"

"Life's a serious business. Certainly my reason for being here with you is."

"Yes," she agreed. "Still, everyone needs to laugh a little now and then."

"Really?"

His expression was deadpan, but the light of laughter twinkled in his eyes. So he had a sense of humor, too.

After a pause, he asked, "Who's Josephine?"

Gray eyes returned her regard unflinchingly, and she was struck once again by their uncanny intelligence, a gift he'd obviously passed on to his daughter. If Anna was his— She halted midthought. It was time to stop hiding behind false hope. In all likelihood, the man sitting across from her would prove to be Anna's father. Why would he go to all this bother if he wasn't certain of the outcome?

"Josephine was my nanny when I was a little girl. She helps me now at the center, and at home with Anna."

"Why does Anna call you 'Binny'?"

She was uncomfortably aware of the intentness of his gaze and overwhelmingly aware of his every movement. He was so close that, even though they weren't touching, she could feel the heat rising from his arms and smell the spiciness of his aftershave. She lowered her gaze and saw a pulse beating in the hollow of his throat, and caught a glimpse of the fine gold hair matting his chest. Her fingers tightened around the foam cup, then loosened when hot liquid threatened to spill over the rim.

"When she first started talking, she had trouble with her v's and called me 'Haben.' Somewhere along the line she shortened it to 'Binny.'"

"So she doesn't call you 'Mommy.'"

His words probed at a wound that refused to heal, no matter

how hard she wished it would. "I'm not her mother," she said slowly, training her gaze at a point over his shoulder.

"Does she know about her mother?"

Haven nodded. "I've told her all about Melinda."

"What about me? Does she know anything about me?"

She looked at him then. "If you're asking if she knows anything about her father, the answer's no. She hasn't asked, and I haven't volunteered."

"Time's running out," he said. "We should have the test results in three to four weeks. When they prove my claim, you're going to have to tell her something."

She stiffened. "I'm aware of that."

"Watch me, Mistuh Woss!" Anna called. When she had his attention, she turned a somersault in the balls.

"That's wonderful, Anna," Brady praised.

Obviously, Anna didn't share Haven's reservations about him. But then, Anna trusted that everyone had her best interests at heart, because that was her experience of the world.

Haven sought for something sensible to say, but her mind wouldn't work along sensible lines. Her emotions were in too much turmoil.

"I think we should get to know each other," she blurted, then inwardly groaned. Lack of sleep had obviously addled her brain.

Brady raised an eyebrow in sardonic inquiry. "Know thy enemy?"

She shrugged. "Something like that."

An uneasy silence settled between them, and Haven busied herself stirring her coffee. When she looked up, she found herself staring straight into his eyes. Eyes that first questioned, then darkened with an awareness as old as time, their expression as searing as a touch. For a long minute, she couldn't think, couldn't even breathe. Hard as she willed herself to, she couldn't look away.

Brady broke the contact first, his gaze roving to Anna. When he looked back at Haven, a change had come over him.

To her surprise, a teasing light had replaced the awareness in his eyes.

"What do you want to know?" he asked lazily.

Everything, unfortunately. Haven bit her lip in dismay and willed her heartbeat to return to normal. This uncontrolled attraction to the man was growing totally out of hand and rapidly turning her from a self-assured, responsible, mature woman into an insecure, trembling, blathering wreck. The only answer was to keep their dealings as impersonal as possible.

"I suppose we should start with what you do for a living," she said, keeping her voice carefully neutral.

He folded his arms behind his head and leaned back against the booth. "Nothing. I'm currently between jobs."

Since none of Anna's other so-called fathers had mastered the art of steady employment, she should have seen that coming. "When you did work, what did you do?"

"I was in the army."

She eyed him skeptically. "What rank?"

"Major." Her surprise must have shown on her face, because he added, "Is that so hard to believe?"

Only that a man like him had advanced so far through the ranks. Judging by the length of his hair, he and the army had parted company some time ago. She wanted to ask if that was where he'd received the injury that had left him with his limp, but decided the question fell under the heading of personal information.

"Are you married?" It wasn't a personal question. If there was going to be another woman exercising an influence over Anna, she had the right to know.

"I'm not into commitments."

Then why was he here? "What about Anna? Isn't she a commitment?"

"No. She's a responsibility."

At the moment, his responsibility was giggling with someone else's responsibility as they played tag in the balls. "To me, they sound like one and the same," she said.

"Actually, they're not. A commitment is something you enter into willingly. A responsibility is often thrust at you—something you have no choice but to fulfill the best way you know how."

She really wasn't attracted to him, Haven thought as she gritted her teeth and counted to ten. She never could be attracted to such an infuriating man.

"That's all Anna means to you? A responsibility you have to fulfill?"

He had the grace to look uncomfortable. "My feelings for Anna are a little more...complex than that."

After a pause, she asked, "So, do you plan on getting a job soon?"

The teasing light back in his eyes, he shrugged. "If the right one comes along."

"But you're not actively looking."

"At the moment, no."

And he wanted her to believe he wasn't after Anna's money. Her voice hardened. "Where have you been since Melinda wrote you that letter?"

The laughter in his eyes died, and a nerve pulsed in his cheek. "Away from Pittsburgh."

The man was impossible. Gritting her teeth, Haven stood up. She had to get out of there. Before she said something she'd regret, something that would alienate him totally and have repercussions she hadn't planned.

"I really do have to get back to the center," she said, grabbing her purse. "Thanks for the coffee."

Chapter 3

It was midafternoon when Brady followed a woman out one of the day care center's rear doors to an open area covered by grass, trees and playground equipment. Cries of children at play filled the air. The woman pointed to a spot about a hundred feet away, and he saw Haven pushing a boy on a swing.

Murmuring his thanks, he set off across the grass, which was worn away in spots from the trampling of feet. Threading his way past slides and sandboxes, he deftly sidestepped the hurtling bodies that chased into his path. As he walked, he mentally rehearsed the speech he'd prepared on the drive over. A speech he promptly forgot when something hit him in the back of the head. Hard.

Wincing, Brady rubbed at the sore spot. When he looked down at his feet, he saw a football.

"Thorry, mithter."

He glanced from the football to a little girl whose thick-lensed glasses made her look like a wise old owl. She stared back at him, arms extended expectantly. Chuckling, Brady picked up the football and tossed it to her. She immediately ran back to her friends.

He turned his attention to Haven. The sunlight transformed the riot of curls on her head to liquid fire at the same time it turned the tip of her nose and her shoulders pink. The sleeveless yellow dress that had seemed so fresh and springlike this morning was now hopelessly wrinkled. A stain on the bodice looked suspiciously like cherry Kool-Aid.

His heart thudded painfully. Lord, but she was beautiful. He'd seen so little beauty over the past few years that she totally dazzled him.

The little boy she was pushing said something, and Haven brought the swing to a halt. A tender smile curved her lips as she watched the child scamper over to the slides. Brady knew the exact moment she saw him, because her smile abruptly faded. Her body grew rigid, and she held her arms stiffly at her sides. With her chin thrust out, she regarded his approach through wary blue eyes.

"What are you doing here?" she asked in a low voice when he drew even with her.

"We need to talk."

The look she sent him was not encouraging. "I think we've done enough talking for one day."

He didn't blame her for being angry. Nor did he blame her for walking out on him earlier. He'd acted like a jerk. A complete and total jerk.

Vividly, he recalled the feelings that had washed over him in front of the lab when Anna had walked up to him and introduced herself. Unable to speak, he'd stood staring at her, sheer panic pulsing through his veins. He hadn't had the vaguest notion of what to do, what to say. She was his daughter. *His daughter.*

Never had he felt more inadequate. He'd jumped out of airplanes into enemy territory without batting an eyelash. He'd planned and led raids on enemy installations, and his pulse had remained steady. He'd survived the torture meted out by the most sadistic SOBs he'd had the misfortune to meet, and he hadn't lost it—well, hardly ever. Yet there he'd stood in front of his daughter, paralyzed by doubt and insecurity.

Like the cavalry, Haven had come along and rescued him. And he'd repaid her by deliberately goading her until she'd been so furious she'd walked out.

He'd had no choice. She made him feel too vulnerable. With just a smile, a mere look, the woman could do things to his heartbeat that should have been illegal. He didn't dare think of the effect she'd have on him if he actually touched her. She'd probably send him into immediate cardiac arrest.

To make matters even more complicated, she was as drawn to him as he was to her. He'd felt it in the air, seen it burning in her eyes, as they sat so close to one another in that booth. That she was fighting it as hard as he was, was equally apparent. Which was why he'd decided to give her the ammunition that would make her keep him at arm's length. If the way she was looking at him now was any indication, the tactic had been enormously successful. The fire was out. Too bad it still smoldered deep inside him.

There was a solution. By most anyone's standards, it had been a long time since he'd taken a woman to his bed. Obviously, his fixation on his daughter's guardian was a direct result of his forced celibacy. Eliminate the celibacy, and the fixation would disappear.

Still, when he thought about going out and searching for a willing woman to satisfy his need, the idea held little appeal. Even though he'd never intended on settling down, his past relationships had all been long-term, with women who knew the score and who'd usually been content not to ask for more than he could give. For practical, as well as health reasons, he'd abandoned casual sex long before his capture. He saw no need, other than the temporary release it would bring, to resume the practice.

The only other solution—embarking on a long-term relationship—was out of the question. Right now, he had nothing to offer any woman. He had no time for anything or anyone but his daughter and his search for a purpose for the rest of his life.

Summoning the rigid self-control he'd cultivated as a child and mastered in captivity, Brady shoved his unwilling awareness of Haven Adams to the back of his brain. His attraction to her wasn't important. His daughter, however, was.

"I know things haven't exactly gotten off on the right footing with us," he said, threading his fingers through his hair. "That's my fault. From the beginning, I've handled this whole thing badly. You may not believe it, but I didn't come here to antagonize you."

Her eyes filled with disbelief, a disbelief that turned to sarcasm when she spoke. "Yesterday you marched into my office, all stern and forbidding, and without warning announced you're Anna's father. Then this morning you act like having a job is about as desirable as catching the bubonic plague. Forgive me if I have a hard time believing you didn't set out to deliberately antagonize me."

He wondered if she knew how expressive her eyes were, how they mirrored her every thought. Despite his rigid self-control, he couldn't help wondering how they would look after making love, wide and filled with carnal knowledge, her lids heavy with satisfaction.

When his body started to automatically respond to his thoughts, Brady gave himself a mental kick in the backside. Now was certainly not the time for such thoughts. In fact, where his child's guardian was concerned, there never would be a right time. His life was chaotic enough. He didn't need any messy complications.

What he did need was to tell her that, although he was unemployed, he wasn't without resources. That he was, in fact, richer than Anna. On second thought, he decided against it. While he wanted to heal the breach between them, it would be better all around if Haven remained wary of him until such time that their only contact occurred when he stopped by to pick up and return Anna. Nurturing her belief that he was an aimless drifter would go a long way toward maintaining that wariness.

"It's not easy for me to let down my guard with other people," he said, instead. "I'm a private person, Haven. I don't give my trust easily. I don't think you do, either."

He waited for her to say something, but she just stood there, staring at him.

Inwardly, he sighed. This wasn't going at all well. "You have every right to be skeptical of my motives. Hell, if I were you and someone like me waltzed into my office the way I did into yours, I probably would have tossed him out on his ear. I never should have made my announcement that way. I should have prepared you first. It's just...I've been as knocked off my feet by this whole thing as you have. I didn't know how to react. Believe me when I say, all I want is what's best for Anna."

She said nothing for a long moment. "What if I tell you that I think your leaving is what's best for Anna?"

He shook his head. "I can't do that."

The tilt in her chin turned mutinous. "Because she's your responsibility."

Responsibility. What an understatement that word was. And totally inadequate regarding his feelings for his daughter.

"Partly," he acknowledged with a nod. "But I also want to get to know Anna, to be there when she needs me. I want her to know me, too. And I want us to find a way to make this possible without turning her life upside down."

Shading his eyes, he looked around the crowded playground. "Where is she, by the way? I don't see her out here."

"Napping. The threes and under always nap this time of day."

"I see." He dropped his arm. "Like it or not, Haven, I'm not going anywhere any time soon. Somehow, we have to find a way to work together. For Anna's sake, if for no other reason. I know I'm asking a lot, but could we start over?"

All the fight seemed to go out of her. Her shoulders slumped, and she looked down at the ground.

"When I got home last night, I compared the letter you gave me with other letters Melinda wrote to me."

She spoke so softly he had to strain to hear. "And?"

Her shoulders rose and fell in a tiny shrug. "If it's a forgery, it's a very clever one."

"It's not a forgery, Haven."

She looked up at him then, and he saw torment in her eyes.

"Melinda said you'd never come. She said you wanted nothing to do with Anna."

"Melinda was mistaken." His gaze held hers as, silently, he tried to reassure her that he wasn't a threat to her. "What about it, Haven? Can we start over?"

A long, sighing breath left her. She extended her hand. "Haven Adams," she said solemnly.

"Brady Ross," he replied, equally solemn.

"Nice to meet you, Brady."

"Nice to meet you, too, Haven."

She opened her mouth to say something more, and was interrupted by a commotion off to her right. Brady heard the sound of angry voices, followed by a cry of pain and a high wailing. When he looked over, he saw a group of children quickly forming a circle around a little boy who lay huddled on the ground.

"Excuse me," Haven said. She hastened to join another woman, who was already crouched at the side of the child on the ground. He'd lowered his arms, and tears streamed down a face sprinkled liberally with freckles.

Outside the circle the children had formed protectively around their fallen comrade stood a young boy, fists balled at his sides. It was this child who drew Brady's attention. He looked to be about six. It didn't take a genius to figure out that he was the cause of his classmate's distress.

The boy had pale-blond hair and blue eyes set in the face of an angel. There was nothing angelic, however, about the look in his eyes. They were jaded and old before his time. And filled with rage.

Brady felt the years rolling away. Gazing at this boy was like looking into a mirror. How well he knew the rage that shone from those blue eyes. He'd felt it himself during the years he'd been shuttled from one foster home to another. If he had to hazard a guess, he'd say the boy's father had disappeared shortly after his birth, leaving his mother, young and undereducated, to fend for herself. If she'd stuck around, she probably worked two jobs just to put food on the table.

Which left the child starved for attention. If he was at all the way Brady had been, he'd do anything to get it. Even if the resulting attention was negative. The things he would do would only grow worse as he matured.

Like Brady, he would probably find himself in and out of juvenile court on a regular basis. Unlike Brady, the odds were prohibitive that, on one of those occasions, a man like Charles Ross would be present to see something redeemable beneath a cocky, unrepentant exterior and offer to act as foster parent. Brady still marveled that Charles had stuck with him despite the hell he'd put them both through that next year, until all the barriers he had erected between them had been broken down. If someone like his adoptive father didn't step forward soon for this boy, his future looked bleak.

While Brady watched, Haven left the injured child to the ministrations of the other woman and walked over to the boy standing outside the circle. Quietly, she spoke to him until the rage left his face, and he seemed ready to cry himself. He nodded in response to something she said, then entered the circle.

"I'm sorry I hit you, Billy," Brady heard him say.

Billy sat up and wiped his forearm across his nose, leaving a streak of dirt on his cheek. "That's okay. Want to play catch?"

"After I go to time-out."

Brady revised his earlier opinion. Maybe the child's future

wasn't so bleak after all. He had a sudden understanding of the importance of the job Haven was doing. Like Charles Ross, she was giving hope, solace and understanding where otherwise there might be none. She was doing the job these children's parents would be doing if they didn't have to work so hard just to provide the basics of survival for their families.

"Sorry about that," she said when she returned. "There's never a dull minute around here."

"What's his name?" Brady asked.

"Who?"

"The boy with the angry eyes and the quick fists."

"Oh. You mean Chad."

"Looks like he needs a stern hand to keep him in line."

Haven sighed. "What he needs, Brady, is a father."

A look of dismay spread across her face, and he knew she regretted the words. He also knew he shouldn't take advantage of the opening, given their new beginning, but he couldn't pass the opportunity by. With Chad's help, Haven had just made his case, far more effectively than he ever could.

"Boys aren't the only ones who need their fathers. Girls do, too."

"What do you want from me, Brady?" Her voice was weary.

"I want you to help me be a father to my daughter."

"I've already told you I'd let you visit with her."

He shook his head. "That's not what I meant. You're a teacher, Haven. I want you to teach me."

"You want me to teach you how to be a father?" Her eyebrows rose.

"Is that such an impossible request?"

"No, just a surprising one."

"So, will you help?"

"It's really very easy, Brady. Just give her lots of hugs and kisses, love her to bits, help her up when she falls—without overcoddling her too much, of course—and listen to her when she speaks."

"That's it?"

She spread her arms. "That's it. Simple, isn't it?"

Simple, yet more complicated than anything he'd ever done. He wasn't sure he was up to it, especially the love part.

"You saw how I was with her this morning. I don't think things are going to be that easy for me."

"Just be yourself, Brady. Kids are smart. They know when someone's patronizing them. They can tell if someone's putting on an act for their benefit. Just relax. You'll be okay."

"Being myself certainly didn't help me with you," he couldn't resist saying.

She surprised him by laughing. "That was different."

How was it different? he wondered. Was it just because he was Anna's father, and therefore an unwanted intrusion in her life? Or was it because, until he'd nipped the feeling in the bud, she'd found him as attractive as he found her?

"Are you going to make me wait until the test results come in before letting me be myself with Anna?"

She seemed to come to a decision. "What are you doing for dinner tonight?"

The rocking chair creaked as Haven, infant cradled on her shoulder, smoothed her hand over the tiny back. A minute later she was rewarded with a loud burp.

"Good boy, Jimmy," she cooed, holding the three-month-old out in front of her. "You didn't even spit up on me this time. Your digestive system must be maturing."

Jimmy smiled and drooled on her, and Haven's heart melted. While she adored all the children in her care, her favorite place was the nursery. She loved everything about babies: the way they looked, so small and helpless; the way they smelled; the way they felt when she held them in her arms; the way they depended on her for their every need. If she'd had her way, she would have had a whole houseful of babies. Forget women's lib. Haven's vision of utopia was herself, barefoot and hugely pregnant, with a baby in her arms and a passel of kids pulling on the hem of her dress.

Unfortunately, fate had stepped in, in the form of an automobile accident when she was sixteen, and made that an impossibility. Fortunately, fate had also given her Anna. And taking care of other women's children ran a close second to having them herself. Though it never quite eased the ache in her heart, it was a comfort knowing that whenever she needed a baby fix, she could just head for the nursery.

Settling Jimmy back on her shoulder, Haven closed her eyes and continued to rock. Almost immediately, her thoughts drifted to Brady Ross and his second unexpected visit. Never had any one man been able to arouse so many conflicting emotions in her in such a short space of time. What on earth had gotten into her? Why had she invited him to dinner that night?

Because he was right. For Anna's sake, they had to work things out. The best course was to start slow, while she could still control his meetings with Anna. Until his paternity was officially confirmed, she would let the little girl get used to being around Brady, to develop a relationship with him, before breaking the news that he was her father.

She could make him wait, she supposed, until after the test results arrived. But that option was dangerous. She wasn't sure if—and how—he would retaliate. No, it was better this way; better to antagonize him as little as possible. No matter how angry he made her.

Haven had a sudden thought. What if he wasn't Anna's father after all? What if this was all an elaborate ruse? The DNA test results wouldn't be in for several weeks yet. That could buy someone a lot of time, especially if that someone's purpose was less than admirable. If his purpose was, say, kidnapping.

Given the size of Anna's inheritance, kidnapping had always been a concern for Haven. Several times—the most recent being after the article in the newspaper—she had considered, and then discarded, the notion of hiring someone to watch over Anna. Melinda had never lived her life in fear, and she wouldn't want her daughter to live that way, either.

Before she died, Melinda had expressed her wish to Haven that Anna grow up as normally as possible. Having a bodyguard underfoot was not what Haven would call normal. While there was always the possibility that some unscrupulous individual would try to kidnap Anna in order to get his hands on her money, the odds weren't that great. After all, they lived a low-profile life in a modest, middle-class neighborhood. Most people had no idea who Anna was, let alone the vastness of her wealth.

No, Haven didn't believe that Brady planned on kidnapping Anna. Scary as the thought was, if that was his goal, he could have already accomplished the task without insinuating himself into their lives. Not to mention that most kidnappers, she assumed, preferred that their faces remain unseen by their intended victim's family. Why would Brady go to all this bother, when it would have been far easier just to snatch Anna and run?

She was still clutching at straws, still hoping that this was all a dream, and that when she woke up it would be just her and Anna again. But it wasn't a dream. Brady Ross wasn't going to go away; he'd as much as told her so earlier. Deep down in her gut, Haven knew he was no kidnapper. And the reason she knew was that she trusted him.

The realization brought her up short, and her eyes flew open. She trusted him. She actually trusted the man. She never would have allowed him near Anna otherwise, nor would she have agreed to take the little girl in for the blood work. She most certainly wouldn't have invited him to her home.

But how could that be? It made no sense. How could she trust a man she didn't even like?

He was arrogant, cynical and totally lacking in work ethic. Plus, he could take Anna away from her. Logic would seem to dictate that she stay away from him. Unfortunately, logic seemed to fly out the window whenever he was near.

She felt her lips twist. He'd really gotten to her with his remark about Anna needing a father, the same way Chad did. Unknowingly, with a few short words, he'd hit her where she was most vulnerable. All those years she'd spent yearning to be closer to her own father, and then in waltzed Brady, offering Anna everything Haven had ever wanted. How could she deny her little girl this gift?

One thing she knew for certain. If he hurt Anna, she'd cut his heart out.

"This is not a date," Haven admonished her reflection four hours later as, leaning forward, she carefully applied her lipstick. "So why are you behaving like it is one?"

Cap safely back on the lipstick tube, she studied her reflection. Gone was the wrinkled yellow dress with its splotch of cherry Kool-Aid across the front. In its place, she'd donned a floral-patterned sundress with a halter top that, to her sudden dismay, exposed a good deal more of her skin than she'd previously realized. She saw also that her shoulders were sunburned. It was time to start applying sunscreen on both herself and the children in her care.

The outfit was too revealing, she decided. She'd have to change. Slacks and a blouse were definitely what the occasion called for. And she'd button the blouse clear up to her neck. After all, she didn't want Brady to think she'd primped and preened just for him.

"Binny!" Anna called up the stairs.

"What is it, honey?" she called back, heading for her closet.

"The stove's makin' a funny noise. It sounds wike a snake."

The stove. Good heavens, the potatoes! She'd forgotten all about them. They must be boiling over.

"Be right there!" she called. No time to change now. As

she ran for the stairs, she was glad Josephine had gone on one of her overnight visits. She wasn't ready yet to tell the older woman about Brady, or the real reason for his visit.

She'd just gotten the kitchen under control, when the doorbell rang. Drawing a deep breath, she mentally steeled herself for the evening ahead. Tonight was the night she started teaching Brady Ross how to be a father. She only prayed she didn't lose Anna in the process.

"Hi," he said with a smile when she opened the front door.

It was the first time Haven had seen him really smile, and for a moment she completely lost her train of thought in the wonder of it. His lips curved upward invitingly, creasing his cheeks and banishing the gauntness from his face. His gray eyes filled with a warmth that had her heart thudding in her chest and the heat of a blush stealing into her cheeks.

"Hi," she replied, mentally cursing the breathlessness she heard in her voice. For Pete's sake, she sounded like a sixteen-year-old greeting her first date!

This is not a date, she reminded herself sternly.

His gaze roved over her, and she couldn't stem a surge of pure feminine satisfaction at the glint of approval she saw in his eyes. "You look nice."

Returning his perusal, she noted that he'd traded in his jeans for a pair of brown chinos and a white cotton shirt. The preppie image was marred somewhat by the shoulder-length blond hair he'd pulled back into a ponytail at his nape. Haven knew that even had his hair been fashionably cut, the ever-present aura of danger that clung to him like groupies to a rock star would never allow him to appear totally respectable.

"Thanks," she said. "You look nice, too."

"Where's Anna?"

"Watching *Sesame Street.* I tape it for her every day."

"May I come in?"

The warmth in her cheeks intensified. She'd been so busy studying him that she'd literally left him standing on her doorstep.

"Of course." She moved aside.

As he crossed the threshold, she saw that one hand clutched a stuffed bear that was obviously for Anna, while the other held a plastic bottle. She closed the door, then turned to face him. He extended the bottle toward her.

"This is for you."

She took the offering. Sunscreen. SPF 30. Bemused, she raised questioning eyes to him.

"I noticed this afternoon that your nose and shoulders were burning."

"Thank you," she said carefully. "That was very thoughtful of you."

If she needed any more proof that her attraction to him was one-sided, this was it. What man besotted with a woman brought her sunscreen? Flowers, candy, even wine. But sunscreen? No, she mused, as she led him down the hall into the living room, this most definitely was not a date.

Carrying the teddy bear he'd brought her, Anna climbed up next to him on the living-room sofa. Though Haven had left them alone together—presumably so they could get to know each other better—the sound of her cleaning up in the kitchen drifted down the hallway and into the room. He found the clatter of dishes oddly comforting.

All in all, he reflected, things hadn't gone too badly. He'd made it through dinner without incident, even if he had eaten with more gusto than the situation had called for. It was the first home-cooked meal he'd had since before his capture, and it had tasted like manna from the gods. After the first bite, he hadn't been able to hold back. Though he'd caught Haven staring at him curiously from time to time, she'd been too polite to ask the questions he'd seen burning in her eyes.

He still felt awkward and unsure around Anna, but it was getting a little easier. With the passage of time, he supposed he would sound less like a robot when he spoke to her and more like a human being. Now, if he could just keep his eyes off her guardian.

Haven hadn't made it easy for him. All he had to do was close his eyes to recall the tantalizing expanse of throat and shoulder exposed by her sundress. Even sunburned, her shoulders were a temptation he found hard to resist.

"Unca Bwady?" Anna asked.

He and Haven had decided on the less formal mode of address, in the hope that it would make the transition to "Daddy" that much easier when the time came. A sudden lump formed in his throat at the thought of hearing that word from his child.

"Yes, Anna?" he said huskily.

"Why doesn't your leg work?"

"I fell and broke it. I limp because it didn't heal properly."

"How did you fall?"

"I jumped out of an airplane and landed wrong."

Her eyes grew round. "With a pawachute 'n' everthing?"

"With a parachute and everything," he said with a nod.

"Wow."

The wonder in the word made him smile. "Would you like to jump out of a plane some day?"

"Um-hmm. But I don't think Binny will let me. She doesn't like danjus things."

"Binny's a very smart lady," Brady said. "You'd do well to listen to her."

He'd thought the subject of his leg closed, but evidently Anna's curiosity wasn't yet satisfied.

"Why didn't it heal popally?"

Because I was captured by a group of guerrillas, and there were no doctors around, so I had to set it myself the best I could.

"It just didn't." He drew a deep breath. "So, what do you want to do?"

Anna jumped off the sofa and ran across the room, where

she grabbed a book from the bookcase. "Will you wead to me?"

At first, his voice was halting and strained. He couldn't seem to concentrate on anything except the child nestled at his side. She was so small, and she gazed up at him with such trust in her eyes. He'd never been more terrified in his life.

Relax. Be yourself. He could almost hear Haven saying the words to him. Surprisingly, he did relax. Instead of concentrating on Anna, he began focusing on the story he was reading, on making it fun for her. Before he knew it, he was lost in the age-old tale of trolls, bridges and billy goats.

When he finished, he looked up to find Haven standing in the doorway. Her eyes were warm and dreamy as she stared at him. Hypnotized, he stared back, his heart thudding painfully in his chest.

"That was wonderful," she said, taking a step into the room. "You really brought the story alive for me, and I've heard it a thousand times."

It was her way of telling him that he was doing okay, without blatantly spelling it out in front of Anna. Grateful for the reassurance, he drew a deep breath and willed his heart rate to slow down.

"Thanks. Can I do anything to help with the cleanup?"

She shook her head. "I'm almost done. Besides, I think someone has other ideas about how you're going to spend your time."

Following the line of Haven's sight, he looked down at the little girl snuggled so closely to his side. To his surprise, her lap was piled high with books. While he'd been staring at Haven, Anna must have taken another trip to the bookcase.

"Can you wead some more, Unca Bwady?" she asked, her eyes bright with pleasure and anticipation. "I wuv the way you wead."

Brady's heart contracted. Right then, if she'd asked him for the moon, he would have gotten a rope and tried to lasso it.

"Sure thing, squirt," he said, his voice gruff. "What do you want to start with?"

An hour later, Anna had been tucked into bed, and he sat a safe distance from Haven on her front-porch swing. The creaking of the swing blended with the chirping of crickets as he watched the sun begin its slow descent in the sky.

"If I didn't know any better, I could swear you'd never seen a sunset before," Haven said. She sounded amused.

"It feels like I'm seeing it for the first time." He turned to look at her in the gathering twilight. "We take so much for granted, you know. The ebb and flow of the tides. The air we breathe. The bloom on a rose." He nodded toward the horizon. "The setting of the sun."

"It is beautiful, isn't it?"

He kept his gaze centered on her. "One of the most beautiful sights I've ever seen."

Haven stared back for a minute before biting her lip and looking away. "So, when are you going to start looking for a job?"

Brady felt his lips twist. Served him right for trying to flirt with her after he'd done everything in his power to put her off. "It really bugs you that I'm unemployed, doesn't it?"

"Yes," she admitted, "it does."

"Why?"

"Chad's mother, for example. She's working herself into a state of exhaustion to provide a better life for her son. It leaves a bad taste in my mouth when I see an able-bodied person just wasting his life away."

"An able-bodied person like me," he said.

"Yes."

"Anna's rich, Haven. She doesn't need me to support her."

The growing twilight could not hide the exasperation in her eyes. "Children learn by example, Brady. What will your not working teach Anna? Just because she's rich, it doesn't mean she's entitled to slide through life."

"I agree."

She blinked. "You do?"

While he might choose not to speak of his past and the reasons for his currently unemployed status, he could reassure her on this issue anyway. "Yes, Haven, I do."

"Then why aren't you working?"

Brady stared out into the night. "I needed some time off. If it makes you feel any better, I'm not on public assistance. And I don't plan on being idle for much longer. By the time Anna's old enough to ask what I do for a living, I'll have an answer for her."

"I'm glad to hear it."

They fell silent. The last rays of the sun disappeared beneath the horizon. In the front yard, primroses unfurled their petals and fireflies flashed.

"I did okay?" he finally asked. "Tonight, with Anna?"

"You did fine, Brady. Matter of fact, you passed the first lesson with flying colors."

He shook his head. "You know, I didn't think it would be so..."

"Easy?" she prompted. "Fun?"

"Both, I suppose."

"When you look at something as a responsibility, it's kind of hard to imagine how it can also be fun."

"Touché," he said to the open challenge in her voice. "Okay, you've got me cornered. I don't just think of Anna as a responsibility. I tried to, but I knew she was more than that the minute I saw her. I hadn't realized there'd be such a...tie between us."

"I've often heard that's the way it can be between parent and child." He heard an odd note in her voice. Wistfulness. And if he wasn't mistaken, pain.

"That's why you were so concerned about me, wasn't it?" he guessed. "It wasn't so much that I'd appeared out of the blue, but that I kept insisting the bond didn't exist."

She nodded. "Anna needs a father who loves her, not one who's only with her out of a sense of duty."

He'd only truly allowed himself to love two people in his lifetime. One had been a father figure; the other was his best friend. Both times, the love had come slowly, grudgingly. Even now, though he felt a bond with the little girl, he wasn't sure he was capable of the outpouring of affection that she would need from him. But he had to try. To do less would be to sully Charles Ross's memory.

"I'm not sure I believe in love," he said. "But I'm here, Haven. And I'm not budging."

"It's a start," she conceded. "I suppose I should warn you that you've got a few lessons to go yet. A three-year-old is a lot easier to deal with than a sixteen-year-old. What are you going to do when Anna comes to you with questions about sex?"

The thought horrified him. "Put her in a convent till she's thirty."

She laughed. "Spoken like a true dad."

The remark pleased him. It also pleased him to sit in the dark with her, to feel the motion of the swing. It pleased him to look at her, to see the way her lips curled, full and inviting, enticing him. It pleased him a lot. Too much, in fact.

He put his feet down, and the swing ceased its motion. It was time to leave. Before he let the magic of the night—and the woman seated next to him—make him do something he'd regret.

Before he kissed her and changed things forever between them.

"Thank you for dinner." He stood up, and she followed suit. "And for the lesson."

"I'll walk you to your car," she said.

"Would the real Brady Ross please step forward?" Haven murmured as she watched his car disappear down the street. What a puzzle the man was. He wouldn't tell her where he'd been since Anna's conception or why he was so reluctant to work, but he'd willingly confided his doubts and fears about his abilities as a father. He was cynical about love, yet he could marvel at the setting of the sun. She wondered if she'd ever figure him out. It would probably be best for her peace of mind if she didn't even try.

She was about to go inside, when a battered car coughed and sputtered its way up her driveway and pulled to a halt. The door opened, and an elderly woman cautiously climbed out.

"May I help you?" Haven asked.

"I'm looking for Haven Adams."

"I'm Haven Adams." She had a sudden premonition of bad tidings. Yesterday, when Brady Ross had spoken the exact same words to her, the news he'd delivered had been less than welcome.

"I was asked to deliver this to you." The woman handed her a manila envelope, then turned to shuffle back to the car. "Have a good evening."

Haven waited until she was inside before opening the envelope and pulling out the sheet of paper it contained. As she read the typewritten words, she felt the blood drain from her face. Her knees threatened to give out on her, and she sank into the nearest chair.

"No!" she cried. "No. This can't be happening."

She read the paper again, convinced her eyes had been playing tricks on her. But they hadn't been. The words hadn't changed. Haven drew a long, shuddering breath.

A petition for guardianship had been filed, and a hearing would be held in six weeks. She was being sued. For custody of Anna.

Chapter 4

In quiet desperation, her heart beating in rhythm to the tapping of her foot, Haven waited while her lawyer scanned the sheaf of papers in his hands. Unable to sit still for more than a few seconds at a time, she shifted in her seat, her gaze roving the large corner office.

Sunlight streamed through a huge bank of windows, throwing shadows across a gray wool carpet. Mahogany paneling and bookcases covered the walls, along with several oil paintings and framed diplomas from the University of Pennsylvania and Harvard Law School. The aroma of good wood, old money and expensive cigars filled the room.

More impressive than the room itself, however, was the man seated behind a massive, gleaming mahogany desk. In his early fifties, Syd Spear was a bare inch under seven feet tall, bald, brawny and eagle eyed. He specialized in estate and family law, and was enormously successful. Haven had met him through Melinda, and he'd been advising her since her friend's death. This morning, she hoped he would advise her that her fears were groundless.

"Well?" she demanded, when she could stand the wait no longer.

With a sigh, Syd laid the papers down on his desk and massaged his right temple. "I haven't had time to review the entire petition in depth, but it appears that Douglas and Pamela Zieglar, Anna's great-aunt and uncle, have filed a petition seeking her guardianship."

"I know all that." Haven had no patience left for long, involved explanations. "Forget the legalese and cut to the chase, Syd. What am I up against?"

"In a minute." He pressed a button on his intercom and spoke into it before leaning back in his chair. "First, I'm going to have my secretary bring you a cup of coffee. After you drink every drop, you're going to take several long, deep breaths. You're wound tighter than an overtuned guitar string, Haven. If we're going to accomplish anything this morning, you have to calm down."

Haven slumped in her chair. "I'm sorry, Syd. I know I'm wound up. I haven't been able to think of anything else since I was served that notice last night. I didn't sleep a wink. I guess I'm just a bundle of nerves."

"I can understand why."

She gazed at him, eyes pleading. "I can't lose Anna. Not to those people. You don't know what they're like."

"I have a fair idea. Remember, I was Melinda's lawyer, too. I know the only reason they took her in after her parents died was for her money. I know they never showed her one ounce of affection. Unfortunately, they are well-known and quite prominent in this community. Regardless of what you or I think of them, they have a sterling reputation."

Haven's fingers tightened around the purse on her lap. "That doesn't make them good people."

"No," Syd agreed, "it doesn't."

The office door opened, and a tall, slim, efficient-looking woman entered bearing a cup of coffee. She handed it to Ha-

ven, who murmured her thanks before taking a sip. The hot
liquid went a long way toward restoring her equilibrium.

"Better?" Syd asked.

"Better," she replied with a nod. "So, tell me what this is
all about."

"Not a word until you drain the cup and take three deep
breaths."

Grudgingly, Haven complied. "All right," she said. "I'm
calm, cool and collected. Now, what's this all about?"

"The Zieglars are charging that you're an unfit guardian."

Shock waves rippled through her body, and she nearly
dropped the empty cup. "That's preposterous!"

She heard the note of panic in her voice and drew another
deep breath, willing herself to remain calm. She needed to treat
this matter the same way she would a crisis at the center. The
minute she lost control, she lost the battle. And this was one
battle she couldn't afford to lose.

"If anyone's unfit to be Anna's guardians," she said, her
voice low and even, "it's them. I could tell you stories that
would regrow the hair on your head. How can they get away
with making such a ridiculous claim?"

"It's all laid out in black and white in the petition," Syd
said.

"How about laying it out for me?"

He flipped through a couple of pages. "For starters, they
claim that Anna's been in day care all her life."

"So are a lot of children of working mothers, and they
aren't accused of being unfit. Anna happens to be in day care
because I run a day care center. And I didn't open that until
she was a year old. She's there so she can be near me."

"The point is," Syd said, "you're not Anna's mother.
You're only her guardian, which changes all the rules."

The words hurt. Haven had wanted to adopt Anna, had
begged Melinda to allow her to do so, but her friend had
refused. Anna was the last of a long line of Dolans, and Melinda hadn't wanted that to end. Besides, in Melinda's eyes,

granting Haven guardianship was the same as making her Anna's mother. Unfortunately, as Syd had so painfully pointed out, the eyes of the law viewed things differently. If Haven had been allowed to formally adopt Anna, in all likelihood she wouldn't be sitting where she was today, terrified of losing the one person who meant more to her than life itself.

"What are the center's working hours?" Syd asked.

"Eight a.m. to 6 p.m., Monday through Friday," she answered wearily.

"That's ten hours a day."

"Yes, it is. Bravo for you, you didn't even need to use a calculator to figure it out." She didn't bother to hide her hurt. "Why are you questioning me like this, Syd? Why are you trying to make me feel in the wrong here?"

"I'm just looking at this the way the Zieglars' lawyer will. Believe me, Haven, it's important. Remember, I'm on your side, even if it may not sound like it. May I continue?"

She gave a stiff little nod.

"I assume you and Anna are there all ten hours?"

"Yes."

"And how much of that time do you physically spend with her?"

Haven spread her arms in frustration. "I don't know. Every minute I can. I don't keep a record. I also spend every evening and weekend with her. Doesn't that count?"

"The Zieglars claim that they're able to give Anna their attention full-time."

Haven felt her lip curl. "You and I both know that if they get her, they'll ship her off to boarding school the minute she's old enough."

"We know it, but the judge doesn't."

"Then why don't we tell him?"

"Because," Syd said, his eyes full of regret, "it isn't a crime to send a child to boarding school."

"I'd be more than willing to testify how they neglected Melinda all those years. They never visited her, or let her come home for the holidays, or even so much as sent her a birthday card."

The lawyer shook his head. "Unfortunately, Melinda is not here to corroborate your story. Your testimony would be considered hearsay. It wouldn't be allowed. Plus, the Zieglars have one card to play that you don't."

"What card is that?"

"The blood card. They're related to Anna, and you're not. That's often a very persuasive argument in matters like these. Most likely, they'll claim that since they already raised their orphaned niece, they're more than qualified to raise her daughter."

Melinda had actually raised herself, but Haven didn't see any point in saying it out loud, since Syd already knew that. She wondered how he would react if she vented her anger and frustration by kicking his desk. Hard. She might have, too, except she was fairly certain the only thing that would get hurt in the process would be her foot.

"What about their age?" she asked. "They're old enough to be Anna's grandparents."

"A lot of grandparents are raising their grandchildren these days," Syd replied. "The key here is that they're family. In most cases, any family, regardless of age, is thought to be better than no family at all. I have to warn you that the judge on this case is well-known for his leanings in that direction."

It took a lot more than blood to make a group of people a family, Haven thought. Love, for one thing. Commitment to a common goal, for another. Why couldn't the court see that?

"What about Melinda's will?" she said. "She specifically stated that she wanted me to be Anna's guardian."

"They'll claim that because of her illness, Melinda wasn't able to truly see what would be in Anna's best interests. The judge might just buy it."

"What if I closed down the center? I could be with Anna full-time then."

"How long would your money last?" Syd retorted. "How

would you support yourself once it was gone? I know you won't touch Anna's money. At least, you haven't so far.''

Haven sighed. "What else?"

"The Zieglars claim that two weeks ago, while in your care, Anna fell and broke her wrist."

For a long minute, she stared at him, uncomprehending. "And this makes me incompetent? Children fall all the time, Syd. That's how they discover their world. Sometimes, when they fall, a bone breaks."

"They say they have a witness who can testify you waited six hours before taking Anna to a doctor."

"Mary," Haven said dully.

"Mary?"

"A former aide. I dismissed her when I found her stealing supplies from the center. She was on playground duty the day Anna fell."

"So you're saying Mary's nurturing a grudge against you, and for that reason she's willing to lie in court?"

Haven felt her heart sink even further. "No, she's telling the truth. Anna didn't receive medical attention until six hours after her fall."

"Why not?" There was no judgment in his voice.

"Anna has a high tolerance for pain, something we learned after this incident. There was no obvious break, and no bruising. She didn't complain of pain until six hours later. When she did, and I realized the wrist could be broken, I took her immediately to the emergency room."

"You do know how this will play in court, don't you?" Syd said.

Haven nodded. She knew. She'd seen enough courtroom dramas on television to have a fair idea of how the scenario would play out. It wouldn't look good. It wouldn't look good at all.

"What else do they claim?" she asked.

"That a year ago you hired a convicted child molester to work at the center."

She squeezed her eyes shut. "Mary again."

"Did you?"

She nodded. "I hired him to be the janitor. Before he started, as is policy with every new employee, I checked his references. I also checked to see if he had a criminal record. That's when I found out about his conviction. Other than his interview, he never set foot in the center. I was with him the entire time. He was never near any of the kids."

"That should be a point in your favor."

His tone of voice told her it might be the only one. Dread formed a hard ball in her chest, and she found it difficult to breathe. Her voice, when she spoke, was barely a whisper.

"Something tells me there's more."

"There is," Syd said. "The petition states that at 2 a.m. on February 10, Anna was found wandering around the neighborhood in just her nightgown and slippers by a neighbor, one June Samuelson, who called Children and Youth Services. A report was filed."

"And the subsequent investigation found nothing," Haven said quickly. "After I explained what happened, June apologized. We'd just moved into the house the day before, and she had no idea who we were. She was only doing what she thought was best for Anna. I don't blame her. Under similar circumstances, I probably would have done the same thing."

"Why was Anna walking around the neighborhood at two in the morning?" Syd asked.

A reluctant smile curved Haven's mouth. "The little imp climbed out the dog door. I'd read her a story before bed about a leprechaun and his pot of gold. There was a full moon that night, and she decided to go searching for her own leprechaun. Afterward, I replaced the door and we had a long talk. There will be no more nocturnal wanderings. Anything else?"

The expression on his face was grave. "For now, that appears to be it."

"You don't look happy," she said slowly.

"I'm not. Fact is, I'm afraid for you, Haven."

She didn't want to believe it. The words stuck in her throat, and she had to force them out. "So what you're saying is, the Zieglars could win."

"I'm saying that I honestly don't know which way this will go."

This wasn't real, Haven thought. Any minute now she'd awake in her bed to find she'd been having a nightmare. How could this be happening? How could those two miserable excuses for human beings take little things, things that, separately, didn't mean much, and weave them together to form a fabric of carelessness and incompetence? Even Haven, with what little she knew of the law, could understand how things might appear to someone who didn't know any better. Someone who didn't know her. Or the Zieglars.

A snippet of an almost forgotten conversation ran through her mind, a conversation with Melinda, one of the few arguments they'd had during those long, last, terrible days. Haven had been trying to understand why her friend was leaving almost half her estate to her aunt and uncle, instead of to her daughter.

"I'm doing it for Anna," Melinda had said. "If they get enough money, they'll leave her alone."

"It's the money," Haven mused out loud. "They must have gone through what Melinda left them. That's why they've waited so long to petition for Anna."

"I think you're right," Syd replied. "I've heard through the grapevine that Douglas has made a few bad investments lately. They're not broke, but they could be doing a lot better."

"Can't you tell the judge this? Surely it proves the only reason they want Anna is for her money."

"All it proves, Haven, is that Douglas Zieglar made a few bad investments. We have to stick to concrete, provable facts, not innuendo and hearsay. The sad truth is that, at face value, things don't look good for you. The Zieglars have a witness, hospital records and a CYS report to back up their allegations.

The hearing will take place in civil court. It will be presided over by a judge, and there will be no jury. Proof beyond a reasonable doubt is not the standard. If there is any question in the judge's mind as to your fitness, he'll give Anna to the Zieglars.''

"So now they want the other half of Melinda's estate," she said dully.

"That would be my take on the situation."

"And we can't prove it."

"No, we can't."

Haven thought for a minute. "What about Anna's father?" she said slowly.

"What about him?" Syd asked. "Far as I know, Melinda would never say who he was."

"What if, until just recently, he didn't know he was a father? What if he showed up and petitioned the court for custody? What if he had DNA tests to back up his claim?"

Syd shrugged. "In all likelihood, there'd be no case. He'd probably be given custody of his daughter. That way, you'd definitely lose, Haven. At least with the Zieglars, you have a chance."

Haven couldn't breathe. It felt as though the walls of the room were closing in on her. She needed to get away from here, to have some time alone to think and sort things through. Taking a deep breath, she carefully set the coffee cup on a brass coaster and rose unsteadily to her feet.

"Where are you going?" Syd asked.

"Out. I need some fresh air. Call you later."

An hour later, after a long walk, Haven was no closer to a decision when she returned to the center to find Douglas and Pamela Zieglar waiting in her office. Swearing beneath her breath, she closed the door behind her and mentally prepared herself for the coming confrontation.

"Pamela, Douglas," she said, resisting the urge to utter a primal scream. "It's been a long time."

It made her skin crawl to look at them. On the surface, they were an attractive couple, having aged well, like a fine wine. Appearances, however—especially in the Zieglars' case—could be more than deceiving.

Both were dressed conservatively, Douglas in a coal gray suit, Pamela in a pale-pink A-line dress. A set of matched pearls decorated her ears and throat. While everything about the pair bespoke money and breeding, inside their chests, Haven knew, beat two identical hearts of stone.

"We're here to save you a lot of trouble," Douglas said.

Since the only altruism he ever practiced was a well-publicized donation to charity every year or so, Haven had her doubts.

"Oh?" She crossed her arms beneath her breasts and raised her eyebrows. "That's kind of you."

"You're aware, aren't you," Douglas said, "that we've filed a petition for guardianship of Melinda's daughter?"

Not for anything would she let them see that she was even remotely concerned about the case. Maintaining careful eye contact, she said, "Yes, I'm aware of that."

"Good. I thought it would interest you to know, also, that the judge in this matter went to Yale with Melinda's father. He and I golf at the same club."

"Meaning?"

"Whose side do you think he'll be on in this matter?"

Haven's blood did a slow boil, but she held the lid on her temper. She didn't want to give them any more ammunition than they already had.

"Are you telling me you bribed a judge, Douglas?" she said lightly. "You could go to jail for that, you realize."

Douglas's smile was about as genuine as a crocodile's. "Of course I didn't bribe him. There really is no need. What I'm telling you is that you can save yourself a lot of time and trouble by conceding the case right now. Like does tend to like, you know."

"That may be true," Haven retorted with a smile that belied

her inner turmoil, "but it didn't stop Melinda from being friends with me. Or from granting me guardianship of her daughter."

The tightening of his mouth was the only indication Douglas gave that her words had hit their mark. "Melinda was a confused young woman," he said dismissively. "She never got over the death of her parents."

"I won't just hand Anna over to you," Haven said.

Douglas shrugged, as if it were no skin off his nose. "I just wanted to spare you a lot of trouble."

"Would you look at this place?" Pamela said, wrinkling her nose in distaste. "Our poor little girl spends most of her life here. Can you imagine it, Doug?"

Pamela had never laid eyes on her "poor little girl" in Anna's almost three years of life. The hypocrisy made the bile rise in Haven's throat.

Suddenly, it was all too much. She couldn't take it anymore. She wanted the Zieglars out of her office, and she wanted them out yesterday.

"I appreciate you stopping by to tell me this," she said stiffly, "but if you don't mind, I have work to do. Please feel free to contact my attorney, if there's anything else."

"Well, really," Pamela said, affronted.

"Mark my words, Haven," Douglas warned, taking his wife by the elbow and shepherding her to the door. "You can't win. The child belongs with us. No judge in the world would choose you over us. You know it, and we do, too."

When they were gone, all the strength drained out of Haven's body, and she started to shake. She slumped into her chair and laid her head on her hands, feeling more exhausted and helpless than she ever had in her life. All she wanted to do was close her eyes and go to sleep, and forget that her world lay in ruins around her feet. What was she going to do?

Slowly, by sheer effort of will, she lifted her head and stared at the picture of the laughing child on her desk. There was no decision to make, really. Douglas and Pamela Zieglar had al-

ready made it for her. She had to do what was in Anna's best
interest. And it would break her heart.

Twenty minutes later, events set into motion, Haven peered
through a small oval window and watched while Anna finger
painted. Her round little face was intent as she smeared a
wedge of blue across her paper. Her tongue poked out of the
corner of her mouth, the way it always did when she was deep
in concentration.

Haven's heart contracted, and she fought back hot tears.
Dear heaven, did she have the strength to do this? A quick
review of her alternatives, and she knew she had no other
choice. For a moment longer she watched the little girl who
owned her heart, the child she would gladly die for. Then,
squaring her shoulders in resolution, she turned away.

A far different emotion from what she'd experienced at the
sight of the Zieglars filled her when she walked into her office
and saw Brady standing there. He looked so big and solid that
she wanted to run into his arms, to feel them close around her
and to hear him murmur that everything would be okay. With
an effort, she walked slowly to her desk and took a seat.

"Thanks for coming so quickly."

He sat down across from her and examined her closely.
"Are you okay?"

"I'm fine."

"You don't look fine," he said.

Haven knew she looked awful. Her hair was an untamed
riot of curls around her face. Except for her sunburn, her skin
was pale, her eyes sunken and haunted. Though she'd taken
the time to dress for work, she hadn't bothered with makeup.
She just hadn't been up to it.

There was, she decided, no delicate way to prepare Brady
for what had to be done. "You're going to have to petition
the court for custody of Anna," she said baldly.

He didn't speak for a long moment. "You want me to file
for custody of Anna?"

"Yes."

"You're asking me to remove her from your custody?"

She swallowed hard. "Yes."

"Why?"

The words spilled out. She told him all about Douglas and Pamela Zieglar and the shameful way they'd neglected Melinda all her life. She told him about the petition for custody and what Syd Spear had said about the natural father stepping forward.

"So you see," she said, shamelessly appealing to his overblown sense of honor, "you have to do this. You have a duty to Anna. You can't let those people get their greedy hands on her."

"I thought I was supposed to be the one with the greedy hands," he murmured.

"Let's just say recent events have altered my opinion on that issue."

"You could win this case, you know. What then?"

She shook her head. "I can't take the chance. I don't want Anna to spend so much as thirty seconds with those people."

His smile was wry. "So, what you're saying is, I'm the lesser of two evils."

"I'm saying you have no choice." She drew a deep breath. "I've got it all figured out. You need to show the court that you can support Anna, so I'm going to give you a job. Temporarily, you're going to be our new maintenance man."

"How can you afford to do that?" he asked. "You're barely making ends meet as it is."

"How do you know that?" She held up a hand. "I know, I know. The private investigator. Don't worry about me coming up with the money. I'll manage somehow. Of course, you're going to have to find a real job as soon as possible. I'll only be able to afford to pay you for a short time. But it should be enough to convince the judge that you're gainfully employed."

"I don't want your money, Haven."

"This is no time for false pride," she told him. "You have to take it, whether you want it or not. You need to have a job."

"I'm rich. I don't need your money. Or Anna's."

Haven did a double take. "What?"

"I said I'm rich."

"You're rich?"

He nodded. "Stinking."

"I don't believe it."

"Ever heard of Charles Ross?"

"The financial wizard? Who hasn't?"

"He was my adoptive father. I'm his only heir."

Her mouth dropped open. "You're Charles Ross's son?"

"That's right."

"But you don't look rich," she blurted.

He seemed amused. "What does rich look like?"

She knew she should be grateful that he was as rich as Anna—richer probably. She knew she should be deliriously happy that he really was here out of a sense of duty to his daughter, and not for her money. If the DNA tests proved his paternity, no court in the land would refuse him custody. She knew all this, yet all she could focus on was one small fact. Yesterday, he'd asked her to start over, but he hadn't felt the need to tell her the truth about himself.

"You lied to me," she accused.

"How did I do that?"

"You told me you were unemployed."

"I am unemployed."

"But you let me think you had no source of income."

He shrugged. "I had my reasons."

What was she doing? Haven asked herself. Why was she arguing with the man when Anna's future was on the line?

"Will you do it, Brady?" she pleaded. "When the DNA tests come in, will you file a petition for custody of your daughter?"

He was silent for so long she knew he was going to refuse.

Her shoulders sagged. She'd been so certain that her appeal to his duty and honor would work. But why should he do this? Though he'd admitted feeling a tie to his daughter, he was only here out of a sense of obligation. An obligation he could carry out regardless of who had physical custody of Anna. By his own admission, he didn't believe in love. She wondered if it was in him to love anyone.

"There is another solution," he offered.

For the life of her she couldn't figure out what it could be. "What's that?" she asked impatiently.

"You could marry me."

Chapter 5

Haven felt as if she'd been plucked up by unseen fingers and dropped into the middle of a Salvadore Dali painting. Everything seemed surreal: her fingers, her toes, her face, the very air she breathed. Even her office furniture seemed to blur around the edges, until she grew halfway convinced that her desk was about to pour onto her lap, like water from a bucket. She had to blink several times before the room came fully into focus.

When it did, she found Brady watching her. He had such a disconcerting way of emptying all emotion from his face, of making his eyes so flat and empty that, for the life of her, she couldn't tell what he was thinking. That he was a complete mystery to her was becoming more of an annoyance than an intrigue. At least he was consistent, she thought.

Despite her anguish over her decision, her fear for Anna, her annoyance that Brady Ross was so impossibly remote and unreadable, her heart beat faster just looking at him. He was so big, so solid, so…damnably good-looking.

And if her ears hadn't been playing tricks on her, he'd just asked her to marry him.

She forced a laugh that was shaky at best. "Want to hear something crazy? It just goes to show how much stress I've been under lately, but I could swear I heard you say we could get married. Isn't that ridiculous?"

"I don't think it sounds ridiculous at all," Brady replied. "Given what you've just told me, it sounds downright necessary."

For the briefest of seconds Haven allowed herself to indulge in the fantasy of what it would be like to be Brady Ross's wife, in the fullest sense of the word. What it would be like to wake up beside him every morning, to feel his possession at night. Desire roared through her veins like a flash fire, obliterating all rational thought and making her weak at the knees.

"You're kidding," she said, her voice deep and husky.

His gaze didn't waver. "I don't kid, Haven. From where I'm sitting, it looks like the only sensible solution."

There was nothing sensible about the graphic images racing through her brain. "Well, from where I'm sitting," she retorted, after clearing her throat and forcing her thoughts back into line, "it looks like the only disastrous solution."

"Why? I'm offering you what you so desperately want. A chance to be with Anna."

"But marriage..." Words failed her.

"What I'm suggesting, Haven, is a temporary measure. A marriage in name only until my paternity is confirmed."

She knew it couldn't be as easy as he made it sound. A person didn't climb in and out of marriage as easily as she did an automobile. The breakup of any marriage, even one as temporary as the one Brady proposed, was never without consequence.

"But marriage..." she repeated.

"Ever hear of Murphy's Law?"

She gave him a patient look. "If something can go wrong,

it will. I've been living it all week. I'm beginning to think Murphy was an optimist.''

"Then you, more than anyone else, should know exactly how wrong things can still go. What happens if they get backed up at the lab, and they can't get to my test before your court date? What happens if someone makes a mistake and the lab loses my sample? Any delay could be costly, both emotionally and financially. Why not settle everything now by getting married? Plus, you could go into court against the Zieglars as a married woman. They couldn't use your single status against you.''

The appeal of his proposal, as far as Anna was concerned, was undeniable. It was the appeal of the man that was giving Haven second, and even third, thoughts. But what good were second and third thoughts when he was offering her the one thing she'd thought she'd lost? She couldn't think of herself right now. She had to think of Anna. She had to do what was best for the precious child Melinda had entrusted to her care.

Lack of sleep, coupled with her constant state of worry, finally took its toll. Haven suddenly felt so weary she could barely hold up her head. Leaning forward, she planted her elbows on her desk and her face in her palms.

"This is impossible," she muttered, shaking her head from side to side.

"You are over twenty-one?" Brady asked.

"Yes."

"You're not legally bound to anyone else?"

Slowly, she looked up. "You know I'm not."

He spread his hands. "Then it's not impossible. Legally, nothing is standing in the way of our getting married. All we need is a license and a judge. It's really very easy. It's also the right thing to do."

Haven stared at him in mounting frustration. What a baffling, infuriatingly enigmatic man!

"Do you always do what's right?" she challenged, ignoring

the fact she'd asked him to do just that when she'd begged him to claim Anna publicly as his daughter.

"I try."

"No matter how hard it is?"

"Doing what's right is rarely easy, but it's always right."

He sounded just like a teacher. Or a parent. "I'll bet you were an Eagle Scout by thirteen," she said.

The glimmer of a smile curved his lips. "When I was thirteen, Haven, I was a hood. I majored in trouble and minored in suspensions. Mothers pulled their kids off the street the minute they saw me coming."

So that was why he seemed so dangerous. His past was still as much a part of him as the hair tied back at his neck.

It took a lot of emotion to be a hood, she thought. It took pain, fury, a sense of injustice, feelings of utter helplessness. Things not usually associated with a child of privilege.

"But you're not a hood now," she prompted, hoping he would volunteer more. "Somewhere along the line you changed."

"Outwardly, anyway," he acknowledged. "So what do you say? Shall we get married?"

He really was serious about this, Haven realized. What scared her silly was that she was seriously tempted to say yes.

"It's a heck of a step to take for someone not into commitments," she remarked.

"Don't think of it as a commitment," he said. "Think of it as a temporary measure."

"What happens afterward?"

"We quietly dissolve the marriage. You retain custody of Anna, and I establish visitation rights. We're right back where we are now, plus the Zieglars are gone for good."

"Why are you doing this?" she asked. "So far, the only people I see benefiting from this situation are Anna and me. What's in it for you?"

His gaze probing hers, Brady studied her, as if carefully considering his answer. As the seconds ticked by, the air seemed to take on thickness and weight, pressing in on them, pushing them closer to each other. Instead of feeling claustrophobic, Haven found herself cocooned in a world of softness and light.

The sensation took her breath away. She couldn't think, much less breathe. He was looking at her as if he were trying to crawl inside her skin, to see into the inner workings of her heart and brain, to read the very essence of her soul. The sensation was as erotic as it was disconcerting. Though she could feel the color rising in her cheeks, she couldn't look away.

"Don't you think I would benefit from being with my daughter?" he finally said in a voice that was slightly unsteady.

"Of course," she acknowledged, her own voice raw with emotion.

"Isn't that reason enough, then?"

She shook her head. "I don't think so. You don't have to marry me to be with Anna. All you have to do is assert your parental rights. There's something else, another reason you're willing to marry an absolute stranger. I want to know that reason before I give you an answer."

His smile was pure sin and upped her pulse rate to dangerous levels. It also effectively broke the spell she'd found herself under and served to remind her how dangerous this man actually was. Somehow, she'd forgotten that.

"Maybe," he said, his voice laden with sex, "I want your body badly enough to make the offer."

Haven refused to let him unnerve her. "The time has long since passed when a man thought he had to marry a woman to get her into his bed."

His eyes darkened. "Are you saying that if I ask, you'll come?"

Heaven help her, she probably would. "I'm saying I don't believe you're offering me marriage just to get me into bed. Besides, you already told me it was to be in name only."

He sighed. "What's in it for me, Haven, is that if we marry I won't be removing my daughter from a stable home. It's as simple as that. I told you before how important that was to me."

Yes, he'd told her. But he hadn't explained why. He was a man who would rather have her believe him a bum than reveal something personal about himself. That his reasoning was somehow tied to his adoption and his self-described years as a hood was obvious. Less obvious was how those two parts of his life fit together.

"Why is it so important to you?" she asked.

His gaze shifted away from hers. "I have my reasons."

She waited until the silence forced him to look at her again. "Please, Brady. I really need to know."

A stillness came over him. He was silent for so long she thought he might not answer. When he finally spoke, his voice was a monotone, and he'd fixed his gaze at a point over her right shoulder.

"When I was three years old, the child welfare authorities found me huddled under a table in a roach-infested apartment. My mother had disappeared a couple of days earlier. From what I've been told, my father fled the picture long before that. When they found me, I was eating a bag of flour because it was the only food in the kitchen."

Haven closed her eyes at the horror of his words. Just three years old—Anna's age—and already he'd known too much of the seamier side of life.

"Oh, Brady," she breathed.

He went on as if he hadn't heard her, as if he'd forgotten she was even in the room.

"After that, I was shuttled from foster home to foster home. I counted them once. Between the ages of three and thirteen, which is how old I was when Charles Ross adopted me, I lived in ten foster homes."

Haven knew that beneath his emotionless words lay an unmeasurable pain. She could only imagine the terror he must have experienced the first time he'd bonded with a new family, only to be wrenched from their arms and sent somewhere else. After the third or fourth time, she supposed, he wouldn't have let himself care. And that was assuming his welfare had been entrusted to decent people. She didn't want to think what he would have endured had the homes he'd resided in been less than caring and sympathetic.

No wonder he didn't want to uproot Anna. That he was willing to marry a woman he didn't love in order to spare his daughter a measure of the pain he'd experienced was a testament to his integrity. Haven felt a fierce surge of admiration for him. Brady truly was putting Anna's needs before his own.

His voice had been so matter-of-fact that when he lowered his gaze and she saw his eyes, she drew in a sharp breath at the turbulence roiling in their gray depths. So alive were they with the pain of remembered emotion that she ached to reach out to comfort him, even as she knew by the way he clenched his hands rigidly to his sides that her comfort would be unwelcome.

The question was, would he ever be able to accept comfort from another person, or would he remain stuck forever in what she'd begun to think of as his emotional hibernation? The sadness of that thought made her want to weep.

"How did a man like Charles Ross come to adopt you?" she asked.

Like a campfire snuffed out by a sudden downpour, Brady's eyes went blank. They were once again the cool gray of a misty morning.

"I went for a joyride in his car. He showed up at my hearing, saw something redeemable in me, and shocked everyone in the courtroom by asking to act as my foster father. The judge agreed. A year later, he adopted me."

"Sounds like he turned your life around."

"Without his intervention, my life would have taken a totally different path. I'd probably be in that prison you thought

I was in.'' He drew a deep breath. "So, now you know why it's so important to me that Anna stays with you."

"Yes," she replied, "now I know."

"Then you agree that the only solution is for us to marry."

He made it sound so logical. So unemotional. But there was nothing logical in the way her body reacted to him. There was nothing unemotional in the way she found herself wishing with all her heart that their marriage could be for a different reason entirely.

"It would only be a temporary arrangement?" she found herself asking against her better judgment.

"Just until we make sure the Zieglars are out of Anna's life permanently," he confirmed. "Which brings up another point. We can't tell anyone why we're getting married."

She blinked. "Why not?"

"For Anna's sake, we have to make everyone believe we're marrying for the same reason most everyone else gets married. It's the only way we'll be able to convince the court of the legitimacy of our relationship."

The rational part of her brain agreed with and even approved of the idea. However, the emotional part wanted nothing to do with it.

"You want us to pretend we're in love?" She heard the note of panic in her voice.

"Yes," he said calmly.

She bit down hard on her lip. "I don't think I can do that."

"Would it really be so hard?" He watched her, his gaze steady. "Do you find me so repulsive you can't even stomach the thought of smiling at me, or holding my hand in public? That's really all we have to do, you know. Give the world the appearance of a loving couple."

Haven only wished she found him repulsive. It would make things so much easier. Until this very moment, she hadn't known that lust could be so powerful, so all-consuming. Her heart faltered at the mere thought of holding his hand, and her pulse hummed so fast she feared she would grow dizzy. What she was most afraid of, though, was that the playacting would become real. For her, anyway.

"Can't I even tell Josephine?" If just one person knew, Haven would be able to stay grounded. The line between truth and reality would not be allowed to blur.

He shook his head. "Not even Josephine. By the way, what does she know about me?"

"Nothing."

His eyebrows shot up. "Nothing?"

"I was going to tell her eventually. I just didn't want to burden her right now."

"That makes things easier anyway."

Yes, she supposed it did. "I guess this means we'll have to live under the same roof."

"I think that goes without saying."

"Where's that roof going to be?"

"Since we don't want to uproot Anna, your house seems the most logical place. That, and the fact I'm renting a one-room efficiency."

She eyed him in surprise. "A one-room efficiency? What's a rich man like you doing in a one-room efficiency?"

"My needs are few," he said dismissively, and she knew she'd gotten all the personal revelation she was going to get from him that day.

"What do we do about Josephine?" she asked. "She does live in my third bedroom, you know."

He shrugged. "We'll work something out."

Thoughts of what that something could be made her mouth go dry.

"What do we tell Anna?" she said quickly.

"The truth. That we're getting married. After all, it would look a little odd if this case went to court and she knew nothing about the marriage. Plus, I think she'll notice me hanging around the house."

"You don't want to tell her you're her father?"

"Eventually, when the time is right."

Could she do it? Haven wondered. Could she enter into a loveless marriage with a man she was far too attracted to for her own good? Could she pretend to the outside world that she was in love with him? When she thought of the alternative, she knew she had no choice.

"Have your lawyer draw up a prenuptial agreement for me to sign," she said.

"No agreement will be necessary, Haven. If I'd thought for one minute you'd take advantage of the situation, I never would have extended my offer."

It warmed her to know that he trusted her. He knew she would never use their short marriage to extort money from him, the same way she now knew he'd never try to take Anna away from her.

"When do you want to do this?"

"How does Saturday sound?"

Entirely too soon. "Can we pull it off so quickly?"

"Allegheny County law requires a blood test and a three-day waiting period, but I know someone who can help us bend the rules a little. How about we meet at lunch and apply for the license? We can also use the time to work up a cover story to tell everyone when we announce our news."

She looked at him with new respect. "How does a man who's not into commitments know so much about Allegheny County's marriage requirements?"

He rose from his chair and walked to the door. "Several years back, I helped a friend of mine elope."

He didn't believe in love, but he'd helped a friend to elope? He didn't believe in commitment, but he was willing to enter into one for the sake of a little girl? Was there no end to the contradictions that went into the making of one extremely puzzling man named Brady Ross?

"I think you should plan on coming to dinner again tonight," she said. "We'd better tell Josephine first."

"I'll be there. See you at noon." He paused, one hand on

the doorknob. "By the way," he said, "are you allergic to cats?"

For hours after the arrangements for his marriage had been completed, Brady walked the city streets. His thoughts raced around in his brain like the three blind mice with their tails chopped off. When his legs threatened to buckle from exhaustion, he reclaimed his car from its parking space and began driving.

From the moment Haven told him about the petition, there had been no question that he would do anything to keep the Zieglars away from Anna. No question that he didn't know the first thing about being a single parent to a little girl. No question that he would not remove Anna from the security of Haven's home. Marriage had been the only option. He'd made the decision willingly and with his eyes open. He didn't regret it.

So why was his mind in such a turmoil?

Because of a woman. A beautiful woman with red hair, creamy soft skin and bottomless blue eyes. A dangerous woman, whose power lay not in her beautiful face, which he enjoyed looking at far more than was sensible, but in her love for a little girl who wasn't even her daughter. To Anna, Haven Adams was everything Brady had ever dreamed of in a mother. That was far more seductive than mere physical beauty alone.

Beginning with his own mother, the women in Brady's life had been anything but gentle and nurturing. Even the women he'd dated hadn't been able to see past his adoptive father's fortune and his bad-boy behavior to the man he was inside. As a result, he'd remained relatively untouched by them. To be fair, a few of his foster mothers had tried to get close, but by that time he'd grown so hardened by his experiences he hadn't been willing to give them a chance. With her fierce protectiveness of his daughter, Haven had revived a part of his heart that Brady had thought long past resuscitation.

Try as he might, he couldn't forget how she'd looked when she'd pleaded with him to assert his parental rights and claim Anna. He couldn't forget the shadows under her eyes that had bespoken her sleepless night and had made her beauty even more haunting and ethereal. He couldn't forget the look of horror on her expressive face when, at her incessant prodding, he'd recounted the events of his childhood.

Still, that didn't mean he was about to behave like a damn fool and fall for the woman. He knew better than to do that, although refusing to be drawn to her was taking on the proportions of a full-time job. Being a part of his daughter's life meant dealing with Haven Adams on a recurring basis. It meant marrying her temporarily to ensure Anna's safety. If they had an affair, it would only make their dealings more difficult once it ended. And it would end, just as their marriage would. It always did.

The last thing he wanted to think about right now was how an affair would be sanctioned legally once they were married.

Surprise jolted through him when he looked out the windshield and saw he'd brought the car to a halt in the driveway of a two-story stone house with green shutters. Then he smiled. His subconscious had directed him to the one place he needed to be right now. Though he and Haven had discussed having people from the center act as witnesses at their marriage, he now knew exactly who he wanted to have by his side on Saturday.

Ambivalence forgotten, Brady climbed out of the car and hurried up the curved cobblestone path. Anticipation filled him as he raised his hand and pressed the doorbell.

The door was flung open by a giant with curly black hair, scowling blue eyes that were almost hidden by bushy black eyebrows, and hands as big as hams. When the giant saw Brady, incredulity crossed a homely face made even more so by the crooked nose that had been broken at least a dozen times. A second later, Brady found himself engulfed in a bear hug so tight he couldn't breathe.

"Careful," he managed to gasp. "My...ribs...aren't as strong...as they used to be."

"Brady, you son of a gun!" Pete Loring roared in a voice deeper than a cellar. "You're back."

Grabbing Brady by the arm, his former foster brother hauled him inside and closed the door. Wincing, Brady gingerly moved his shoulder to make sure it hadn't pulled loose from its socket, while Pete boomed, "Eileen, come quick. Brady's here!"

Eileen Loring was as round as her husband was tall. She'd been born with a happy face that was a perfect circle, with warm brown eyes, a button nose and a mouth that tilted upward even when she was angry. Her hug was just as fierce as her husband's.

"Look at you," she groused when she stood back to examine him. "You're so thin! There's no meat on you. Come on out to the kitchen this minute. I have an apple pie just waiting to be sliced."

"We couldn't get much out of the army, other than you'd been taken hostage," Pete said after he and Brady had taken a seat at a rectangular oak table. "Every time I called, they gave me the same runaround. Said you were okay, that they were negotiating for your release, and no, they couldn't give me a definite date for your return."

Pete looked him over from head to toe. "You seem to have survived your adventure well enough."

Leave it to Pete, Brady thought gratefully, to downplay the entire ordeal. It was, he knew, out of deference to his wife's tender sensibilities, and not to a lack of caring. Eileen had the gentlest heart Brady had ever encountered. Pete refused to take her to see any movie that wasn't a comedy, because dramas made her sob so much. She cried at the news, and when she heard a sad story. She even grew misty-eyed when someone stepped on a bug.

"Yes," Brady said, "I survived." He gazed at the big man

seated across from him and felt a lump lodge in his throat. "Damn, Pete, I've missed you."

They'd known each other since they were twelve and both had been sent to the same foster home. If possible, Pete Loring had been even wilder and more uncontrollable than Brady. It was a wonder his foster parents had survived the two of them. Or put up with them for longer than twenty minutes. Popular opinion at the time had held that they'd both come to a sorry end. But, by some miracle, they hadn't. They'd both been turned around: Brady by Charles Ross, and Pete by a strong, spirited, tenderhearted young woman named Eileen Tobias.

"I've missed you, too, bro," Pete said. "What happened to the mission?"

"I don't really know for sure. Everything went wrong from the beginning. The weather was bad, and the plane went off course. I broke my leg when I parachuted. Next thing I knew, I was staring up the wrong end of a submachine gun."

"Did they treat you badly?" Eileen asked, her concern obvious. "Is that why you're so thin, why you're limping?"

Not even for Eileen would he recount the horror of those years. "I limp because my leg was never set properly. As for my accommodations, let's just say they weren't the Ritz. But I made it through. A few didn't."

"I prayed for you every night," she said softly. He could see the tears gathering in her eyes.

Emotion made it difficult for Brady to speak. "Thanks. I appreciate it."

Pete cleared his throat, and Brady knew the professional wrestler known as Killer was as moved as he'd been by Eileen's words. "Let's not talk about this anymore," he declared. "Brady's back, and that's all that matters."

The slice of pie Eileen placed in front of him was large enough to feed three men. "I want you to eat every bite," she ordered as she took her seat at the head of the table.

"What are you going to do now?" Pete asked.

"For starters," Brady said, picking up his fork, "I quit the army."

"Hallelujah!" Eileen cried. "Does this mean you've finally had your craving for danger knocked out of you?"

"Like candy from a piñata."

"It's about time," she said with satisfaction.

"What are you going to do with yourself, now that Uncle Sam has released you to your own devices?" Pete asked.

"I haven't the faintest idea."

"Talk about a midlife crisis." Pete took a bite of pie and chewed.

Brady followed suit. The home-baked pie tasted so good he thought he'd die from the sheer pleasure of it. "Tell me about it." Eagerly, he forked up another mouthful. "And I'm only thirty-two."

"You'll figure out something to occupy your time," Eileen said. "I have faith in you."

Brady wished he had that much faith in himself.

He surprised himself by polishing off the entire piece, plus seconds. He waited until he'd swallowed the last crumb, placed his folded napkin on top of the table and loosened his belt a notch before dropping his bombshell.

"I'm getting married this Saturday. I was hoping the two of you would stand up for me."

As he'd expected, a deafening silence greeted his announcement. Eyes wide and mouths hanging open, Pete and Eileen stared at him.

"Hey," he joked, "what's going on here? You two look like I just asked you to rob a bank."

"You're getting married?" Pete asked at the same time Eileen sputtered, "You're in love?"

"To a woman?" Pete added, while Eileen said, "With a woman?"

This was it, Brady thought. His first test. He smiled what he hoped was the smile of a man looking forward to his coming nuptials. "Yes, I'm getting married to a woman. And yes, we're in love. Isn't anyone going to congratulate me?"

Pete reached out a meaty hand to cuff Brady on the arm. "Congratulations, brother," he said heartily. "This is great news. Isn't it, honey?"

Eileen still looked bewildered. "Who is she? How'd you two meet? I thought you just got back."

Rubbing his now-sore upper arm, Brady related the story he and Haven had concocted on the drive to apply for their marriage license. They'd decided that, to allay suspicion, they would tell everyone they'd met years ago, when he was dating Melinda. Thank goodness Haven was a runner. The story they'd fashioned was that they'd run into each other again while both were out jogging, and had struck up a conversation. A conversation they'd continued for the next twenty days, at which point they realized they were in love. He made no mention of Anna, other than to say she was Haven's ward. Nor did he mention his paternity or the custody suit. The truth would come out soon enough. When it did, hopefully their saying that their initial meeting had been through Melinda would explain the strange coincidence of his turning out to be Anna's father.

"I don't know," Eileen said when he'd finished. "It's too soon. What if this Haven person breaks your heart?"

Brady choked. He'd expected her to demand that he have a prenuptial agreement drawn up to protect his fortune. Her question about his emotional welfare caught him completely off guard. Could Haven break his heart? A few days ago he would have said he didn't have a heart to break. But a few days ago he hadn't met Anna or Haven.

"Hey," he said. "This is me you're talking to. The one who helped you elope, remember?"

"Come on, honey," Pete said. "Give the guy a break. After what he's been through, he deserves a little happiness, don't you think?"

"Of course I do." Her expression cleared, and she reached

across the table to give his hand a hard squeeze. "Congratulations, Brady. I'm very happy for you. But I'm warning you right now. Come Saturday, I'm going to have my eye on this Haven person of yours. If I don't like what I see, when the justice of the peace gets to the part about anyone objecting, expect to hear my voice loud and clear."

"All I expect to hear," Pete told Brady, "is a lot of loud sobbing. You may or may not be making a mistake, but my wife is most definitely a sucker for weddings."

Haven's nerves were stretched to the breaking point by the time Brady arrived that evening. She didn't know how she was going to make it through dinner, much less pull off the act she and Brady were slated to perform. She could tell from the questioning looks the older woman kept tossing her that Josephine knew something was up. But so far, her former nanny hadn't pried. Haven knew better than to think that state of affairs would last for long.

Brady took one look at Haven after she opened the door and asked, "Are you okay?"

The smile she gave him was shaky at best. "The truth? I think I'm going to be sick."

"No, you're not," he stated confidently. "This is for Anna, remember? Don't worry, you won't be alone. I'll be right by your side."

Strangely enough, his words comforted her.

"Ready?" he asked.

She drew a deep breath and straightened her shoulders. "As I'll ever be."

"Let's go, then."

"Hi, Unca Bwady," Anna said when they reached the dining room. "Did you bwing me sumfing tonight?"

"Anna!" Haven admonished, bending down to the little girl. "It's not polite to ask for gifts."

"Sowwy."

"That's all right. Why don't you go sit down while I introduce Uncle Brady to Josephine. Scoot."

Obediently, the little girl skipped over to the table and climbed into the booster seat that had been set atop a chair. Haven straightened. When her gaze met Josephine's, the woman's raised eyebrows let her know that she was now aware that Anna had already met Brady, and that he'd obviously been to the house. Frankly, Haven had been surprised to get through breakfast that morning without Anna mentioning her newfound uncle and the teddy bear he'd brought her. Coward that she was, she'd been vastly relieved when all the little girl could chat about was the clown they'd booked for her birthday party next week.

Taking Brady by the arm, she walked him over to Josephine. "Josie, this is Brady Ross. Brady, this is Josephine, my right hand."

"Hello, Josephine," Brady said with a smile. "I've heard a lot about you."

Josephine looked Brady up and down. "Well, I, for one, certainly haven't heard enough about you. Have a seat, child. Let's chat."

Things were going well, Haven thought later, as dinner drew to a close. In fact, they were going much better than she'd anticipated. Oh, Brady didn't seem to have much of an appetite, which wasn't surprising. And he was still hesitant around Anna, treating her as if she were a porcelain doll who might break if he didn't handle her just right. But Josephine seemed genuinely charmed by him. Yes, things were going well. Maybe all Haven's worries had been for nothing.

She waited until Anna had climbed down from the table and disappeared into the den to play before summoning up what she hoped was a brilliant smile. "Brady and I have an announcement to make, Josie. We're getting married this Saturday."

Josephine's fork clattered to her plate. "What?"

Brady reached over and threaded his fingers through hers. "We're getting married."

The older woman was silent for a long moment before directing her gaze at Haven. "May I speak to you in private, please?"

The way she was feeling, if Josephine got her alone, her story would fall apart in less than thirty seconds. She had a feeling Brady knew that, too, because he gave her hand a supportive squeeze.

"Anything you have to say to me, you can say in front of Brady."

"All right, then. I don't like it, child. I don't like it one bit." Josephine glanced at Brady. "No offense."

"None taken," he said. "I understand your concern."

Haven felt awful. She hated lying, especially to the woman who'd been more of a mother to her than her own mother. What distressed her even more was how skilled she was becoming at it. Even though she kept telling herself it was all for Anna, it didn't make her feel any better.

"Why are you so upset, Josie? You certainly seemed happy enough a couple of days ago, when you found out there was a man in my life."

"A couple of days ago you said nothing about marriage. You two first met, what, four years ago for a very brief time? And then you ran into each other again just three weeks ago? Child, you don't begin to know thing one about him. And he doesn't know you. What's the rush?"

"I know it seems sudden," Haven said. "But we love each other. I'm twenty-eight years old. I think I'm old enough to recognize love when it finally comes my way. My mind is made up, Josie. I know I'm doing the right thing."

"You really love him?"

Would there be no end to the lies she would have to tell? And would Josephine ever speak to her again when she found out about Brady's paternity and the custody suit? She was doing this for Anna, Haven reminded herself. Right now, that was all the justification she needed.

"Yes, Josie, I really love him."

Josephine turned her gaze to Brady. "You love her?"

"With all my heart," he replied solemnly.

"You don't have to worry," Haven assured the woman. "You'll always have a place here. We both want you to stay."

Josephine shook her head. "No, child. The minute you two marry, I'm moving out."

Stunned, Haven stared at the older woman. "But...why?"

"Because of an old saying. Remember the one about two being company and three a crowd? Once you're married, you're on your own. You two have to build a life together. I'd just be in the way."

"But you can't..." Haven protested.

"Can't what?" Josephine asked.

Leave me alone with him. "Nothing," she replied. Deep down, she felt a sense of relief that Josephine would be leaving. That way, Brady could bunk down in the spare bedroom, instead of having to share with Haven.

"Where will you stay?" she asked.

"With Jackson, of course. He's been asking me to move in with him for months now." The woman smiled. "Who knows, I might even be able to get him to follow your example."

Haven was happy for her friend. She hoped things worked out the way Josephine wanted them to. "I know you don't approve, but will you stand up for me? Will you be my maid of honor?"

Josephine's brown eyes filled with the warmth of love. "Of course I will, child. You know I'd do anything for you. What time's the wedding?"

"Saturday at noon."

"I'll be there in my best dress." The woman cleared her throat and stood up. "Now, come on, you two. Help me clear this table."

Chapter 6

Saturday morning arrived with indecent haste. After spending a couple of hours playing with Anna, Haven left the little girl to Josephine's gentle ministrations and retired to her room to dress. It didn't take her long to get ready, which left her some much needed time to compose herself before facing the man who would shortly become her husband.

Her husband. Haven drew a deep breath as desperation hummed through her.

"Talk me out of this," she whispered to her reflection in the mirror.

The face that gazed back at her remained mute. Instead of looking drawn and pale with anxiety, she appeared almost serene. The only hint that something out of the ordinary was happening was the flush in her cheeks and the sparkle of—could it be anticipation?—in her eyes. Anyone who wasn't in the know—which was everyone, really—would think she was actually looking forward to this marriage.

"Ridiculous," she said out loud. The color in her cheeks was surely the result of too much sun, and the sparkle in her eyes could be explained as a desire to get this farce over with as soon as possible. If she was looking forward to anything, it was to getting the Zieglars out of Anna's life forever.

A glance at her watch told her it was almost time to leave. Haven ran a comb through her unruly curls and checked to see that her lipstick was on straight. Then, squaring her shoulders and taking a deep breath, she went downstairs.

The living room was empty, but she heard a low murmuring coming from the kitchen.

"You two ready?" she called in a voice that wasn't quite steady.

"Be there in a minute," Josephine called back.

Too restless to sit, Haven walked to the window and parted the drapes that had been drawn to protect the dark-blue carpet from the midday sun. To her surprise, sheets of rain pounded the earth. When she'd gone upstairs to dress an hour ago, she could have sworn there hadn't been a cloud in the sky.

"Happy is the bride the sun shines on," she murmured.

A stirring of unease flitted up her spine. At least it wasn't lightning and thundering, she told herself. That would have been too much.

She wasn't superstitious, and she didn't believe in omens. But if the rain that was falling with a force greater than a waterfall wasn't a sign, she didn't know what was. It didn't take a genius to decipher its meaning. She was making a mockery out of the institution of marriage, and there most certainly would be a penalty to pay.

Haven allowed the curtain to fall back into place. She'd gladly pay any penalty, no matter how steep, if it guaranteed Anna's safety and happiness.

"Pwetty, Binny," she heard Anna say.

Whirling, she turned to face the doorway, where Josephine stood in her Sunday best, Anna beside her. The little girl looked adorable in a pink cotton dress and white patent leather shoes, her hair pulled back with a lacy bow. Josephine had used matching lace to fancy up the cast on the child's wrist.

"You look pretty too, sweetheart," Haven said, her heart squeezing with love. Seeing the child gave her renewed courage. She was doing the right thing. She wouldn't allow herself to falter again.

Standing in silence, she waited while Josephine's brown eyes narrowed shrewdly to study the pale-blue silk dress Haven had bought the day before. She hadn't set out to buy anything new for the ceremony, hadn't wanted to make more of the occasion than it really was. But when she'd seen the dress hanging in the store window, she hadn't been able to resist. It was sleeveless, with a curved neckline dipping low enough to reveal a hint of cleavage, and the soft silk fell in layers from an empire waist to swirl around her calves. Haven felt almost like a princess wearing it. That she'd chosen to wear it this day was a puzzle she didn't care to solve just now.

When Josephine finished her inspection, there were tears in her eyes. "Oh, child," she said softly, "you are the most beautiful bride I've ever seen." She sniffed. "I think I'm going to cry."

To Haven's dismay, she felt tears welling in her own eyes. She'd been counting on Josephine's no-nonsense approach to life to get her through the ordeal with some modicum of dignity.

"Don't you dare go getting sentimental on me," Haven warned sharply, "or I swear I'll...I'll..."

"You'll what, child?"

"I'll fire you, that's what."

"Never happen," Josephine said with a confident smile and a shake of her head. "I'm indispensable. Surely I've taught you that by now. You couldn't manage without me."

Relieved that the emotional moment had passed, Haven chuckled. "What can I say? When you're right, you're right."

"Ready to go?" Josephine asked.

"Ready as I'll ever be. Guess we'd better grab some umbrellas, though. It's raining like crazy out there."

A quizzical look crossed Josephine's broad features. "What rain? It's not raining."

Sure enough, when Haven parted the curtain again, the sky had cleared and the sun blazed down. Bemused, she shook her head. Had she just imagined the downpour? No, the puddles on the sidewalk bore mute testimony to the fact that it had been raining just minutes earlier.

"Must have been a cloudburst," she murmured. The kind that was over almost as soon as it had begun.

A gentle hand squeezed her shoulder. "Let's go," Josephine said tenderly. "We don't want to keep your bridegroom waiting."

"Come on, Binny," Anna added. "Let's get mawwied."

The guilt that had been her constant companion for the past few days stabbed at Haven again as she followed Josephine and Anna outside. If only Josephine were still suspicious, still leery about the wisdom of this marriage, the whole ordeal might have been easier for Haven to bear.

But Josephine no longer opposed her marrying Brady. The act she and Brady had put on must have been more convincing than she'd realized at the time, because somewhere during the last three days, Josephine had taken it into her head that this wedding was the most romantic happening since King Edward VIII had abdicated the throne for Wallace Simpson. The older woman's unexpected reaction had made Haven feel so miserable she'd nearly blurted out the truth a dozen times. Only the knowledge that she was carrying out this charade for Anna's sake had kept her quiet.

Last night, though, had nearly broken her. While she was making a last minute run-through of the center prior to locking up, she'd heard voices coming from what should have been an empty cafeteria. A chorus of "Surprise!" when she'd opened the door to investigate had nearly scared ten years off her life. It had taken the better part of a minute to understand that she'd stumbled upon a surprise wedding shower, a shower arranged by Josephine, and that she was the guest of honor.

Haven had spent the next two uncomfortable hours oohing and aahing over beautiful presents she didn't deserve and receiving well wishes from the people who mattered to her most. Her deceit had become unbearable. Small wonder she hadn't fallen asleep until after four in the morning.

"Are you sure you two don't want to get away for a while?" Josephine asked as Haven buckled Anna into her car seat. "A weekend honeymoon with a toddler underfoot just doesn't seem romantic."

The thought of a real honeymoon with Brady made Haven's stomach dip and sway.

"It's our first weekend as a family," she replied. "Brady and I want to spend it that way, with all of us together." Lord, but she was becoming an accomplished liar, she thought in dismay.

Josephine shrugged. "Whatever you say."

They were the first to arrive. The office of the justice of the peace, which was located in a six-story brick building, seemed deserted when Haven and Josephine entered, Anna between them.

"Hello?" she called. "Anyone here?"

"Be right with you," a man called back, his voice filtering through a crack in a door to her right. "Make yourself at home."

The reception area was small and cramped. An old battered metal desk, matching file cabinet and four cracked vinyl armchairs the color of rusty water took up most of the floor space. The carpet beneath their feet, a fraying and faded imitation Oriental, released a musty odor with each footfall. Not exactly the surroundings Haven had pictured whenever she'd imagined what it would be like to get married. But then, in those same fantasies, she'd always dreamed she would marry for love.

A glance at her watch told her it was five minutes after twelve.

"He's late," she murmured. "Maybe he's standing me up."

She didn't know whether to feel relieved or disappointed at the thought.

"That's just bridal jitters talking," Josephine stated with confidence. "He's probably on his way up in the elevator right now. Don't worry, child. He'll be here." She snapped her fingers. "Before I forget, I brought you something."

Haven suppressed a groan of dismay. "Oh, Josie," she protested, "you shouldn't have. You've done too much already."

Josephine waved away her protest with one hand while rummaging through her purse with the other, and the old saying about tangled webs and lies echoed in Haven's head. It really was true that one small lie could snowball into something as big as the national debt. If she somehow managed to untangle herself from this mess with any friends left, Haven promised herself she would never tell another lie for as long as she lived.

"Here it is," Josephine cried triumphantly. She pulled a black velvet jewelry box from her purse and thrust it at Haven. "Your dress covers the something new and blue. I thought you might also like something old and borrowed."

Reluctantly, Haven lifted the lid of the velvet box. Nestled inside was a set of perfectly matched silvery white pearls. She stared at them wordlessly for a long moment before raising tear-filled eyes to her friend.

"I don't know what to say. They're beautiful."

"They're my mother's," Josephine replied with an understanding smile. "She wore them the day she married my father, and they've lived happily together for almost fifty years. I thought they might bring you luck."

She'd need more than luck to make this marriage last, Haven thought as she blinked back her tears. She'd need a blooming miracle.

Josephine lifted the necklace from the box and clasped it around Haven's throat. The pearls felt cool and smooth, and oddly comforting.

"One more thing," Josephine said. Like Mary Poppins pulling a brass lamp from her carryall, Josephine reached into her purse and withdrew a small bouquet of red roses and baby's breath.

"I know you didn't want to make a big production out of this," she said, handing them to Haven, "but you can't have a wedding without flowers."

Haven couldn't take it any longer. She couldn't keep on lying. Not to this woman who had done so much for her. Determined to set the record straight, she drew a deep, bracing breath.

"Josephine, I—"

The words caught in her throat when the door opened and a man and a woman entered, followed closely by Brady. Haven barely had time to register that the man was built along the lines of Paul Bunyan and that the woman had a round, sunny face, before her gaze became riveted on her husband-to-be.

For one long moment she couldn't breathe, couldn't move, couldn't think, couldn't do anything but stare while a disconcerting warmth suffused her. Brady was here. And he looked magnificent in a black tuxedo and crisp white shirt.

When she saw that his shirt was open at the collar, and that his black tie hung loosely around his neck, she was blindsided by an overwhelming urge to fasten it for him. She had to curl her fingers into her palms to keep from reaching out to do just that.

But what really took her breath away, and robbed her of her composure, was his hair. He'd gotten it cut. It had been clipped in a military style, not quite a buzz cut, but certainly shorter than the current fashion. Though she hadn't thought it possible, the close-cropped hair made him look even more masculine, more dangerous. It accentuated the planes and angles of his face, making his presence seem even more powerful. What it didn't do was make him look more respectable, and for that she was fiercely glad. She would have hated to see that part of him diminished, the way Samson's strength had been diminished by the loss of his hair.

"Excuse me," the man who looked like Paul Bunyan said as he stepped forward, "but I have the feeling I could grow old and die before my friend here introduced us. I'll forgive him, though, since he's so obviously taken with the beauty of his bride-to-be." He held out his hand. "I'm Pete Loring, and this is my wife, Eileen."

Absently, Haven shook the proffered hand. She didn't speak. She couldn't. She was too busy staring at Brady.

"Josephine Clark," she dimly heard her maid of honor say. "As you've already guessed, the woman with her mouth hanging on the floor is the bride."

Haven gave herself a mental shake and snapped her mouth shut. "Thank you for coming," she said, offering her hand to Eileen Loring.

For the briefest of seconds, the woman appeared to hesitate, her probing gaze raking Haven from head to toe. Whatever she saw must have reassured her, because she gave Haven a broad smile before pumping her arm vigorously.

"Happy to be here," she said. "I wouldn't have missed this for the world." She turned to Brady and added, "I don't think I'll be protesting this afternoon."

Haven wondered what the woman meant, but didn't feel free to ask.

The door to her right creaked slowly open on hinges that hadn't been oiled in years. When she looked over, she saw an elderly man framed in the doorway. His reed-thin body seemed so frail, and his shoulders so stooped, she almost expected his bones to creak in protest when he moved, the way his office door had.

"Good morning, everybody," he boomed in a voice that was anything but frail. His step, too, when he approached them was surprisingly spry, and his brown eyes sparkled with intelligence and humor. "I'm Christopher Eriksson. I assume you're my wedding party?"

"Yes, Mr. Eriksson," Brady said, reaching into his suit jacket for the necessary paperwork.

"'Christopher' will do just fine. 'Mr. Eriksson' sounds so stuffy, don't you think? Makes me feel like an old man." He grinned, then looked at the papers Brady had handed him. "Everything appears to be in order. Are the witnesses here?"

"All present and accounted for," Josephine said.

"Excellent, excellent." He beamed down at Anna. "And who's this lovely lady? The bride?"

Anna giggled. "No, silly. I'm Anna. Binny's getting mawwied to Unca Bwady."

Christopher Eriksson nodded. "So she is. So she is. Shall we proceed?"

"Just a minute," Eileen said, then busied herself with Brady's shirt and tie. When she finished, she patted Brady on the chest and smiled her approval. "Now we're ready."

"Will the bride and groom please join hands?"

Brady moved to stand next to her. Eyes hooded, he gazed at her and offered his hand. "You look beautiful," he murmured.

His words made her heart pound. "I like your haircut," she murmured back.

Brady's hand closed over hers, and a rush of heat surged through her. Though she tried, Haven couldn't suppress the tremors that shook her body at the contact, especially when he squeezed her hand tightly and the pad of his thumb caressed the inside of her wrist.

He lowered his head so that only she could hear him speak. "It's not too late, you know. We don't have to do this if you don't want to."

Grateful that he'd mistaken the source of her trembling as nerves, she shook her head. "I want to."

"Dear friends," Christopher Eriksson intoned, "we are assembled here today to witness and celebrate the joining of two lives in marriage. Brady and Haven have asked us to be with them, to rejoice with them in the making of this important commitment...."

Haven tried to remain unmoved. She tried to remain level-headed and objective. *This isn't for real,* she told herself over and over like a mantra.

But when, in a tone of awed reverence, the justice of the peace spoke the age-old words about love and the joining of two into one, she forgot her surroundings and became caught up in the spirit of the simple ceremony. Would it be so terrible to just, for one minute, pretend this was real, that she and Brady were pledging their troth to each other? she wondered dreamily. Who would it hurt? The outcome would be the same regardless.

"Do you, Brady, take Haven to be the wife of your days, to love and to cherish, to honor and to comfort, in sorrow and in joy, in hardship and in ease, to have and to hold from this day forward?"

Brady's eyes glittered down at her. "I do," he said, his voice strong and even.

Behind them, she heard Josephine sniffle.

"And do you, Haven, take Brady to be the husband of your days, to love and to cherish, to honor and to comfort, in sorrow and in joy, in hardship and in ease, to have and to hold from this day forward?"

"I do," she whispered.

"Who has the ring?" Christopher Eriksson asked.

Pete Loring fumbled in his pocket, then handed the smooth gold sphere to Brady, who placed it on her finger.

"With this ring," he repeated after Christopher Eriksson, his voice low and husky, "I marry you and pledge my faithful love."

He really was a marvelous actor, Haven thought. The tone of his voice and the look in his eyes almost had her convinced that he meant every word of the vow. If she didn't know firsthand exactly how much rigid self-control he exercised over his emotions, she could almost believe he had become as caught up in things as she had.

And she'd do well to remember that they were *both* play-acting.

The justice of the peace spoke above their heads to the trio behind them. "For as much as Brady and Haven have consented together in wedlock, and have pledged themselves each to the other in the presence of this company, I do now pronounce that they are husband and wife. Let all others honor their decision and the threshold of their home." He looked meaningfully at Brady. "You may kiss your bride."

Bride, Haven thought fuzzily. She was a bride. The significance of Christopher Eriksson's words penetrated her bemusement, and she felt her eyes widen. She'd forgotten all about the first, obligatory kiss.

Brady's gaze, dark and restless, dropped to her mouth, and she caught her breath. Slowly, he reached out to her, his hands sliding up her bare arms and gently pulling her toward him. Helpless to fight the rush of desire that coiled in her stomach at his touch, Haven tilted her head back, closed her eyes and mentally steeled herself for the brush of his lips against hers.

It's just a simple little kiss, she told herself. *Nothing to get excited about. One second, and it'll all be over.*

She wasn't prepared for the jolt of electricity that shot through her at the gentle pressure of his mouth. Nor was she prepared for the way every nerve ending in her body roared to full, throbbing life.

When Brady lifted his mouth from hers, she felt bereft. Time hung suspended as he gazed at her, his eyes questioning. Then, a low moan escaping his throat, his mouth crushed hers with an intensity that made Haven's heart ricochet against her ribs. Her knees went so weak she had to clutch at his lapels to keep from falling.

The world turned upside down as his hands moved from her shoulders to her waist, molding her body to his so tightly she could feel the beating of his heart. Of their own accord, her hands lifted from his lapels to slide across his broad shoulders. She wound her arms around his neck and buried her fingers in the springiness of his hair.

No man's kiss had ever made her feel this way. No man's

touch had ever reduced her to such a mass of quivering need. At that moment, if Haven had had three wishes, the first would have been that the kiss go on forever.

"Now, that's what I call a kiss," Pete Loring said, his voice threaded with amusement.

Haven felt Brady's body jerk. The next thing she knew, he was prying her arms from around his neck and thrusting her away from him. Lips throbbing, she stared at him in stunned silence. He stared back, his breathing ragged.

It dawned on her then. The emotion in his eyes was real. For once in his life, Brady Ross had lost control. He wasn't playacting. He was as affected by the kiss as she was.

This was not good. Just how were they expected to live under the same roof—alone but for Anna—without giving in to the passion that still vibrated in the air like a tuning fork? A passion that was now sanctioned by law.

It would be sheer folly to surrender to the emotions swirling through her. Because of Anna, she and Brady would always be in contact. If they slaked their passion for each other, once it was extinguished—as it inevitably would be—they would still have to deal with each other. It would only make things more difficult than they needed to be. And when Haven did give herself to a man, she wanted him to be able to share his deepest thoughts and feelings with her openly.

No one could accuse Brady of being an open book.

Embarrassed by her loss of control, Haven pulled her gaze away, only to discover Christopher Eriksson beaming at them with paternal approval. As for the women, it was painfully obvious they were both hopeless romantics. It was a toss-up who was sobbing louder, Josephine or Eileen.

He was a married man. Brady turned that thought over and over in his brain as he followed Josephine on a guided tour through Haven's house. He saw little and absorbed even less. The only reality that mattered to him was that he was now married, and all he could think about was making love to his bride.

What had gotten into him? he wondered in disgust as desire roared through him. Everything was supposed to have been so simple. A short wedding, followed by a short marriage, and then a quickie divorce. But nothing, from the moment he awoke that morning till he said "I do," had gone the way it was supposed to. He had the sinking feeling the near future held more of the same.

It all started when he'd opened his closet door and realized that barring his military dress blues, which were inappropriate for the occasion because he was no longer in the service, the only other suit he owned was a tuxedo. He'd felt ridiculous putting it on, even more so when he'd looked into a mirror and seen his hair.

It probably had something to do with his military training; whatever the case, he hadn't been able to reconcile the formality of a tuxedo with long, flowing hair. Since he'd had only an hour until the wedding, he'd jumped into his car, tux and all, and driven straight to a barbershop.

He'd withstood Pete's teasing about the monkey suit well enough on the drive to the justice of the peace. He'd even taken the sudden rain in stride, although the rapid change from clear sky to raging downpour and then back again had been more than a little disconcerting. But it had all fallen apart when they'd arrived at their destination and he'd seen Haven in that dress. He'd known then he was in trouble. Big trouble.

That dress. Brady's mouth went dry all over again at the memory of how the folds had clung to her body. She'd looked like a fairy princess, so chaste, and yet so provocative. His imagination had gone into overdrive trying to envision the precise dimensions of the curves the dress so teasingly covered.

As disquieting as his overwhelming desire for Haven had been, it was nothing compared with his reaction to the wedding ceremony itself. What he'd never expected in a million years was that he would get so caught up in the whole thing. He wasn't a sentimental man. Even so, he'd been moved nearly to the point of tears by the eloquent words spoken by the justice of the peace. So moved that he'd found himself repeating his vows with a conviction that had been downright alarming.

And then, of course, there was the kiss. He hadn't meant to kiss her like that. He certainly hadn't meant to lose all self-control. But there had been that look in her fathomless blue eyes when he'd lifted his head after the first brush of his mouth against hers. The look that had begged him for more. And her skin, where he'd touched her, had felt like silk; her hair had smelled like flowers. Everything about her had gone to his head, and he hadn't been able to stop himself. He'd had to taste more.

So here they were, married, the two of them suffering from self-consciousness and going to great pains not to meet the other's gaze.

"This is the guest room." Josephine's words broke into his thoughts.

The walls of the room were pink, as were the rugs scattered across the hardwood floor. A flowered chintz spread covered the brass bed. Matching valances hung at the windows. Feminine, was the only word Brady could think of to describe it adequately. Ultrafeminine. His room, though Josephine couldn't know that.

They were going to have to come up with an excuse for his using it, he realized. Just in case Anna let slip that he and Haven weren't sleeping together. He was fast learning that one couldn't always predict what would come out of a toddler's mouth.

"It's...frilly," he said.

"Haven likes frills."

"I noticed," he replied, dimly recalling the ruffled gingham curtains hanging in the kitchen and the floral wallpaper that had been liberally applied to the walls throughout the house.

He turned to the older woman. "You don't have to leave, you know. Haven and I would be more than happy to have you stay." Although how he would preserve his sanity sharing a bedroom with Haven was anyone's guess.

"Yes, child, I do have to leave. You and Haven have to build a life together, and you'll do it better without me underfoot. I'm giving you fair warning, though." Her eyes and voice turned fierce, protective. "You hurt my girl, you'll answer to me."

What was it about Haven that brought out the protective instinct in everyone? he wondered. Not that she needed protecting. Brady had never met a more self-sufficient woman.

Still, he couldn't deny that he felt the urge to protect her, too. Truth was, he suddenly realized, he hadn't married her to shield Anna from harm. He could have achieved that purpose adequately without marriage. No, he hadn't married Haven to protect Anna. He'd married Haven to protect her from the Zieglars.

"Believe me," he said, "the last thing I want to do is cause Haven any pain."

Josephine nodded. "See that you don't."

Her smile returned then, and she led the way back downstairs. As he followed her into the den, where Haven and Anna played with the kittens he'd found, Brady wondered who was going to protect him.

Chapter 7

This was torture, sheer torture, Haven thought as she pounded her pillow and laid her head in the indentation. Closing her eyes, she willed herself to sleep, but her brain kept ticking away. She couldn't take much more of this. If she didn't fall asleep soon, she was going to lose what little was left of a mind that insisted on playing images of entwined bodies like a screen at an adult movie theater.

Never in all her life—except for a brief period in her early teens, which she discounted as a normal part of the growing-up process—had she obsessed about sex. Yet from the minute her head had hit the pillow at eleven o'clock until now, three hours later, all she'd been able to think about was making love. Specifically, making love with Brady. Why?

Because it was her wedding night, even if her marriage was one of convenience and destined to be short-lived. And because the object of her fantasies was asleep in the room across the hall. He was so close she could swear she heard him breathing.

The thought of Brady's body all tangled up in the pink-and-

white striped sheets adorning the brass bed in her guest bedroom should have brought a smile to her lips. If there was
anyone who would be out of place in that bastion of femininity, it was her brand-new husband.

Instead of making her laugh, however, whenever she pictured his long limbs spread across the mattress, a throbbing
heat gathered in her abdomen. Did he sleep in the nude? she
wondered, then flung one arm across her closed eyes and
groaned when the heat in her lower body intensified.

If only he hadn't kissed her. With one soul-shattering kiss,
he'd awakened a passion in her she hadn't known existed. A
passion only he could slake.

For just a moment, she indulged herself in the fantasy that
she could be the one woman to reach Brady's heart, to make
him open up to her. With gentle love and patient understanding, she would take away all the pain and disillusion. Together,
they would build a life filled with passion and love.

And pigs might fly.

With a sigh, she opened her eyes and stared up at the shadows flitting across her ceiling. So many conflicting emotions
had ebbed and flowed through her body since meeting Brady
Ross she was beginning to feel like an electronic transmitter
that had gone on the blink. Added to the mix were her fears
for Anna and her guilt at deceiving Josephine. Haven no
longer knew what was right or wrong or which way was up.
She didn't even know how she was going to survive the next
five weeks until the hearing—or until the DNA test results
were in and Brady could get his lawsuit heard, whichever
came first—with Brady living under the same roof.

"One day at a time," she murmured. "I'll take it one day,
one minute, one second, at a time."

Nine hundred interminable seconds later, Haven tossed back
her covers and sat up. Obviously, sleep wasn't going to come
any time soon. She might as well do something productive.
What she needed was something brainless, something that
would keep her hands busy while at the same time occupying

her mind so that it wouldn't be distracted by any more unwanted thoughts.

As she slipped silently down the stairs and made her way to the kitchen, she knew just what she was going to do. She was going to bake a cake.

It was quite possible, Brady thought, that before this farce of a marriage was over, he would go stark raving mad.

Shifting restlessly in the brass bed, he folded his arms beneath his head and gazed at the ceiling. If he concentrated hard enough and the limbs of the tree outside his window bent just so in the breeze, he could swear the shadows on the ceiling formed the outline of a woman's face. Haven's face.

Groaning, he closed his eyes. He needed sleep. Badly. Given his current state of mind, however, he had about as much chance of getting it as he did of being struck by lightning where he lay.

Never before had he had any problems sleeping, not even when his bed had been a hard dirt floor. Maybe that was it. Maybe the unaccustomed softness of the mattress was what had kept him awake for going on four hours now. Or maybe the room was just too blasted feminine to give any self-respecting male a peaceful night's rest.

He grimaced. Yeah, right. He could lie to himself all he wanted, but it still wouldn't change the truth. The reason for his insomnia had nothing to do with the softness of the mattress or the femininity of the room's decor. It could be summed up in three short words: Haven Adams Ross.

What brainiac had dreamed up this cockamamy marriage idea anyway? What Einstein had thought marriage and cohabitation the perfect solution to their dilemma?

He groaned again when the answer came to him. It had been him. All the way. He had only himself to blame for his current, miserable, aroused state. He never should have insisted that they marry, and he most certainly never should have moved into her home.

Unfortunately, here he was, married, and here he would stay, until his daughter's future was assured. And Haven Adams *Ross,* his wife, was asleep in the room across the hall.

How could she sleep?

Muttering an oath, Brady tossed the covers aside and sat up. Sliding his legs over the edge of the bed, he looked around the ruffle-bedecked room and decided that this was no place for a man to spend his wedding night.

He knew where he wanted to be: in the room across the hall. More specifically, in Haven's bed. With Haven. He wanted to feel her in his arms, to taste every inch of her. He wanted to bury himself inside her and take them both to a place where nothing mattered but the moment. Barring that, he just wanted to hold her while she slept.

Which shot to hell his theory that it was his more than three years of abstinence ruling his arousal.

This was not good. Nowhere were his developing feelings for Haven included in the plans he'd made. It had taken Charles Ross a full year to break down the defenses he'd erected to protect himself from further pain. It had taken his daughter and Haven Adams just six days to breach those same defenses. Anna's breach he could accept. She was his child; he had a responsibility to give her whatever she demanded from him.

But Haven—if he allowed his feelings for her to deepen and grow, and if she returned them—would make a whole different set of demands. Demands impossible for him to meet.

He was a man at a crossroads who should be trying to determine what his future held, instead of obsessing over a beautiful woman. He didn't need to take a course in psychology to realize that he was also a man who, after too many abandonments, had made a habit of sidestepping all personal involvement. Even Charles's death, involuntary though it had been, had felt like another abandonment and had served to underscore that he did best when he had few emotional ties. With the exception of Anna and the Lorings, Brady had no intention of breaking a habit that had served him so well over the years. Not even for a woman as alluring as his temporary wife. The biggest favor he could do both Haven and himself was to stay out of her way.

He rubbed his palm along the stubble on his cheeks while he tried to figure, at a minimum, how much time he'd have to consciously find a way to keep his distance. Excluding the hours she spent at the center, time they would both spend with Anna, and sleep—if he could ever get any—that left roughly three hours a day that he'd have to spend alone in her company. Considering his three years plus of imprisonment, three hours a day was a snap of the fingers. A cinch. No problem at all.

The only snag was, when he was being held prisoner he hadn't had the added torture of being attracted to his captors. Erotic images flashed through his mind again. Did she wear frilly, lacy things to bed? Or did she favor flannel or, better still, nothing at all?

Yes, Brady thought grimly as his arousal made itself painfully felt, he was well on his way to losing his mind. Otherwise, why would he imagine he smelled a cake baking at three o'clock in the morning? He crinkled his nose and took a deep, appreciative sniff. His stomach rumbled. Chocolate cake, if he wasn't mistaken.

Barefoot, he crossed the room and carefully opened the door. Across the hallway, the door to Haven's bedroom stood ajar.

He felt a moment's satisfaction. She hadn't been able to sleep, either.

The light from the kitchen drew him. As he neared, his footsteps muffled by the carpet, he heard Haven humming softly to herself. It was an old tune, one that had been popular when they were kids, and it was definitely off-key. Way off-key. He grinned at the realization that she was totally tone-deaf.

His grin died when he rounded the corner, and Haven came

into full view. Her back to him, she stood on tiptoe, reaching into an open cupboard. She wore an oversize white T-shirt that fell to midthigh. A riot of auburn curls rested in tangled splendor on her shoulders. Like him, her feet were bare. Beneath the T-shirt he saw the outline of her panties and the long, long legs that seemed to go on forever. There was no outline where her bra should be.

Suddenly, those three hours a day seemed an eternity.

She turned, a box of confectioners' sugar in one hand. The swell of her unbound breasts beneath the thin fabric of the T-shirt was as alluring as it was unmistakable. A smudge of cake batter decorated the tip of her nose.

Brady couldn't move, couldn't think. He couldn't do anything, because all the blood had left his brain to gather in one particular part of his anatomy. A part that throbbed and ached with unbearable intensity. Closing his eyes, he struggled for self-control. When he opened them, he found Haven staring at him, her gaze riveted to his bare chest. Had it been riveted any lower, she would have had irrefutable evidence of the direction his thoughts had turned.

As quickly as he could in his current state, he took a seat at the kitchen's center cooking island, where two layers of chocolate cake sat cooling on a wire rack. To his relief, the countertop hid his lower anatomy from view.

"Hi," he said gruffly.

"Hi," she replied. "Sorry I woke you."

She reached back to close the cupboard door, then moved to stand opposite him. Fascinated, he watched her every movement. With deft fingers, she ripped off the box top and dumped the confectioners' sugar into a stainless-steel bowl.

"You didn't wake me." Striving for nonchalance, he asked, "What are you doing?"

After adding a stick of butter and some vanilla to the bowl, she placed it beneath a mixer. "Making icing for the cake," she said over the whine of the blades.

"You always do your baking at 3 a.m.?"

"Not usually."

He waited, but she didn't elaborate. Not that he needed her to. He knew exactly why she was down here. While it would please his ego to think that an answering desire for him was what was keeping her awake, he was fairly certain her insomnia had a far different cause.

"Does it bother you so much?" he asked.

She placed a cake layer on a white porcelain plate, then dipped a knife into the bowl and began icing it. "Does what bother me?"

"Having to share Anna with me."

The knife stilled for a moment before continuing in its circular motion. "At first, it did."

"And now?"

She lifted her gaze to his. "I'd rather share her with you than the Zieglars. Actually, with the Zieglars there'd be no question of sharing. They'd never let me near her."

He felt his mouth twist. "So I was right. I *am* the lesser of two evils."

She shook her head. "No, Brady," she said softly. "Even if the Zieglars weren't in the picture, I wouldn't mind sharing Anna with you. You're her father. She needs you. I think you'll be good for her. I know she'll be good for you."

The admission was more, far more, than he'd expected. Or deserved. Gratitude, and an emotion that defied definition, warmed him.

She'd never looked more beautiful to him than she did at that moment in her plain white T-shirt, face free of makeup, hair tousled and blue eyes weary from lack of sleep. The cake batter on her nose had been joined by a streak of icing that ran from beneath one eye to one corner of her mouth.

Unable to resist, Brady leaned across the counter and traced his finger across her cheek.

"Icing," he said, holding his finger out in answer to the question in her eyes.

Gaze squarely on hers, in a motion that was deliberately

sensual, he slipped his finger into his mouth and slowly licked off the icing.

Haven's soft gasp was audible. Beneath her T-shirt, her nipples hardened. Her chest rose and fell in a rapid rhythm, as if she'd just run a mile in record time. Brady knew the feeling well. He experienced it each time he looked at her. He was experiencing it now.

Dimly, he heard the knife she was using clatter to the floor as, helpless to obey anything but the elemental impulses in control of his brain, he rose and purposefully strode around the counter. She gasped again, much louder this time, when he stood directly in front of her, and she saw the way his arousal strained against the fabric of his pajamas.

The ache in Brady's groin intensified. He didn't care that he was courting danger. He didn't care that his actions were in direct opposition to his decision to stay away from her. Nothing, short of the sprinkler system turning on or an earthquake, could stop him from kissing her.

Slowly, his arms slid around her waist. She seemed to melt at his touch, her body becoming soft and pliant as he pulled her toward him. Reaching up a hand, not in resistance but to brace herself, she splayed her fingers against his bare chest. Their touch made his blood surge wildly, and he crushed her to him until he felt the hard nubs of her nipples boring into his skin. The rigidity of his arousal came to a rest in the soft hollow between her legs.

Her eyes widened at the intimate contact before growing slumberous with desire. Lids drifting closed, she tilted her head back, allowing him full access to a tantalizing length of throat.

Starting with the hollow at the base of her neck and moving upward, Brady planted teasing little kisses over every inch of exposed skin. The soft little sighs of pleasure she made went straight to his head. When he reached the line of her jaw, he followed it to one ear. Taking a lobe gently between his teeth, he nibbled.

She smelled like cocoa and felt like sin. "I want to kiss you, Haven," he murmured in a husky voice that was barely above a whisper. "Really kiss you."

"Yes." The word was a sigh and an entreaty rolled into one.

Her lips parted. Needing no further invitation, Brady captured the mouth raised expectantly to his own, and marveled that it could feel even better than it had that afternoon. She kissed him back hungrily, her arms curling around his neck while her agile tongue tangled with his in slow, delicious strokes.

Brady felt as if he'd been torched. He struggled to breathe, but his lungs wouldn't cooperate. They refused to allow him to inhale anything but short, shallow breaths. Against his chest, he felt Haven's heart beating an irregular rhythm. The roaring in his ears told him his heart was keeping the same rhythm.

Making a low, hungry sound, he deepened the kiss. While his mouth continued to plunder hers, one hand moved to cup her bottom. Blatantly, deliberately, he rubbed his aching erection against the juncture of her thighs, eliciting a low moan from her throat. His heart threatened to burst from his chest when she moved her hips in an answering motion, her body arching against his.

Lord, she felt good. Brady couldn't remember wanting any woman the way he wanted Haven at that moment. Just kissing her made him ready to explode.

His movements urgent, he shoved her T-shirt out of the way to slide his hand up the smooth skin of her back, skin so hot to the touch it burned. When his fingers grazed the side of her breast, she shifted in his arms, giving him easy access to the object he so eagerly sought.

Her breast was small and fit perfectly into the palm of his hand. Cupping its weight, he brushed the pad of his thumb across her hard nipple, and took delight in the way his touch made her tremble.

He wanted to make love to her with a desperation that was soul shaking. He ached to sweep her into his arms and carry her upstairs to her bed; to strip the clothes from their bodies and ease his hardness inside her. The only thing holding him back was the tiny grain of self-preservation that still remained in his consciousness.

This would not be a casual coupling. At least, not on his part. He wouldn't be able to indulge his need and walk away, unscathed, when it was over. In the cold light of day, he would regret his actions. And so, too, he knew, would Haven.

It had been a long, stressful week for both of them. Their defenses were down. Neither one of them was thinking clearly. Hell, he could barely think at all. And to top it all off, they were exhausted.

"No, don't," she protested when he lifted his mouth.

It took every ounce of willpower he possessed, but after pressing his lips briefly, chastely, to her forehead, he set her away from him.

"Go to bed, Haven," he said in a strangled voice.

Her eyelids fluttered open. "What?" She looked dazed.

"Go to bed." He knew he sounded angry, but frustration tended to put a little harshness in a man's voice.

"But...you...I...the cake..."

He balled his hands into fists at his sides to keep from reaching out to her. "I'll ice the blasted cake. Go to bed, Haven. Now." He paused. "Unless, that is, you want what's going on here to continue to its logical conclusion."

She stared at him for a long, tortured moment. "I think I'll go to bed," she finally said, as he'd known she would. Careful to give him a wide berth, she walked around him and out of the room.

Body aching, Brady watched her until she disappeared from view. A minute later he heard the soft whooshing sound of her bedroom door as it closed. Heaving a regretful sigh, he bent to pick up the knife from the floor. After washing it off in the sink, he set to work on the cake.

Five minutes later, he stood back to survey his work. The cake was a little lopsided, and the icing was obviously thicker in some spots than others. It certainly wasn't anything to brag about, but what the heck, it was iced. And he'd kept himself out of trouble. For now, anyway.

After cleaning up the kitchen, Brady went upstairs and took a long, cold shower.

The bed bounced. Brady grumbled a protest and pulled the covers up over his head.

The bed bounced again.

Lowering the sheet and cracking one eyelid, he saw Anna perched at his side, a kitten in each arm. He had just enough time to wonder where the third kitten was, when he felt the tiny flick of a sandpaper tongue against his cheek.

"Are you awake?" Anna asked.

"Depends," he croaked. "What time is it?"

She shrugged. "Don't know."

Brady struggled up onto his elbows and groaned when he saw the clock. Six-thirty. It was only six-thirty.

"Do you always get up this early?"

"I gets up when I wakes up," Anna said with a child's simple logic. The kittens in her arms moved restlessly, and she placed them down on the bed.

He stifled a sigh. "What about Binny? Does she get up when you wake up, too?"

"Binny's sleeping. I twied to wake her. She won't move."

Small wonder, Brady thought, considering the two of them had gotten to bed less than three hours earlier. With one last, regretful glance at his pillow, he rubbed his hand over his eyes and determined to wake up. Haven needed the sleep, and this would give him time to spend with his daughter. Time for the two of them to get to know each other better.

Brady stared at the little girl sitting on the side of his bed and felt his heart twist. For the first time, he realized how hard it was going to be to leave once his marriage to Haven was over. Not that he was actually leaving Anna. He and Haven would set up a regular schedule of visitation. Still, it wouldn't be the same as living under the same roof. He wouldn't wake up in the morning to find her bouncing on the side of his bed.

"I'm hungwy, Unca Bwady," Anna said. "Will you make me bweakfast?"

He scooped the kittens off the bed and stood. "Sure, squirt. What do you want? Cereal? Toast?"

"Pancakes," she said promptly. She rubbed her belly. "I wuv pancakes."

His culinary skills were a little rusty from disuse, but Brady thought he could manage a batch of pancakes. He reached for the pajama top he'd slung over the footboard the night before. "Pancakes it is. Lead the way."

Anna stood her ground. "You haf to make your bed first."

Brady glanced at the sheets. In his restlessness the night before, he'd pulled them completely from their moorings beneath the mattress. The bed would have to be totally remade from scratch.

"I do?"

The little girl nodded solemnly.

"Right now?"

She nodded again. "It's a wule. When you wakes up in the morning, you has to make your bed."

He sighed in resignation. "Can't go breaking the rules now, can we?"

Anna leaned over and patted his arm reassuringly. "I'll help."

A sudden thought occurred to him while he tucked in the sheets at the foot of the bed. "You don't need help going to the bathroom, do you?"

Anna pointed with pride to her chest. "I go all by myself. I'm a big girl."

Brady felt a surge of relief. While he was feeling more at ease with his daughter, he wasn't sure he was up to that particular part of parenting just yet.

The first thing he saw when he entered the kitchen with Anna was the cake he'd iced just hours before. At the sight, memories crowded his brain. Memories of the way Haven had looked in her skimpy T-shirt, of the way her mouth had tasted and how it had felt having her body pressed up against his. With ruthless determination, he shoved the images to the back of his mind. He was making breakfast for his daughter; this was not the time for inappropriate thoughts.

"Can I help?" Anna asked.

"Sure, squirt," he said, grateful for the distraction.

Together, they measured out the flour, baking powder and sugar, getting as much on the table as they did in the bowl. He let Anna break the eggs, and they laughingly picked out the pieces of shell that landed in the batter. While Anna stirred the mixture, Brady fired up the griddle he found in a bottom cabinet. Five minutes later, they were seated at a table, munching contentedly.

"These are the bestest pancakes I ever had," Anna said around a mouthful, syrup dripping down her chin.

"That's because I had such a terrific helper," he replied, feeling unaccountably touched at how little it took to please her.

After he cleaned up the kitchen, he spent the next two hours playing Candyland, reading whatever book his daughter chose from the living-room bookcase, and laughing with Anna as they watched the antics of the three kittens. To his surprise, instead of feeling restless or bored, he genuinely enjoyed every minute.

At nine-thirty, he decided it was time to wake Haven.

"How about helping me make Binny some breakfast and taking it to her in bed?" he asked Anna.

"She likes pancakes, same as me."

While Brady tended to the cooking, Anna prepared the tray. He'd just slid the pancakes on a plate and covered it with a napkin to keep them warm, when he felt a tug on his pajamas.

"Yes?"

Anna lifted a finger and motioned for him to lean down. When he did, she kissed him on the cheek.

"I wike you, Unca Bwady. I'm gwad you mawwied us."

His heart swelled with pleasure. "Thank you, Anna. I'm glad I married you, too. Now, are you ready to take this upstairs?"

Anna nodded toward the tray and asked, "Can I cawwy it?"

"As long as you're careful."

When they entered Haven's bedroom, all he could see was a lump in the middle of the bed. A lump that was totally covered by bedclothes. A lump that snored.

"Rise and shine, sleepyhead," he called in a loud voice.

The snoring stopped. With a grunt, Haven burrowed deeper beneath her covers. "Go 'way."

Grinning, Brady walked to the window and ruthlessly drew back the curtains so that a stream of light hit the middle of the bed.

"Someone has a sadistic streak in him," Haven muttered.

"And someone else isn't a morning person," he retorted.

"We've been up for hours and hours," Anna said.

Blinking, Haven pulled the sheet from over her head and pushed the hair out of her eyes. "You have? What time is it?"

"Nine-thirty," Brady supplied.

Haven's dismayed gaze flew to his. "Nine-thirty? Tell me she didn't get up at six-thirty."

He shook his head. "Afraid I can't do that."

"I twied to wakes you up, Binny," Anna said, "but I couldn't. So I wakes Unca Bwady, instead."

The look Haven flashed him was full of gratitude and made him want to kiss her again. "Thanks for letting me sleep in."

"We made you breakfast," he said, nodding at the tray in Anna's arms and trying to forget how lusciously tousled Haven looked lying in her bed.

"You did?"

"It was Unca Bwady's idea," Anna said.

Her gaze searched his face. "It was?"

"I thought you might like breakfast in bed," he muttered with a shrug, feeling self-conscious.

Anna placed the tray across Haven's legs. "Sit up, Binny," she ordered. After placing Haven's robe around her shoulders, the little girl fluffed up the pillows so Haven could lean comfortably against the headboard.

"You can eat now," the little girl announced.

Brady wanted to leave Haven to eat her breakfast in peace. But before he could move, Anna reached out and slipped her hand into his. It was plain she was going to stay and make sure Haven ate every bite. Since he didn't want to let go of the hand that had so trustingly taken hold of his, he had no choice but to remain.

The scene was intimate, he and Anna standing over Haven like guardian angels. So this was what it felt like to be a family, he thought. It had been so long since he'd experienced the feeling, he'd forgotten. For just one minute, he felt a longing so strong it made his knees week. With determination, he pushed it to the far recesses of his mind. While he could build a family with Anna, doing the same with her guardian was out of the question. Giving himself one hundred percent to a woman was one risk he'd never been willing to take, even when his life had been full of risk.

"That was wonderful," Haven said when she laid her knife and fork down for the last time. "You two can make breakfast for me anytime."

"Tomowwow?" Anna asked eagerly.

Laughing, Haven reached out and rumpled the little girl's hair. "Tomorrow's a school day, so there won't be any time. Speaking of time, you need to get dressed for church, young lady."

"Aw, Binny, do we haf to go?"

"Yes," Haven said firmly, "we do."

Anna turned to him. "Are you coming, too, Unca Bwady?"

He hadn't been in a church since he'd turned to it for help as a child, and his prayers had gone unanswered. But when he looked into his daughter's eyes and saw the appeal there, he didn't have the heart to refuse.

Haven rose with the rest of the congregation to sing the closing hymn. Instead of concentrating on the words of the song, all she could think about was the kiss she and Brady had shared in the kitchen earlier that morning. And the fact that, had he not pulled back, she would have made love with him. It horrified her that she could stand in such a holy place and still think such thoughts.

What horrified her even more was the helplessness she felt against the desire Brady aroused in her. All he had to do was look at her with those steel gray eyes of his and she lost all power to think rationally, all power to resist. Why?

The answer left her senses reeling. Her feelings for him were beginning to go beyond the physical. She was beginning to care for him. Far more than was either sensible or safe.

Dismayed, she glanced to her right, where Brady stood holding a hymnal at Anna's eye level, even though the little girl couldn't read. His deep bass voice rumbled on the air.

As if sensing her regard, he turned his head. The look in his eyes made her cheeks burn, and she quickly pulled her gaze away. How could she have been so foolish? How could she have let down her guard and opened up her heart to him?

"Good morning, Anna. Good morning, Haven," the priest said as they exited the church a few minutes later.

"Good morning, Father," Haven said.

"Brady Ross," Brady said, extending his hand. "I'm Haven's husband. We were married yesterday."

Inwardly, Haven groaned. Drat the man! Couldn't he have stopped after his name? Why had he felt compelled to add the husband part?

She felt the priest's curious gaze on her. He knew she hadn't been married in this church yesterday. She knew he was wondering exactly where the marriage had taken place.

"We were married by a justice of the peace," she confessed, deciding to get it over with as quickly as possible.

"I see. Congratulations, you two." The priest leaned in so that his words could be heard only by Haven and Brady. "You might want to think about having another ceremony here, just to do things up right, hmm?"

That was a subject she just couldn't allow herself to think about. Doing things up right would mean their marriage had passed beyond the convenience stage and into the committed stage. Much as that thought was starting to appeal, she knew it wasn't going to happen. Because Brady Ross was a man who was definitely not into commitments. She'd be a fool to delude herself otherwise.

Chapter 8

The grandfather clock chimed the hour. Eight p.m. Haven kicked off her shoes and collapsed onto the green leather love seat in the den. With any luck, Anna would be asleep momentarily. And she could finally relax and unwind. Or come as close to that desired state as possible with Brady in residence.

Heaving a grateful sigh, she closed her eyes and decided to think positively. She'd survived her first full day as a married woman. That was cause for celebration.

Now all she had to do was make it through the night.

She felt his presence before he uttered a word. She hadn't heard him approach, but when her eyes suddenly flew open and her gaze traveled to the doorway, there he stood. He looked big and handsome, and more weary than a new mother who'd spent the night pacing the floor with a colicky baby.

Unbidden, longing stirred and swelled within her. She ached to reach out to him, to gather his head to her breast, to smooth the grooves of exhaustion from his forehead. What truly amazed her was that she could feel this way and act as if she felt nothing at all.

"Tired?" he asked.

"I feel like I could sleep for a week."

She closed her eyes again. It hurt too much to look at him, in light of her growing feelings. No matter what, she could never allow herself to forget that, one day, all too soon, he would be gone. Her only contact with him would be when he came to visit Anna. It would be beyond foolish to nurture her longing for him, to hope it would grow into something else. Something lasting.

For her self-preservation, she couldn't allow herself to hide from the truth. Brady was a man who didn't want to care for anyone. A man who, whenever those feelings threatened to arise, fought them with the fierceness of a samurai warrior.

But he did care, deeply, about Pete and Eileen. She'd seen that yesterday at their wedding. He'd cared enough about Anna to enter into a bogus marriage. He'd taken three abandoned kittens and given them a home. And she'd heard the love in his voice when he spoke of his adoptive father. Was there hope that he could care for her, too?

Maybe, she conceded, if a miracle occurred. Unfortunately, she'd ceased believing in miracles long ago.

"I'm exhausted, too," he said. She heard the leather of the matching sofa give as he stretched out on it. "It's been quite a day. Two days, really."

"You can say that again." She was surprised she was still awake. She must be running on fumes.

"Anna asleep?" she asked.

"Finally. Although if I never read about Evangeline and that blasted stranger again, it'll be too soon for me."

Haven chuckled. "How many times did she make you read it?"

"Three."

"Only three? You got off easy. Usually it takes four or more for her to nod off."

"I must have the magic touch."

He certainly did, so far as Haven was concerned. "Where are the kittens?"

"Sleeping with Anna. By the way, she's named them. Care to take a guess?"

Eyes still closed, Haven snuggled deeper into the love seat. "I'm too tired to try to figure out the workings of a precocious toddler's mind. You'll just have to clue me in."

"How do Praise Be, Glory Be and Hallelujah strike you?"

Surprised laughter bubbled out of her. "What?"

"She heard the words in church this morning and thought they would make lovely names. I didn't have the heart to disagree with her."

"They sound like good names to me," Haven said.

His answering chuckle warmed her to her toes. "Me, too."

For several minutes, the only sounds in the room were the distant hum of the dishwasher and the ticking of the grandfather clock. Haven thought he must have fallen asleep, but when she opened her eyes she saw Brady studying her, his gaze frankly curious.

"How do you do it?" he asked. "How do you manage to run the center and take care of that little girl all by yourself?"

She took advantage of his open perusal to do a little surveying of her own. When an unruly lock of hair fell over one eye, obstructing her view, she impatiently brushed it away.

"I don't do it all by myself." She spoke absently, absorbed by the way the fabric of his jeans clung to his thighs. "I'm really lucky to have a lot of wonderful people in my life, people who support me and offer help when I need it."

"That's not luck, Haven," he said softly. "You give of yourself, and people respond to that. You're like a magnet. People are automatically drawn to you."

Her gaze flew upward. *Are you?* she wanted to say, her heart pounding.

She searched his face for any evidence that it might be so, and was struck by the sincerity in his eyes. His voice had held a wistfulness that made her wonder if he wasn't a lot lonelier than he let on, and her heart went out to him. Aside from the Lorings, whom she liked very much, she hadn't seen any evidence that there was anyone else in Brady's life. Of course, there had to be. No one lived in a vacuum. Still, there were times when he seemed so utterly alone.

It was the pain, she thought. The pain of abandonment that he'd felt over and over again throughout his childhood. He was still so full of that pain it kept him from being close to anyone else. If only he would let her, she would gladly do what she could to take it away.

But he wouldn't let her. He had made that abundantly clear.

"What about your parents?" he asked.

The question caught her off guard. "What about them?"

"I was just wondering. You haven't said much about them. Do they live far from here?"

"They live near the airport," she said carefully.

"It must be nice having them so close. I assume they're part of your support system?"

"No, Brady," she said softly, "they're not."

In answer to the quizzical light that formed in his eyes, she gave the standard excuse she always gave whenever someone asked about their absence. "They're research scientists. They're devoted to their work and practically live at the lab. They don't have time for much else."

Even to her the words sounded rehearsed and false.

"Have you told them about us?" he asked. "About our marriage?"

"No, I haven't. And I'm not planning to."

He raised his eyebrows. "Ever?"

"Not ever," she confirmed.

"Why not?"

She looked away so he couldn't read in her eyes what the sight of him was doing to her. And so that she could concentrate on framing her answer. Tilting her face toward the ceiling, she studied a crack she saw there. How exactly could she explain the conundrum that was her relationship with her parents? It would be far easier to explain the theory of relativity.

"My parents and I…" she began, then lapsed off as she searched for the right words. "We're not exactly close. A long time ago we made the decision to live independently of each other. They go their way, and I go mine. I only share with them the things they need to know. Since our marriage is temporary, I didn't feel it was something they needed to know. Believe me, it's better this way."

"So," Brady said, "you're not telling them in order to spare them a lot of unnecessary grief?"

She had to smile at the absurd notion that anything she did would cause her parents grief on anything other than a superficial level. "No. I'm not telling them in order to spare *me* a lot of unnecessary grief."

He smiled back at her, and her heart flip-flopped.

"What happens when they find out anyway?" he said. "People do talk, you know."

She grimaced, imagining the discussion that would result if they were to learn of her marriage. She'd endured similar "discussions" many times over the years. Her parents hadn't supported her when she'd minored in education. To their way of thinking, it served only to steal time from what was truly important, which was her chemistry studies. They hadn't supported her decision to act as Anna's guardian after Melinda's death. They most certainly hadn't supported her decision to open the day care center. Though they were brilliant scientists, emotionally they were as stunted in their growth as the bound feet of the Chinese women whose tradition had kept them in servitude for thousands of years. Haven's marrying Brady for Anna's sake was something they would never understand. To them, it would represent just one more failure on her part.

Haven had accepted long ago that she was a disappointment to them. It had been only in the last year or two that she'd stopped trying to curry their favor.

"I'll deal with that when the time comes," she said. "Can we change the subject please?"

"Okay. Why don't you tell me about you and Melinda?"

What Haven wanted to know was about Brady and Melinda. From the letter her friend had written, she knew they had met in a bar and had been together just that one night. But the knowing raised more questions than it answered. At this point, the only thing she was sure of was that Melinda had been certain Brady wouldn't be bothering Haven because he hadn't replied to the letter. Melinda had had no way of knowing he never received it.

"What do you want to know?" she asked quietly.

"For starters, how did you two meet?"

Haven struggled up on her elbows, the better to see his reaction to her words. "We met in boarding school, when we were six years old. One of the older, bigger girls was picking on me, and Melinda told her to stop. When she wouldn't, Melinda punched her in the nose. We were inseparable after that."

"Sounds like she was quite a character."

Memories washed over her, and Haven smiled. "She was an original. She was so rebellious she made James Dean look like a conformist. She liked to say that she never met a rule she didn't break."

"That must have landed her in trouble."

"Constantly."

"Funny," he said, "I don't see you with a person who flouts authority just for the hell of it."

"Melinda wasn't like that," Haven defended. "When she broke a rule, she had a reason for doing so. She was the most moral person I ever knew."

"Morality and rebellion don't normally go hand in hand."

"They did with her. You see, her rebellion had more to do with a sense of injustice than with the notion of just making trouble. When she saw something wrong, she felt it her duty to fix it."

"Like the way she evened the score with the girl who picked on you," he murmured.

Haven nodded. "Exactly. I think it was because of her guardians. Douglas and Pamela Zieglar are about as amoral as you can get, and she hated the thought that people might think she was like them. Whatever the reason, Melinda always owned up to everything she did, even when she didn't get caught. She was scrupulously honest and always faced up to her responsibilities."

"Now that," Brady drawled in a sarcastic voice, "is a rarity. Someone actually wanting to take responsibility for her actions."

Haven knew he was thinking of his childhood, of the way his parents had abandoned him and the way the foster care system had failed him.

"Not everybody walks away from responsibility," she said softly. "I don't. You don't. Melinda didn't. That makes at least three of us. I bet out of all the billions of people in the world, if we looked hard enough, we'd find a few more."

He ignored her comment. "What about you? Were you a rebel like Melinda?"

"Me?" She had to laugh, although to her ears the sound held a tinge of bitterness. "No, I wasn't a rebel. I was the ever-dutiful daughter. I was so boring people yawned just looking at me."

He raked his gaze over her from head to toe, and her skin heated up about ten degrees. "'Boring' is not a word I would use to describe you," he said.

She felt warmth crawl up her neck and into her cheeks. "Thanks...I think."

"So," he said, "what does an ever-dutiful daughter do?"

Haven sat up and crossed her legs Indian-style. "She lets herself be shipped off to boarding school without a word of complaint and without shedding a tear, although her heart is breaking and she's so scared her knees knock. She works hard and gets good grades. She doesn't break any rules."

"Does she also get a degree in chemistry to please her parents?"

Haven hesitated a moment before answering. He was too perceptive by far. If he could read her so easily, how long would it be before he discovered her growing feelings for him? She'd just have to work hard to see that he didn't.

"Yes," she admitted, "she does." She cleared her throat. "But we were talking about Melinda, not me. And I'm still more than a little confused. She wasn't into one-night stands. In fact, I'm surprised she was even in that bar. She didn't drink."

"Well, she was drinking that night," Brady said. "Heavily. So was I."

"Did you approach her, or did she approach you?"

He sat up and wearily ran a hand through his hair. "I don't remember who said hello first. Does it really matter? All I know is, I glanced across the bar and there she was. And she looked as desperately alone and torn apart as I felt."

"You were upset that night?" She kept her voice as neutral as possible, afraid to let him see how important his answer was to her, afraid that he might go back inside himself and not answer her at all.

He drew in a heavy breath and gazed deeply into her eyes, as if searching for something. "Yes, I was. You see," he said slowly, "I'd just gone to visit my birth mother. And she'd tossed me out on my ear."

Haven stilled. It was the first time he'd willingly offered anything personal about himself. It was just exhaustion, she cautioned against the hope blooming in her heart. No breakthrough had been achieved. He was just too tired to realize he'd let his guard down.

At least now she knew the key. Keep the man a victim of sleep deprivation and he'd tell her anything she wanted to know.

"I'm so sorry," she said when she could find her voice. "That must have hurt."

His lips twisted in that mocking half grin of his that held entirely too much appeal. "Don't be sorry. It was entirely my fault. I was old enough to know better."

"There's no shame in wanting to believe the best about people," she said softly. "No shame in hoping that maybe things could be different."

"Isn't there?" he challenged.

What could she say to him that wouldn't sound like a platitude? People are inherently good? If you expect the best out of people, they usually give it to you?

"So you went to the bar after seeing your mother."

He nodded. "As you've probably already guessed, my goal was to drink myself senseless."

"And that's where you met Melinda."

"Yes."

"And she was drinking," she murmured to herself. It still didn't make any sense, until she remembered the date on the letter. Then everything clicked.

"I think I understand now," she told him. "That must have been the day Melinda found out she was sick. She was at the bar for the same reason you were, to forget. She told me she'd thought about ending it then, but that something had happened to make her change her mind. That something must have been you, Brady."

He shook his head in denial. "You give me too much credit. I was too absorbed in my own pain to be of much use to anyone else."

"But you spent the night together. You two made love. You conceived a child."

A dozen emotions flitted across his face, and she wished she could read them all. "We didn't make love. We barely spoke. All we knew was that we were both hurting. Instinctively, we reached out to each other in the only way we knew how. We…comforted each other. I don't even remember what she looks like."

"Don't move," Haven ordered, jumping up and crossing to

the oak armoire that held her television set. She rummaged inside the cabinet until her fingers found the tape she sought. Grabbing the remote control, she inserted the tape into the VCR before returning to the love seat.

"After Melinda died, I gathered up all the pictures I could find and took them to a photographer. He put this film together for Anna, so that she would have a way of knowing her mother." Haven bit her lip, then said, "I haven't watched it yet."

The look in his eyes told her he understood the reason for her hesitation. "Are you sure you're ready?"

She drew a deep breath, then nodded. "Yes. I want you to know her the way I do."

She pressed the play button. For a second, the television screen went black. Then music filled the room, soft and haunting, as a series of photographs slowly rolled across the screen. The first images were of an attractive young man and woman beaming in obvious pride as their newborn grew into a delightful toddler.

"That's Melinda and her parents," Haven said. "They died in a plane crash when she was two."

There was an obvious gap in time as the next picture to appear showed a group of school-age children.

"Let me guess," Brady said. "The Zieglars weren't into photography." The irony in his voice was plain.

"Not of Melinda anyway," she confirmed. "I'm sure they have plenty of pictures of their own children. This photo was taken at Willowhurst."

"The boarding school you both attended?"

Haven nodded. "It's our first-grade class picture. Melinda's the one on the far right, bottom row."

"Who's standing next to her?" Brady asked. "The little girl Melinda has her arm around. The one with the black eye and the skinned knees."

Haven remembered that day vividly, her first day at the school. "Me."

"I thought so. How'd you get the black eye?"

"Julie Hodgkiss hit me."

"And the skinned knees?"

"She tripped me."

"Is she the one Melinda punched?"

Haven nodded.

"Good," he said. "I'm glad she did. If I'd been there, I would have punched her, too."

His obvious concern filled her with warmth as Haven continued to narrate while the pictures rolled across the screen. Together, she and Brady watched Melinda grow up. There were prom pictures and graduation pictures, both high school and college. There were also pictures of Haven and Melinda that had been taken on their trip to the Grand Canyon two years before Melinda became ill.

Then came the footage Haven had been dreading. She'd filmed it the morning of Anna's birth. It was the only videotape on the cassette.

Haven caught her breath when Melinda's face filled the screen. She was in a hospital room after giving birth to Anna by cesarean section.

As weak and frail as she'd been, Melinda had still glowed with the delight of new motherhood. Emotion caused Haven's throat to close while she watched her friend unwrap the blanket from around Anna and exclaim over the perfection of her daughter's ten fingers and toes.

When the television screen went black, they sat for a long moment in silence. "That's all," Haven said thickly as she rose to turn the television off. "Melinda died a week later."

She didn't realize she was crying, or that Brady was by her side, until he reached out and brushed a tear from her cheek. Embarrassed, she looked away.

"Don't," he said roughly. "Don't turn away from me, Haven."

She tried to move out of his reach, but his arms went around her, stopping her. Blindly, she moved into them as she fought to hold back the tears.

"I miss her so much," she said against his chest.

"I know," he soothed, his lips brushing her forehead in the instant before his chin settled on top of her head. "But she's not gone. She's still with you. She'll always be with you. You see her every time you look at Anna."

Surprise made her pull back in his arms. If there was one person in the world who she would have sworn would not speak those words of hope, it was Brady Ross.

When she saw the compassionate understanding on his face, it was too much. The floodgates opened, and she sobbed her heart out. When her racking sobs had turned to intermittent hiccups, his shirt was wet from her tears, and she clung to him, weak and exhausted.

"I'm sorry," she said.

"For what?"

"For getting you all wet."

His voice held humor and a tenderness she'd never heard before. "I'll dry."

Haven had no strength left to protest when he gathered her up in his arms and carried her to the sofa. Stretching out beside her, he pulled her close once again.

"I'm glad you were there for Melinda," she murmured in a sleepy voice, feeling warm and cozy and safe in his embrace. "I think you saved her life that night."

"You're wrong, Haven." His voice was muffled in her hair. "She saved mine."

She was asleep.

Brady watched as Haven's chest rose and fell in an even rhythm. Soft and warm, her breath brushed across his throat like a feather. In repose, her face was serene. There was no visible evidence of the grief that had tormented her a short while ago.

The weight of her head was making his arm go numb, but

he didn't want to move. Not just yet. A feeling of tenderness and a longing he couldn't identify swelled his heart as he gazed at her.

He liked the way she looked, snug in his arms. He liked the way she felt, curled trustingly against him. He liked the way she smelled, like roses and apples. For a forbidden moment he allowed himself to wonder how it would be to hold her this way every night.

Brady felt like a rope in a tug-of-war contest as his fear that he would always be alone warred with his fear of letting anyone close. He wanted to reach out to Haven with a fierceness that shook him. If he did, he knew she would reach back.

And he would be lost.

In the past, he'd risked life and limb—first, on the streets during his reckless youth, and later, while serving his country. But during all that time of risk taking, the one thing he'd always refused to endanger was his heart.

With the exception of his adoptive father, and of Pete and Eileen, he'd always been careful not to get close enough to another person to care. He'd learned at a young age that the fewer people you cared about, the less you could be hurt and disillusioned. Already, his daughter had blasted a chink in the armor surrounding his heart. And now Haven was close to doing the same thing. Dangerously close.

The choice was simple: stay and be hurt, or leave and feel the emptiness. Since he couldn't leave, at least not until Anna's future was assured, he'd have to be very careful.

His years in near-solitary confinement were easily worth ten years on an analyst's couch, he figured. Brady understood the way he was, and why. And though intellectually he'd accepted the arguments of those who claimed it was never too late to change, emotionally he knew he was a hopeless case. He was the way he was, and there was no changing him.

What he didn't understand was why he'd confided in Haven the way he had. Before tonight, he'd never told anyone about his meeting with his birth mother, not even Pete. The surprise he'd seen in Haven's blue eyes when he'd told her about the visit had equaled his own when the words had spilled out of his mouth.

Perhaps it was because she'd revealed so much about herself, and, in his exhausted state, he'd felt compelled to reciprocate. Or perhaps it was simply because she was more like him than he'd realized. Now that he thought about it, their similarities were striking. Neither one of them had close ties to their biological parents. They'd each had to rely on themselves to make their own way in the world.

There was one major difference, though. Haven was a hell of a lot braver than he'd ever be. There were those, Brady knew, who thought of him as a hero because of his exploits in the military. But Haven was the true hero. She allowed herself to believe in the goodness in people.

No matter how hard he tried, Brady couldn't make himself do the same.

What he could do, in the dark of night, was permit himself this one little weakness. In the dark of night, he could believe whatever he wanted, whatever he wished. He could believe she was his, and that what they felt for each other would last.

But after night came the day. And in the light of day, he knew better than to fool himself.

With a sigh, he shifted his numb arm. Then he lowered his head against hers and closed his eyes.

Chapter 9

Haven had a crick in her neck. But when she tried to move, something big and hard and very warm was in her way. She opened her eyes and saw stripes. Blue and white stripes. Brows furrowing in concentration, she tried to figure out what the stripes were.

Realization dawned at the same time as full wakefulness, and she caught her breath. The stripes made up the pattern of Brady's shirt. Which meant that the something big and hard and warm that was in her way was none other than Brady himself.

Now that she was awake, she became aware of much more. She was lying on her side, facing him, and Brady's arms were wound tightly around her. Her legs were entwined with his, and her nose was buried in the hollow of his throat. Her mouth was open against his skin. The heat radiating from him warmed her more thoroughly than a thermal blanket. His male scent filled her nostrils, making her shiver.

She must be dreaming. A wonderful, miraculous, fairy tale

of a dream. Because, for the life of her, she couldn't recall how she came to be in his arms like this.

The clock chimed the quarter hour, and the veil obscuring her memory lifted. The pictures of Melinda and the videotape. The way she'd cried like a baby in his arms. The way he'd held her, soothed her. They must have fallen asleep.

She should wake him, she told herself. She should send him upstairs to the comfort of the guest-room bed, where he could get a decent night's sleep. Yes, she should wake him.

But she didn't move, didn't want to move. Even with the crick in her neck, it felt wonderful to be in his arms. It felt heavenly to have the length of his body against hers and to hear the reassuring beat of his heart in her ear. Selfish though it might be, she simply wasn't ready yet to move.

Besides, it wasn't every day she was presented with an opportunity like the one literally staring her in the face. An opportunity to study Brady without his being aware of her regard.

She bit her lip. Okay, so it was sneaky and just the slightest bit underhanded, and she felt a pang of conscience at taking advantage of his vulnerability. Still, a vulnerable Brady was not something she was witness to all that often. A vulnerable Brady was something that streaked across her horizon about as frequently as Halley's comet.

Leaning back as far as his arms would allow, Haven let her gaze rove over his face. In sleep, his forehead was smooth and unlined, the planes of his cheeks less angular and defined. Even his jaw seemed rounder, less determined, his nose less regal. He looked impossibly young and heartbreakingly sexy, and when her gaze landed on his mouth, she found herself fascinated by the tiny lines and grooves making up the fullness of his lips.

When the urge to press her mouth against those lines and grooves grew overpowering, Haven forced herself to continue her examination. The stubble on his chin was thick and heavy. Unlike most blonds, Brady would grow a beard easily. He also had the longest eyelashes she'd ever seen on a man. She hadn't noticed that tantalizing fact before, because they were the same golden color of his hair.

She was still drinking her fill of him when his eyelids fluttered open. Caught in the act, Haven held her breath and was rewarded when, in the first few unguarded moments of half wakefulness, he looked at her with a combination of hunger and possessiveness that made her mouth go dry.

Heart pounding, she moistened her lips. "Hello."

She knew the moment he became fully awake, because the warmth left his eyes and their expression grew carefully neutral. She could almost feel the wall go up between them as he laid it, brick by brick. Where it touched her, his body tensed.

"Hello," he replied.

Bittersweet regret pierced her. She knew what the look in his eyes and the tension in his body meant. The closeness she'd felt to him earlier, the unexpected gift of his sharing, was not to be repeated. From now on, he'd be doubly on his guard. Though she told herself it was probably for the best, her heart ached for what might have been had Brady been a different person.

"Looks like we fell asleep on the sofa," she said inanely, because she could think of nothing more intelligent to say.

He started to stretch, but when the movement brought a certain part of his anatomy into close contact with a certain part of hers, he stopped abruptly. "Looks that way." His voice sounded strained.

"Thanks for the shoulder to cry on." She was feeling the strain, too. "It appears to have dried."

He looked more uncomfortable with the memory than he did with the closeness of their bodies. "No problem. What time is it?"

Slowly, regretfully, Haven disentangled her limbs from his and sat up. One hand tried to straighten out her clothing, while the other smoothed her hair. She must look a fright, she realized. Not that Brady noticed, since he was looking everywhere but at her.

A glance at the grandfather clock told her it was too late for them to retire to their respective bedrooms. Which was probably a good thing, because right now sleep was the last thing on her mind. "Almost six o'clock."

She saw him wince as he pulled himself upright beside her. "Something wrong?"

He shook his head, then winced again. "My back," he said. "I think I pinched a nerve."

"Lie down," she ordered.

He blinked. "What?"

She nodded to the sofa. "On your stomach."

When he just looked at her as if she'd lost her mind, she explained, "Melinda had terrible back pain during the last few months of her illness. I took a course in massage to help her manage her pain. I thought maybe I could make you feel better."

"That's okay," he said quickly. "I'll be fine."

It was obvious that he wasn't fine. Why were men such babies about aches and pains?

"Come on, Brady," she challenged. "What are you afraid of? You're obviously in pain, and I can help. Would you turn down the heart surgeon who offered to unblock your six clogged arteries?"

He looked away, and for a minute she thought he wasn't going to answer. Seeming to come to a decision, he squared his shoulders and met her gaze again.

"Never happen," he said with a confident shake of his head.

"What wouldn't? You having clogged arteries, or a surgeon offering to fix them?"

"Me having clogged arteries."

She knew he was getting at something, but she hadn't figured it out yet. "How can you be so sure?"

He shrugged. "It's elementary, really. I don't have a heart."

His words hit her like a projectile, and she drew a sharp breath. She must have given away a lot more last night than just her pain at Melinda's loss. Somehow, she'd let him know that her attraction to him went beyond the physical. Just thinking about it made her heart go into palpitations. This whole exercise was obviously Brady's way of warning her off in the nicest way he knew how.

After all, a man without a heart couldn't fall in love.

And a woman would have to be a total idiot not to realize it.

"You mean you're a zombie?" she said.

He looked startled. "A what?"

"A zombie. I have a master's degree in chemistry, remember? I'm not unfamiliar with human biology. Unless there have been radical developments that I haven't heard about within the last couple of years, the only people walking around without beating hearts in their chests are zombies."

When he spoke, his tone was defensive. "What I meant was—"

"I know what you meant, Brady," she interrupted, feeling a mite on the defensive side herself. "I got your message, loud and clear. Must be lonely, though, going through life a zombie."

"I'm used to being alone," he said. "It's the way I like it best."

Her laugh held little humor. "I'm used to being alone, too. Far as I'm concerned, it's not all it's cracked up to be."

He looked at her with open confusion. "Why is it that every conversation I have with you always gets turned around in a direction I never intended?"

She had to smile and take pity on him. Poor guy. He didn't have a clue.

"I'll give you a hint. You're a male. I'm a female. We don't think the same. There've been lots of books written on the subject. Maybe you should read one."

A ghost of a grin tugged at his lips. "Maybe I should."

And maybe she should remember that the only reason they were together was for Anna, and not keep complicating the issue with her silly dreams. It was simply a matter of focus. She just had to stop focusing on the wrong things. Like the way his eyes crinkled when he smiled. Or the way his mouth felt on hers. Or how good it felt to have his arms—

Haven drew a deep breath and let it out slowly. "I don't want your heart, Brady," she lied. Another lie to add to the seemingly hundreds she'd told since he entered her life. "I apologize if I've said or done anything that gave you that impression. So you don't have to worry about me anymore. I'll be just fine. Now, does your back still hurt?"

Still eyeing her somewhat warily, he nodded.

She kept her tone deliberately crisp. "Then stop being such a baby about it and flop onto your belly."

Once he was on his stomach, Haven straddled his hips. Since his shirt had already pulled loose from his jeans, she pushed it up, exposing his bare back. Flexing her fingers, she positioned her hands. The intimacy of the pose registered, and she hesitated. Maybe Brady had the right idea after all. Maybe this wasn't wise.

It took a full minute, but she finally managed to put all thought, other than giving him a release from his pain, out of her mind. "Upper or lower back?" she asked.

"Lower."

Fingers curled, she squeezed his muscles against the balls of her hands, her thumbs gently kneading his spinal cord. At her touch, a low grunt of protest escaped his throat. It quickly changed to a sigh of relief as she continued her ministrations.

Slowly, Haven made her way up his back, squeezing and kneading, until she felt all the tension drain out of him.

"How am I doing?" she asked.

His answer was a groan of pleasure.

She shifted her body weight off of him and moved so that she was sitting beside him. After massaging his neck, she made her way down his left, then his right, arm.

''All done,'' she announced when she was finished.

She could feel beads of perspiration on her forehead. Her body felt as if she had just run a marathon. All her energy had gone into soothing away his pain, leaving her drained and weak. She hadn't realized it would be so physically debilitating to touch him, while schooling her thoughts not to feel anything at that touch.

He looked over his shoulder and smiled at her. ''Thanks. I feel much better.''

With an effort, she summoned up a carefree laugh. ''Just doing my wifely duty,'' she said dismissively.

It was the wrong thing to say. She knew it the minute the words left her mouth, because her next thought was of another, much more intimate, wifely duty. By the look on his face, Brady was thinking the same thing.

Haven froze as his smile died, and he stared at her with mounting intensity. He moved so swiftly that before she knew it, she was on her back, her hands trapped in his, and he was the one gazing down at her.

No longer were his eyes flat and unreadable. On the contrary, they were blazingly alive with emotion. The passion in his gaze nearly undid her. Mesmerized, she couldn't look away.

''It always comes back to this, doesn't it?'' he asked.

She could see the hunger in his eyes, felt an answering hunger building in the pit of her stomach. He didn't love her, would not allow himself to care. But, hard as he tried not to, he did want her. And oh, how she wanted him.

''It seems to,'' she replied shakily.

He shook his head. ''What am I going to do with you, Haven?''

Love me, need me, stay with me. Since none of those options were open, she chose the only one available to her. ''Kiss me?''

She heard him suck in a sharp breath. Then, eyes heavy with desire, his intention unmistakable, he lowered his head.

Haven's heart beat a furious rhythm as she parted her lips in anticipation and closed her eyes. She didn't care about morning breath. She didn't care that her hair was probably standing up in five different directions on her head. She didn't care that yesterday's mascara was most likely a black smudge beneath her eyes. And she didn't care about the doubts and fears and worries clamoring in her brain. The only thing that mattered was that Brady was going to kiss her.

Again.

His mouth was hard and hot and searching, and his tongue teased and taunted her until she was a whimpering mass of need in his arms. Mindlessly, her bones turning to water, Haven wrapped her arms around his neck, her fingers seeking out the soft springiness of his newly cut hair.

She couldn't remember wanting anyone so much. She felt ambushed by her desire and need and want. But it was more than wanting, she realized, more than mere desire and need. It was a yearning. A yearning to belong to Brady totally, body and soul, and to have the lonely shadows gone from her heart forever.

The knowledge that she couldn't belong to him, would never belong to him, only served to make the shadows loom larger.

She would not feel sorry for herself, she decided. She would not moan and groan and bewail the fate that surely awaited her. Not now, anyway. Live for the moment was the mantra she would adopt for the duration of her marriage.

Brady's hand slid up the front of her blouse to graze her breast, and liquid heat shot through her. Moaning, she arched her body closer, abandoning all thought. Her hands roved over his hot skin on a search of their own.

"What are you doing?" a small voice asked.

The words dashed her desire more effectively than a bucket of water. With a start, Haven pulled away from Brady. Breathing heavily, she looked over her shoulder. Anna stood a few feet away. The three kittens frolicked at the little girl's feet.

After tossing a helpless look toward Brady, Haven returned her gaze to her ward. Her brain sought desperately for the right words to fit the occasion.

"Wrestling," was all she could think of to say.

Brady make a choking noise.

"Can I westle, too?" Anna asked.

"Sure." The word was a strangled sound from her throat.

Without hesitation, the little girl leaped on top of them and began tickling. Haven stole a glance at Brady, who simply shrugged before doing some tickling of his own. Relieved that the situation had been defused so easily, Haven joined in the fun. A minute later, they rolled onto the floor, a tangled mass of arms and legs, with the kittens getting into the act, too. The sound of laughter filled the room.

Haven was breathless when they finally rolled to a stop. The smile on her face felt a mile wide as she picked herself up off the floor. Brady reached out a hand to help her, and their gazes met. His eyes were full of laughter, and the grin on his face matched her own. As her heart skipped a beat, she couldn't help thinking how like a normal, happy family they would seem to any outsider looking in.

Her smile faltered. The one thing they would never be was a normal, happy family.

Live for the moment, she reminded herself as she brushed away the cat hairs from her slacks while symbolically brushing the sadness from her heart. *Live for the moment.*

"That was fun," Anna proclaimed. "Can we do it evwy morning?"

"I don't know about every morning," Haven replied carefully. "But maybe every now and then."

Taking the little girl by the shoulders, Brady turned her around and aimed her for the doorway. "Playtime is officially over, squirt," he said in a no-nonsense voice. "Time to get ready for the day. March.''

Haven wondered if he knew what a terrific father he was.

"So what's on the agenda?'' Brady asked an hour later. He'd fed Anna breakfast while she'd gone for a quick jog, and now he was helping her clean up the kitchen.

A glance over her shoulder told her that the little girl was safely out of earshot in the den. ''I have a meeting with the Zieglars' lawyer this morning.''

His head shot up. ''What for?''

''I have to give my deposition for the hearing.'' She gave what she hoped was a nonchalant shrug. ''It's just routine.''

''Why didn't you tell me about it before now?'' He sounded irritated.

She smiled apologetically. ''I'm sorry, Brady. In all the go-ings-on the past few days, I guess I just forgot.'' And the minute she'd seen the notation in her appointment book a few minutes ago, her palms had gone clammy with fear.

''I'm going with you.''

''There's no need. My lawyer will be there.''

''I'm going with you, Haven,'' he repeated, his tone brooking no resistance. ''I'm your husband. We're in this together. They might as well know it from the start.''

A wave of gratitude washed over her. ''Thanks. To tell you the truth, I'm a little nervous about it.''

''Why? If things go according to schedule, the hearing will never take place.''

''I know.'' She chewed on the inside of her cheek. ''I guess I've just had too much experience with things not going ac-cording to schedule. You must have, too, or else we wouldn't be married.''

''Well, take my word for it,'' he asserted. ''This is one time they're going to.''

''I hope you're right.''

For several minutes the only sound in the kitchen was the clatter of dishes as Brady filled the dishwasher.

''Haven?'' he asked.

"Hmm?" she said absently as she wiped down the table.

"About the kiss…" he began, then hesitated.

The hand holding the dishcloth stilled as she slowly looked up. One glance at the troubled look on his face, and the gratitude she'd felt toward him vanished. So help her, if he apologized for kissing her, she'd punch him.

"Which one?" she said through gritted teeth, not bothering to hide her irritation. "The one at our wedding ceremony? Or the one when I was icing the cake? How about the one this morning on the sofa? Which particular kiss would you like to dissect?"

He had the grace to look uncomfortable. "All of them, I guess," he mumbled.

She settled her hands on her hips, not caring that the wet cloth was leaving a nice round spot on her dress. "What about them?"

"I just don't want you to get the wrong idea."

"I think I have exactly the right idea," she shot back. "You can't keep your hands off me."

He gave a surprised laugh. "That's true enough."

She decided to take things one step further. "And I like them on me. I like it a lot."

For a second, before he hooded them from her gaze, she saw desire flare in his eyes. "That's what I want to talk about," he said seriously.

All the fight went out of her. He was, after all, simply being honest. He didn't want to lead her on. She had to admire that. It wasn't his fault she wanted more than he could give. And it made no sense being angry about something she couldn't change.

"It was just a couple of kisses, Brady," she said with a sigh. "I'm an adult. I'm perfectly able to handle an adult encounter. Don't worry, I won't stake a claim on you. I won't expect you to put down roots and stay here forever just because we exchanged a few kisses. You don't have to run away."

He raised an eyebrow. "Run away?"

Okay, so maybe she was still a little peeved. First, there had been the discussion about his not having a heart, and now this. She was getting tired of being warned away.

"Isn't that what you always do when a person gets too close? You know, I bet that's why you chose the army. You knew you'd never be in one place long enough to put down roots."

His shoulders squared defensively and his chin jutted out. "I chose the army because I wanted to. That's all. I'm not running from anything."

She shrugged and aimed for wide-eyed innocence. "If you say so."

She finished wiping down the table, then hung the washrag over the faucet. As she walked out of the room, she could feel his stare burning a hole through her back. She'd shaken him up. Good. Now he could be as rattled as she was whenever they were together.

Brady glanced at Haven as they stepped into the elevator that would take them to the lawyers' offices on the tenth floor. She looked coolly beautiful in a slim-fitting navy blue dress. She also looked pale, so pale that for a minute he was afraid she might faint. When he reached out and took her hand in his, it was icy cold.

"You okay?" he asked.

She turned her face to him, and he saw the shadows in her eyes. She summoned up a wan smile. The gesture tugged at the heart he'd told her was nonexistent. She looked tired, lost and uncertain, and he was filled with an overpowering urge to protect her.

"I'm just a little nervous," she said.

If only she didn't turn his world upside down every time they had a discussion. If only her kisses didn't make him feel things he didn't want to feel. If only her touch didn't make him yearn for the impossible—to put down roots; to stay and build the family he'd never had. For the first time since his adoptive father's death, he didn't want to be alone. And it scared him spitless.

Which just proved that the sooner this whole situation was resolved, the better for all of them.

He gave her hand a reassuring squeeze. "Don't be nervous. I'll be right by your side."

Her grateful smile made his heart slam in his chest. "Thanks."

The elevator doors slid open. Still holding her hand in his, Brady led Haven into a huge foyer boasting a fifteen-foot ceiling and a massive crystal chandelier. Overstated elegance was obviously the order of the day. A plush, pristine white carpet lay beneath their feet; oil paintings of stiff-looking men hung on the walls; small groupings of Chippendale sofas and side chairs were sprinkled around the room. In the center of all this poshness, a lone woman sat guard behind an immense, highly polished desk.

If the reception area was any indication, Brady knew that the offices of the lawyers who had paid for the decor, and which were hidden from view behind the closed mahogany doors inset in the back wall, would be straight out of *Architectural Digest*.

"Looks like the Zieglars are sparing no expense in their battle to take Anna from you," he murmured into Haven's ear.

"Why do you think I'm so worried?" she whispered back. She looked around her. "How can I compete with this?"

"Don't forget, you have me in your corner. Remember the game Rock, Paper, Scissors?"

She nodded.

"Well, think of this as just another variation. But in this version, blood wins out over high-priced lawyers every time. My blood. And Anna's."

The receptionist directed them to a far corner of the room, where a man rose to his feet as they approached. A giant of a man at least seven feet tall, with a head as bald and shiny as polished brass.

"Hello, Syd," Haven said, taking the giant's hand. "I'd like you to meet my husband, Brady Ross. Brady, this is my lawyer, Syd Spear."

The only outward sign that Haven's words took the man by surprise was a slight narrowing of his eyes. His many years in the courtroom had obviously taught Syd Spear how to disguise his feelings well. When he extended his hand, Brady expected the grip to be punishing. What he received instead was a firm, measuring handclasp. The message was clear: Syd Spear didn't need to use brute force to make his presence felt.

"Husband?" the lawyer asked after Brady had released his hand.

"We were married on Saturday," Haven said.

Syd Spear turned his eagle eyes on Brady. A gaze that was merciless in its appraisal raked him from head to toe. Brady was glad the man was on their side. He was certain the lawyer's eyes missed nothing, from the way he parted his hair to the brand of shoes he wore.

"Is this the man you spoke to me about last week?" Syd asked in a quiet voice.

"Yes," Haven replied.

"Anna's father?"

"Yes. We're waiting for the DNA test results so that he can file for custody."

"And while you were waiting, you decided to pass the time by getting married?"

Haven opened her mouth to reply, but Brady thought it was time he put his two cents in. Syd Spear was their most important test. If they could convince him that their marriage was real, and not one of convenience, the battle, should it come down to one, would be half won.

Putting his arm around her shoulders, Brady pulled Haven to his side and gazed down at her with what he hoped was an expression of pure adoration. He must have succeeded, because her mouth dropped open and her eyes grew round.

"It was the most amazing thing," he said, looking deeply into her eyes. A man could get lost in the magic of those big blue eyes, he thought, and promptly forgot what he was going to say.

"Yes?" Syd prompted.

Clearing his throat, Brady tore his gaze from Haven's. "See how it is?" he addressed the older man. "I just look at her, and my brain goes to mush. Nothing in my life prepared me for the moment I first saw her. You see, we fell in love. At first sight. Isn't that right, honey?"

He squeezed Haven's shoulder hard in warning. "What?" she stammered. "Oh. Oh, yes." She batted her eyes up at him before leaning her head against his shoulder. "It's true. It was love at first sight. We just couldn't wait to be together."

"Well, then," Syd said, "I suppose congratulations are in order."

"Thank you," Brady replied. "I'd appreciate it, though, if you didn't say anything to the Zieglars or their lawyers about my being Anna's father. Once we have proof in hand, there will be plenty of time to confront them with the news."

The lawyer gave him a look that told him he hadn't been born yesterday. "As you wish."

"You may go in now," the receptionist called to them.

"Remember," Syd instructed Haven when they were on the other side of the mahogany doors, "this is just routine. They'll ask you questions pertinent to the complaints outlined in the petition. Answer everything honestly. Whatever you do, don't lose your temper. I'll be there to make sure they don't veer off track."

Haven glanced at Brady, her face pinched with worry.

"For Anna, remember?" he encouraged.

She nodded and squared her shoulders. "For Anna," she repeated, plastering a smile on her face.

Brady felt a spark of admiration. Haven Adams Ross was one gutsy lady.

As he'd expected, they were shown into a conference room that made the reception area look like a poor relation. The walls were covered with intricately carved mahogany paneling; the carpet was pure Persian, and the center of attraction was a gleaming banquet table that could easily seat twenty. Already seated were two men dressed in black suits and conservative ties who were obviously lawyers, and a couple Brady presumed to be the Zieglars. The lawyers rose when Brady, Syd and Haven entered. The Zieglars remained seated.

His first impression of the pair who had wreaked such havoc in his and Haven's lives was that Douglas and Pamela Zieglar seemed harmless enough. Except for their obviously expensive clothing, they looked like any other couple in their late fifties. But then, his captors, the few times he'd been allowed a glimpse of their faces, had looked like little boys barely old enough to shave. The brutality they'd meted out, however, had been anything but childish.

Yes, Brady knew all too well that looks could definitely be deceiving. And if half of what Haven had told him about the Zieglars was true, these two were piranhas in human clothing.

"Who is this person?" Pamela said with a disdainful nod toward Brady once they were all seated.

Witch, he thought, forcing a smile to his lips. "Allow me to introduce myself. My name is Brady Ross. I'm Haven's husband."

He hated the pretension of people who used their wealth as a means of obtaining clout. But in this case he deemed it necessary. Since money was the only thing the Zieglars understood and respected, it was important for them to realize at the outset that, in this particular arena, Brady held the upper hand. Which was why he added, "I'm sure you've heard of my late father, Charles Ross?"

"The financier?" Douglas said sharply.

"The very same."

Pamela's eyes narrowed. "Is this true?" she asked Haven.

"Yes," Haven said. "He's Charles Ross's son."

Her eyes snapped with impatience. "I was talking about the two of you. Are you married?"

"As of Saturday," Haven confirmed.

"Sorry you weren't invited," Brady said. "But it was just a small, intimate affair. You see, she swept me off my feet, and I couldn't wait to have her all to myself."

Pamela Zieglar was less than moved by his protestations of love. She glared at Haven malevolently. "Don't think having a rich husband by your side is going to change anything," she snapped, rising to her feet. "Anna belongs with us, and you know it."

Douglas Zieglar shot a warning glance at his wife, and she settled into her chair. "You'll have to excuse Pamela." He addressed Brady in a smooth voice. "She tends to get a trifle emotional where her great-niece is concerned. By the way, congratulations on your marriage. I hope you and Haven will be very happy together. I think, though, a new marriage would get off to a better start without a youngster underfoot. Don't you agree?"

"On the contrary," Brady replied, his voice as smooth as Douglas's. "Anna isn't in the way at all. As a matter of fact, I love her like a daughter."

He wasn't sure, but he thought he heard Syd Spear smother a laugh. When he glanced over, he could swear he saw the glimmer of a smile on the giant man's lips.

The Zieglars' emotions were far easier for him to read. If the looks on their faces were any indication, they'd found his words about as palatable as dining at a fast-food restaurant. It gave him immense satisfaction.

Syd Spear laid his briefcase on the table and opened it. "Shall we proceed?"

For the next two hours, Brady sat and listened while Haven answered the questions the Zieglars' lawyers hurled at her like punches. He sat with his hands balled into fists on his lap and his teeth gritted while they tried to twist and turn her words around in an effort to trip her up and make her admit she had been negligent in her care of Anna. He sat filled with a helpless rage that he could do nothing to stop what appeared to his eyes a gross miscarriage of justice.

Disgust left a bitter taste in his mouth. They were little more than bullies, the whole lot of them. Big, overgrown bullies. The fancy, high-powered lawyers might be wearing custom-tailored suits and demand hundreds of dollars an hour in fees, and the Zieglars might envision themselves to be high society, but they were no better than the playground hooligans who used their size and strength to intimidate the small and the weak.

Haven handled herself magnificently. She didn't lose her temper, despite plenty of provocation, and she refused to incriminate herself. Though it wasn't obvious to anyone else, except maybe Syd Spear, Brady could see the effort it cost her. That made him even madder. At the same time, he'd never been prouder of anyone in his life.

By the time the meeting ended, his head throbbed from the strain of being civil and his heart pounded with fear. He now understood the desperation that had driven Haven to beg him to assert his parental rights. He understood it, because he felt it himself.

And he felt it himself because he knew that what had just occurred in this highfalutin law office was a mere prelude to what would come later. In the courtroom, it would be far worse. The Zieglars' lawyers would twist and torture the truth until it was anybody's guess what the outcome would be.

Before, when he'd thought of the threat to Anna, he'd always dismissed it with a shrug. He'd found arrogant security in the knowledge of the type of home Haven provided for his daughter and the fact that the DNA tests would bear out his paternity. The threat had never felt real enough to spend much time anguishing over.

But now he had seen the enemy in action, and they were

indeed formidable. He was no longer so cocky. The threat was very much real, and Anna was truly at risk.

This will never go to trial, he told himself. The minute the DNA tests came back, he'd have Syd Spear file the necessary papers that would ensure Anna's welfare permanently.

But what if something did go wrong? What if something unforeseen happened?

The unforeseen had happened in a South American jungle when he'd been taken prisoner. The unforeseen had happened when he'd returned to safety and had received the letter telling him he was a father. The unforeseen had happened when he'd married Haven and had found himself drawn to her.

The unforeseen happened every day.

Whether the unforeseen happened or not, the one thing Brady knew for certain was that he'd move heaven and earth to protect his daughter. There was no way he was going to allow the Zieglars to get their moneygrubbing hands on her. He wasn't without connections himself. Charles's name would open doors that would remain otherwise closed.

Soldier that he was, Brady was ready to dig a trench and fight with any ammo he could get his hands on. If the Zieglars had an Achilles' heel, he'd find it. And he wouldn't hesitate to shoot an arrow straight into it.

Chapter 10

Juggling a bag of groceries in one arm and her briefcase in the other, Haven hooked a finger around the screen door and pulled it open. Anna raced ahead of her into the front hallway.

"Hello," she called as the screen door banged shut behind her. "We're home."

Home. How easily the word tripped off her tongue. How right it sounded. How foolish to think of that word in conjunction with her temporary husband.

Because her home wasn't his home, she reminded herself. For Brady, her house was just another place to rest his slippers for a while, like the many foster homes he'd stayed in over the years. Nothing permanent. His options were open, and he could leave whenever he wanted.

"In the kitchen," Brady called back.

Anna dashed down the hallway. A minute later Haven heard the murmuring of voices. After placing her briefcase at the foot of the stairs, she set the groceries down on the library table to leaf through the pile of mail that Brady had obviously brought in earlier.

Anna came racing back down the hall. "Unca Bwady made dinner," she announced excitedly. "Sketti and meatballs. Can I watch *Sesame Stweet*?"

Haven was suddenly aware of the delicious aromas of garlic, tomatoes and oregano floating on the air. Her stomach rumbled, a reminder that she hadn't eaten anything since breakfast.

"Only if you promise to turn the television off the minute it's over," she said.

"I pwomise." The little girl took off at a run for the den.

"Slow down," Haven called after her, "before you break another bone."

"Okay, Binny," Anna dutifully replied, slowing her gait to a fast walk.

Shaking her head in mock exasperation, Haven gathered up the grocery bag and headed for the kitchen. Unaccountably, she found herself smiling. It had been a lousy day filled with worries and tension, and all she could do was smile like an idiot at the thought that Brady was in her kitchen, and that he'd made them dinner.

Oh, she didn't actually think he'd cooked the meal. If he was like most of the men she'd dated, he'd probably gone to the nearest Italian restaurant and purchased everything they needed. Still, it was the thought that counted. And any meal she didn't have to prepare was okay with her.

Haven rounded the corner and stopped dead in her tracks. Her mouth dropped open, and the grocery bag in her arms tilted precariously for a moment before she hastily righted it. Never had she seen such a mess in her life.

Every cupboard door in the room hung open. Pots and bowls covered all available surfaces. A thin layer of flour lay over the pots and bowls and countertops, and even dusted the floor. In one corner, the kittens played with a pile of pot holders.

"What's all this?" she said faintly.

Brady turned from the stove, and she saw that he'd wrapped

one of Josephine's aprons around his middle. With the sleeves of his denim shirt rolled up to his elbows and his face liberally streaked with flour, he looked like a cross between the Galloping Gourmet and Brad Pitt. Her heart set up a sturdy pounding at the sight.

"I made dinner."

Out of the corner of one eye, she caught a glimpse of the dining room. Her best linen tablecloth covered the table, which had been set for three with her best china. Beside the china, gleaming brightly in the late-day sunlight, sat the silver flatware that had lain, forgotten and unpolished, for several years in a buffet drawer. In the middle of the table stood a vase of long-stemmed red roses surrounded by a sprig of white baby's breath.

Slowly, feeling dazed, she let her gaze return to the devastation that was formerly her kitchen. "You did this? All by yourself?"

"Don't look so amazed." There was a hint of a smile in his eyes. "I thought you deserved a good meal after the meeting this morning."

"But..." She'd been going to say, "How could one person make such a mess?" before realizing how critical the words would sound.

It was second nature for her to gauge the mood of the children she supervised and to act accordingly. She did so now with Brady. He looked so proud of himself she would hate to say anything that would take the wind out of his sails, anything that would make him retreat behind the wall he usually put up between him and the rest of the world. Instead, she substituted lamely, "I bought groceries."

He relieved her of her burden and began storing the food in the refrigerator. "They'll keep."

She looked around her again. Picasso had never made such a mess, not even when he'd hurled paint at his canvasses. "I still can't get over all this."

"Why?"

Since she couldn't tell him the truth, she thought fast. "Most men aren't any good in the kitchen."

"I made you pancakes yesterday. Remember?"

"But all that amounted to was pouring mix from a box and adding water." *And you didn't make near the mess you did today.*

He drew himself up in mock haughtiness. "I'll have you know, I made them from scratch. How could you not taste the difference?"

Because all she'd been aware of was his presence in her bedroom. And all she'd been able to think about was the kiss they'd shared just hours before. She could have been eating sawdust, for all she'd tasted them.

In the middle of the mess, she saw the pasta machine she'd bought a couple of years ago on impulse, then never used. "You made the spaghetti from scratch?"

"It isn't homemade unless it's from scratch."

That explained the flour that was everywhere. What she couldn't quite understand were the streaks of tomato sauce on the ceiling. She didn't have the strength to ask.

"I didn't know you were such a purist," she murmured while mentally calculating how long it would take to clean up. If she helped, they might make it out of there by, oh, say, midnight.

"Well, I am."

She eyed her navy blue linen dress, which had looked crisp and professional that morning but was now looking the worse for wear. "I think I'll go upstairs and change into something more comfortable."

"Take your time. Dinner won't be ready for a little while yet."

When Haven returned to the kitchen ten minutes later, she wore a pair of kelly green slacks and a bright print blouse. She hoped to find that her eyes had been playing tricks on her, and that things weren't as bad as she'd thought they were.

Unfortunately, that wasn't to be. If anything, the room looked messier.

And the maker of the mess had never looked sexier.

"Don't worry, I'll clean it up," Brady said, obviously picking up on her distress.

It wasn't the mess that bothered her. Not really. While she was meticulous about the state of her home, she never had been the kind of person to dog other people's footsteps, cleaning up behind them. No, it wasn't the mess; it was the idleness that was driving her crazy. With nothing to occupy her hands, her mind had free rein to think whatever it wanted. Right now it persisted in reliving in vivid detail every kiss she and Brady had shared.

"I'll just give you a head start on it now," she said quickly, bending over to pick up the pot holders that the kittens had abandoned in the middle of the floor.

A flicker of annoyance passed over his face. "I'm perfectly capable of cleaning up my own mess."

"I know you are," she soothed. "I'm just not the kind of person who can sit still while someone else does all the work. Indulge me, please. Just this once."

He shrugged. "If it means that much to you."

"Thanks." She made a beeline for the center cooking island, where the worst of the devastation was located. "Who taught you how to cook? One of your foster mothers?"

Steam surrounded his face when he lifted the lid on a boiling pot of water. "I learned as an adult, when I was out on my own. It was a matter of self-defense. I got tired of eating TV dinners and macaroni and cheese out of a box."

She understood completely. When she'd lived on her own, she'd eaten more than her fair share of macaroni and cheese, too. She paused in the middle of rinsing a bowl to glance at him curiously. "Why didn't you take the easy way out and just hire someone to cook for you?"

"I don't believe in taking the easy way out. Besides, I couldn't afford it."

She raised her eyebrows. "You couldn't afford it?"

He dumped a handful of spaghetti into the boiling water, stirred and replaced the lid. Then he picked up a knife and began cutting a loaf of Italian bread into thick slices.

"My adoptive father was a wise man. When he knew he was going to die, he redid his will. You see, he figured all that money might go to an eighteen-year-old's head. So, when he died, the house, along with all his properties, were sold and the money put into trust for me. I received just enough to pay for college. I didn't come into the bulk of my inheritance until I was thirty. By then—"

He stopped abruptly. She waited, but he didn't continue. "By then, what?" she prompted.

The knife in his hand stilled. He held her gaze for a long moment before looking away and resuming his slicing. "By then I was being held prisoner."

His voice was pitched so low she could barely hear it. When the significance of his words penetrated, she drew a quick breath and studied the face he kept averted from her. He didn't look exhausted. He didn't look as if he were walking in his sleep. Which meant only one thing. He was volunteering this information of his own free will.

Her heart surged with hope. She wondered if he realized the magnitude of the step he'd just taken. Still, she'd have to tread warily. It wouldn't take much for him to retreat again.

"Where were you held prisoner?" she asked carefully, trying to keep the excitement out of her voice.

"South America. I was a member of Special Forces. We were on a mission, when I was taken prisoner by a band of guerrilla soldiers."

"How long were you held there?"

"Three years, seven months and seven days." He paused. "I was released a month ago."

A month ago. It explained so much: his limp, the paleness of his skin, the reason he'd never received Melinda's letter.

"What are you thinking?" he asked.

That he was the most extraordinary man she'd ever met. At a time when he should be relishing everything he'd missed, he was here with her, fighting for his daughter. Guilt surged through her when she remembered how she'd hounded him about not working. If anyone deserved a little R and R without being badgered about it, it was Brady.

"I'm thinking I'm glad you told me."

He gazed at her thoughtfully. "Guess I no longer have any secrets from you."

If only that were true. After all she'd just learned, he was still such a mystery. How could a person endure what he had and not be profoundly affected? It gave her nightmares just thinking about it. And if the thought of it was enough to give her nightmares, what had actually living through it done to Brady? No wonder he couldn't sleep at night. There was still so much she wanted to know. She told herself not to ask. She did anyway.

"What was it like, being held prisoner?"

For a moment, his eyes took on a shadow, as if some cloud had passed in front of the sun. Whatever he was thinking, his thoughts weren't pleasant.

"I swore to myself, once I returned, that I'd never think or speak about it again."

"I'm sorry," she said quickly. "Forget I asked."

"No, Haven," he surprised her by saying. "I'd like to tell you. Know something? In all the debriefing I went through when I returned, no one once asked me what it was like. Oh, they wanted to know what had happened to me, but they never asked how I felt about it. You're the first person to care enough to do that."

His knuckles turned white as his hand clenched the handle of the knife. "What was it like? Picture being lost deep in a cave without food, blankets or batteries for your flashlight, and then magnify that picture a million times."

She shivered. "Were you alone?"

"Most of the time."

Where would she be if she'd spent over three years in a dank cave with no company? Probably in a padded cell somewhere. If she'd survived. "What did you do to pass the time?"

"Lots of things. I exercised to keep up my strength. I tried to recall every word of every book I'd ever read. I built houses and skyscrapers brick by brick. I spent a lot of time dreaming about what I'd do when I got home." He smiled his irreverent, irresistible and decidedly sensuous half smile. "I finally narrowed the list to three things."

Admiration for his strength and sheer will to live humbled her. She'd known before that he was a man like no other. What she hadn't known was how truly heroic he was.

"What were they?"

"Number one was to visit my father's grave and explain why I was away so long."

Tears pricked the back of her eyes. "Number two?" she prompted huskily.

"Charter a plane and fly to a steak house I know of in New Orleans, where I would order the biggest steak on the menu. Medium rare."

"And number three?"

"Go for a long run."

"Did you get to do all of them?"

"I haven't yet gone to New Orleans."

"Because you came to see me," she guessed.

He nodded. His tone turned brisk. "Now, if you don't mind, I don't ever want to talk about that time in my life again. I wasted over three and a half years in that hellhole. I refuse to waste any more time thinking about it."

"It's that easy?"

"Mind over matter."

She wished she found it so easy to ignore the way he made her feel inside. She wished she found it so easy to forget about the threat the Zieglars posed. But that was one of the major differences between men and women, wasn't it? In the face of a problem, men could compartmentalize their emotions and get on with what needed to be done. Facing the same problem, women became emotionally paralyzed and could do nothing until it was resolved to their satisfaction.

"You're worried about the meeting this morning, aren't you?" he said.

She looked at him in surprise. "Among other things." Drawing a deep breath, she asked, "What did you think of them?"

"The Zieglars? They both need a character transplant."

His accurate assessment made her laugh, and she decided to put her worries behind her. For this evening, at least. She'd certainly done her share of worrying that day, and it had taken its toll. Tonight, she was determined to relax and enjoy the unexpected luxury of having her dinner cooked for her. And she wouldn't even think of the cleanup that faced them once it was over.

"Is dinner weady?" Anna asked from the doorway. "I'm hungwy."

As if on cue, the oven timer went off, signaling that the pasta was done.

When they were seated around the table, steaming plates before them, Haven took one last look at the pristine white tablecloth that had cost her a small fortune. With a mental shrug, she pushed away all thoughts of what spaghetti stains would do to it, and decided it would just have to wash. Some things were more important than spaghetti stains.

"How'd you get the spaghetti sauce off the ceiling?" Brady asked.

Haven paused in the middle of scrubbing down the stove top to glance over her shoulder. Still wearing Josephine's apron, and managing to look impossibly sexy in spite of it, he stood in the doorway, eyeing her quizzically. He no longer looked pale, she realized as her heart skipped a beat. His skin had taken on a golden hue from the sun, and his body had filled out. In all the right places.

"I stood on the counter."

"The counter," he murmured, shaking his head. "I should have thought of that."

"You would have, given time."

"I wouldn't be too sure. You see, my plan was to scour your garage for a ladder so I could reach it that way."

"I don't have a ladder," she told him.

The warmth in his eyes took her breath away. "I did take that possibility into consideration. It might interest you to know that I had a backup plan in place for just that contingency."

Crossing her ankles, she leaned back against the stove. "I can't wait to hear it."

"It's kind of hard to put into words, but it involved standing in the middle of the floor, dishcloth in hand, and jumping as high as I could."

The mental image made her smile. "And if that didn't work?"

He shrugged. "I'd probably just throw a bucket of water at it and hope that did the trick."

He really was changing, Haven thought as she laughed. Little by little. He probably didn't even realize it himself, and the casual observer would have no way of knowing. But she wasn't a casual observer. As each day passed, she saw less and less of the stern, forbidding man who'd first walked into her office. His eyes were no longer cool and remote, but filled with warmth and laughter. His smile came more easily, and he joked and teased. On occasion, as he had before dinner, he even offered information about himself without being begged or threatened. Slowly, one by one, the barriers were coming down.

It was all because of Anna. The little girl, and her outpouring of love and affection, was rounding the rough edges on him, making him softer. If a man like Brady Ross could ever be called soft. Oh, he wasn't ready for the big leagues yet, like love, commitment and trust. Given his past, he probably never would be. But it still pleased her to no end to see him this way.

She turned back to the stove and tackled a particularly stubborn stain. "Do you always have a backup plan?"

"Always."

"Why?"

"So that I never wind up with my back to the wall, with all escape routes cut off."

She knew he was talking about more than just his experiences in the military. He was talking about a way of life. No matter what happened, he would do what he had to in order to protect himself.

Some of the happiness leaked out of her heart. Maybe he hadn't changed as much as she'd thought. After all, it was one thing to let a little girl lower your reserve, and another thing entirely to make yourself vulnerable to a full-grown woman.

When the stove was clean, she rinsed out the dishcloth, folded it in half and laid it over the spigot to dry. Turning, she inspected her now-gleaming kitchen. It hadn't taken nearly as long as she'd expected to put it to rights.

"As you can see," she said, "no backup plan is necessary. I'm all done."

"You really should have left the cleanup for me," he said.

Pushing all gloomy thoughts from her mind, she forced a smile. "What, and have you bouncing all over my kitchen like a Mexican jumping bean? Think of the scuff marks that would leave on the floor. Besides, much as I might have paid to see that spectacle, Anna did want you to bathe her and read her a bedtime story." Haven's grin broadened as she remembered Brady's look of terror at the prospect. Then, when Anna had gazed at him pleadingly, he'd given a resigned shrug and followed her up the stairs. "And I dare you to look me square in the eye and tell me you're not thrilled to bits you don't have to spend the next couple of hours on KP."

He grinned, and a tiny thrill shot through her. "I probably wouldn't have done it to your satisfaction anyway."

"Probably not," she agreed, grinning back.

His grin faded, and an emotion she couldn't read filled his eyes. "Thanks for cleaning up."

She shrugged. "It's the least I could do after that magnificent meal. You really are a good cook."

To her amazement, a dull flush colored his cheeks. She couldn't believe it. He was actually blushing. Never, in her wildest dreams, would she ever have imagined she could make him blush.

From the look on his face, she would have thought nobody had ever paid him a compliment before. A pang pierced her as she remembered his upbringing. Maybe no one had. At least, during her formative years, when it mattered most, she'd had Josephine to cheer her on and buck up her confidence. But until Charles Ross came along, who had Brady had? No one.

Well, all that was about to change, she decided. For as long as they were together, she would make it her business to see that he got the praise he deserved.

Of course, she'd have to be subtle about it. He might be changing, but she knew he wasn't ready to be overwhelmed with praise. Maybe a little more lighthearted teasing was what the situation called for.

"I can't believe it," she said, her gaze fixed on his ruddy cheeks.

"What?"

"You're blushing."

"I am not." His cheeks grew even redder. "I never blush."

"Then why is your face so red?"

"For your information, Anna likes her bathwater hotter than Hades. There was more steam in that bathroom than at a boiler convention. If my face is red, blame it on that."

She wasn't about to let him get away with that flimsy excuse. "Anna was done with her bath ages ago. Your cheeks are red because you're blushing." She tilted her head to study the phenomenon some more. "I thought you were too cynical to blush."

"I am."

She ignored his denial. "Let's see if this has any effect. You're a wonderful father."

His reaction surprised her. Instead of more color flooding his cheeks, his body grew as rigid and unyielding as a petrified tree. "Am I?" he asked in a tight voice.

She could feel the tension rolling off him like a fever, and she knew how important her answer was to him.

"Yes," she said, abandoning her teasing. "You most definitely are. You spend time with her. You listen to her. You make her feel important. I always wanted a dad like you when I was a kid."

He swallowed hard and looked away. "At least your father was there. Mine couldn't even be bothered to stick around for my birth."

"But don't you see," she explained, "that's what made it worse. Yes, my father was there, if by 'there' you mean he provided me with a roof over my head and clothes on my back. He fulfilled his obligations as far as I was concerned. But there was never any question that his research came first, my mother second and me a distant third."

"Maybe he just didn't know how to express his feelings for you," Brady said.

"Maybe," she acknowledged, although she didn't really believe it. "But I wasn't asking for flowery phrases of love and adoration. I was just a kid. It would have been enough for him to read me the funny pages on a lazy Sunday morning. Or take me to the zoo. Or play bucking bronco and let me ride on his back. Or simply ask how I was doing. I can't tell you how many meals I ate at the same table with him without his even acknowledging my presence. It made me feel invisible."

"He was still there," Brady maintained. "He didn't leave you."

A forgotten memory flashed in her brain, and she drew a

shuddering breath. She gazed at a point over his shoulder, her focus turned inward, remembering.

"He kept a diary, wrote in it religiously every day. Once, when I was twelve, I snuck a peak. I found the volume that contained the entry for the day I was born. There was a detailed description of the project he was working on at the time, but absolutely no mention of me. My birth wasn't important enough for him to write down."

She heard Brady's harsh, indrawn breath. "What did you do?"

Her throat grew tight with remembered emotion. "Closed the book and put it back. Tried to pretend it never happened. I never told anyone."

She crossed the room until she stood in front of him. Her gaze level with his, she said, "You see, Brady, there are ways of abandoning people without physically walking out on them. But the thing is, I survived. And you did, too. We both made it. Do you know what an accomplishment that is?"

He reached out an unsteady hand to brush the hair back from her face. "You're so brave," he murmured. "I wish I had some of your strength."

His gesture melted her heart.

"Careful," she said, blinking back sudden tears. "Much more of this and you'll have a weeping woman on your hands."

He recoiled in mock horror. "Not that, please. Anything but that."

Impulsively, she threw her arms around his neck and hugged him. "Thank you for caring," she whispered in his ear.

He went stiff in her arms, and she knew she'd gone too far. To suggest to Brady that he cared was to threaten his very existence. In his mind, she knew he'd convinced himself that to care for anyone else was to leave him vulnerable to being hurt. That was why the military had appealed to him so much, she figured. It kept him on the move, kept him from settling down in any one place. It kept him from forming close ties with anyone who might tempt him to care. Already Anna had squeezed under his defenses. He wasn't about to let her squeeze past them, too.

"You're all wet," she said, in an effort to change the subject.

"I am?" He sounded dazed.

She nodded, pulling back just far enough to get a good look at him. Unabashedly, she ran her gaze from his broad chest, over his flat abdomen and down his powerful-looking thighs. The apron covering them was soaking wet.

"Just who was bathing who up there?" she asked, amused.

He grimaced. "Anna and I played battleship. I lost."

He really was a terrific father. Haven wondered if he knew just how seductive that was.

Impulsively, she threaded her arms around his waist so that her fingers could untie the knot in the back. The movement brought her body up against his, and she was all too aware of how her breasts brushed and swelled against his chest, how hard his thighs felt against hers.

"You still have your apron on," she said breathlessly.

"Do I?" His voice sounded strangled.

She nodded. The knot gave, and she helped him lift the garment over his head, then let it drop, unheeded, to the floor. Underneath, his shirt was as wet as the apron had been.

Without thinking, she reached out and began unfastening buttons. "Here, let me help you take that off. It can't be comfortable—"

His hands shot up to still hers. Slowly, she looked up into his hot, hungry eyes. The longer she looked at him, the faster her heart beat.

"My pants are wet, too," he said softly. "Are you going to help me take them off?"

She gulped. The images racing through her brain were making her knees weak. "Do you want me to?"

His eyes glittered down at her. "What do you think?"

What did she think? She thought she'd go stark raving mad with the desire pulsing through her body like lava flowing down a hillside.

Instead of giving him an answer, she slipped one hand from his and slid it inside his shirt and across his chest. Her fingers tangled in the blond hairs covering his warm skin, then moved to brush the hard nub of one nipple.

Brady's arms closed around her. She felt his need as if it were a separate being—alive, breathing, pulsating. Everything had been building to this moment, she realized. From the second she'd seen him standing in her kitchen with that ridiculous apron wrapped around his waist and a look of happy expectation on his face, this was what she'd been waiting for. Every touch, every glance, every thought, every shared word, had been but a prelude to the desire that vibrated in the air around them like a tuning fork.

She couldn't fight it any longer. She wanted him. She would die if she didn't have him.

A jolt of pure joy shot through her when his lips claimed hers. His kiss was hot and wild and deep, and her mouth opened willingly in response, her tongue seeking and finding his. Nothing else existed but the sound of her breathing and his, coming faster and faster as their need grew. Warmth pooled in her belly, gathering and tightening into a hard knot of desire that would not be denied.

All too soon, kissing was not enough. Needing to feel closer to him, she strained toward him, her hips rocking against the rigid shaft of his arousal. Brady groaned. His hands slid to her bottom, pulling her even closer and making her senses spin out of control.

Then, with one last flick of his tongue and a ragged sigh, he set her away from him.

"No," she groaned in protest after gulping in a breath of air. "Don't stop. Please don't stop."

"I have no intention of stopping," he replied, chest heaving, his gray eyes glittering with a need that matched hers. "Is the house locked up?"

She nodded.

"Good." Catching her behind the knees, he swept her up into his arms. "Because we're going to bed."

He whisked her up the stairs as if she were a featherweight. Shouldering her bedroom door open, he set her gently on her feet. Neither one of them bothered to reach for the light switch; the moonlight shining through the window provided all the illumination they needed.

They shed their clothes with indecent haste. Haven caught her breath at the magnificence of Brady's naked body, at the unashamed way he stood before her, his desire evident.

"You are so beautiful," he murmured, his eyes dark with arousal. His gaze felt like a flame licking hotly over her naked body.

"So are you," she croaked.

He took her into his arms. Instead of kissing her, he sought her gaze and held it for endless seconds.

"It isn't because it's been so long for me, Haven," he said huskily. "I want you to know that."

He was telling her that he truly desired her, that, in his own way, he cared. She laughed softly, triumphantly, deep in her throat. "I know."

His mouth scorched her then with its heated demands. His hands cupped her bottom and pulled her close. His hot, hard body pressed against hers until Haven felt he would melt into her and they would become one where they stood.

She never remembered crossing to the bed, so busy was she luxuriating in the sensations she was feeling. She'd turned into a mindless, tactile being, shutting out everything but that which stimulated her senses.

Never in her life had she experienced such an intense feeling of abandon, of freedom. She basked in the feel of cool cotton sheets against her body, the touch of Brady's fingertips on her skin, the feathering of his mouth on her lips, her throat, her breasts. She thrilled to the scent and taste and touch of him. The groans he made when she pleased him set her afire.

When he entered her, they moved together as if they'd known each other a lifetime. Eyes open, they watched each other's faces, sharing the intimacy of the pleasure they were both giving and receiving. Slowly, steadily, the pressure built into an exquisite agony. Haven closed her eyes then, her movements becoming hotter, more urgent. Moments later, Brady's hoarse cries followed hers as they both went over the edge and spiraled out of control.

It was a long time before the thudding of her heart slowed. Sated and happy, she felt the lack of sleep she'd gotten the past week finally catch up with her. She barely had time to snuggle her head onto Brady's chest before falling into a deep, dreamless sleep.

Chapter 11

Brady's arms tightened around Haven as he tried to think of a word to describe his feelings. She was sound asleep, her face tilted up toward him, her sweet breath brushing his cheek and her flame red hair floating in a halo of curls against his arm. His heart tightened painfully as he looked at her and remembered the passion they had shared.

He'd never known lovemaking could be like that. In the past, his couplings had been perfunctory, a release of pent-up tension. Afterward, his only desire had been to find an excuse to leave. He'd certainly never enjoyed holding a woman in his arms the way he was holding Haven right now.

In all honesty, he had to admit he'd been the one thing women complained about most: a selfish lover. When he'd taken a woman to bed, *his* pleasure had been uppermost in his mind. Feelings of love, or even affection, had never entered the picture. That the women he'd bedded had also seemed to feel pleasure in his touch had been merely incidental.

But tonight, with Haven, had been different. For the first time in his life, he'd put her pleasure ahead of his own. And in so doing, he'd multiplied his pleasure a thousandfold. After his release, a release that had felt more spiritual than physical, he'd experienced a falling away, a healing almost, as if a part of him had died and been reborn.

Poleaxed. That was the word he'd been searching for. He'd been poleaxed. The word described his feelings perfectly. He'd been struck down. Twice. And he was reeling.

The first time happened a few short hours earlier, while he was giving his daughter a bath. Anna had been laughing at him and dousing him with water, when he was suddenly seized with a regret that squeezed his heart like a vise. All he'd been able to think about was that he'd missed so much of her life: her birth, her first steps, her first words. That was when he knew he loved her. He loved her, totally and completely. The intensity of that love had taken his breath away, and he'd vowed he wouldn't miss any more milestones in her life.

He'd been poleaxed again when he'd walked into the kitchen after Anna was safely asleep and Haven had seduced him with her beauty and her sweetness.

How his life had changed in the space of eight short days. Was it just a month ago that he'd slept on a dirt floor? It seemed like a lifetime. Certainly the person he'd been then was entirely different from the person he was now. The person he'd been then, and had been long before his capture, had been solely concerned with his own survival. Now all he cared about was the welfare of two females, one little girl and her beautiful guardian, whom he hadn't known until a long-overdue letter had catapulted him into their lives.

What a fool he'd been. Eight days ago he'd stood on the pavement outside the Melinda Dolan Center for Children and cockily vowed he wouldn't get involved. He'd thought himself above such things. He was self-sufficient. He didn't need anyone or anything. And then he'd seen Haven and Anna, and suddenly nothing had been the same.

He cringed when he remembered the canned speech he'd given Haven that morning. The I-enjoy-your-kisses-but-I-can't-get-involved speech. He was surprised she was even speaking to him after that.

Haven had been quick to reassure him that she didn't want his heart. Now that he really thought about it, why should she? *He* was the one who'd bulldozed his way into *her* life. *He* was the one who had threatened the safety of the little world she'd built for herself. In all probability, she held him in the same esteem she did the Zieglars. No, that wasn't exactly true. She trusted him with Anna. He knew for a fact that she wouldn't let the Zieglars within a mile of the little girl.

Okay, so maybe he was one step ahead of the Zieglars in the food chain. Or was it one step behind? The question was, what had it gotten him?

It had gotten him into her bed. It had gotten him heaven on earth. That was one good thing, at least.

She'd also reassured him that she was perfectly able to handle an adult encounter, and that he didn't have to run away because they'd shared a few kisses. Well, now they'd gone and shared a lot more than kisses—and the last thing on his mind was running away. What truly poleaxed him was the reason he didn't want to run. He didn't want to run because he'd gone and done the one thing he'd sworn he'd never do. He'd fallen in love. With his daughter, and with his wife.

Haven made a little sighing noise and burrowed her head deeper into his chest. Kissing her warm forehead, he tangled his fingers in the soft curls of her hair.

He would have seen it sooner if he hadn't been so busy hiding from the truth. Haven was right. He'd always told himself he'd joined the army for the danger. But the truth was, the allure of the constant movement from one place to another had been the real draw. In the past, he *had* run whenever someone, particularly a female, had gotten too close. His legacy, he knew, from his runaway mother.

When he was eight years old, and the social workers had come to remove him from yet another home, he'd vowed to himself that he would never love anyone again. He'd broken that vow only twice: first with Pete Loring and later with his adoptive father. It wasn't uncoincidental that both times he'd broken the vow it had been for men. Oh, he cared for Eileen Loring as much as he did Pete, but she didn't count. She was married to his best friend, so she wasn't a threat to his carefully protected heart.

After Charles had died, he hadn't even let men close. There was a limit to the pain a person could take, and he'd reached his.

Pete would always laugh at him and shake his head whenever Brady had asserted he would never fall in love. "When you meet the right woman, there'll be nothing you can do to stop it," he'd say. But Brady had never believed him. Until now.

In eight short days, Haven and Anna had obliterated the defenses he'd built around his heart and stolen it clean from him. And instead of being terrified, he was elated. Poleaxed, but elated.

He knew the exact moment he'd fallen for Haven. It had been when she'd come to him and begged him to assert his parental rights in order to save Anna from the Zieglars. Throughout his years in the military, he'd witnessed many acts of self-sacrifice and bravery. What Haven had done had surpassed them all.

But then, she was like no other woman he'd ever known. She was caring. And giving. While the best of her was already out there, shining brightly for the whole world to see, just being near her brought out the best in him.

If he could get her to love him back, he knew she would never lie to him. She would never leave him. She would never let him down.

So how did he get her to love him back? And how did he manage to stay by her side until that mythical day arrived?

Brady drew a deep breath and slowly let it out. He wouldn't let his doubts get the best of him. A man who did that had already lost the battle. He knew that much at least.

He knew one other thing. He was good at making plans. And executing them. All he had to do was come up with a plan to make Haven love him, eliminate or overcome all the obstacles that could possibly stand in his way, and he'd make her his.

Why, then, did he think it wasn't going to be as easy as it sounded?

Haven opened her eyes and strained to see in the blackness. For a moment, she felt disoriented. Memory returned, and she automatically reached out for Brady. But the space next to her was empty, the sheets cool to the touch.

A soft sound alerted her, and she slowly turned her head. Profile to her, Brady stood absolutely still at the window, staring out into the night. Moonlight streamed over his shoulders, making his body look like a carved alabaster statue. Hungrily, she ran her gaze over one broad shoulder, down a muscled arm, past a lean hip and curved buttock, until it rested, finally, on the curve of one calf. She'd never seen anything so perfect. Her gaze climbed again, and her heart raced as she mentally replayed in exquisite detail every moment of that beautiful body's possession of hers.

Without warning, he turned his head to look at her. Holding the sheet protectively to her naked body, she struggled up onto her arms, pushed the pillows against the headboard and leaned back against them.

"Hi," she said softly.

"Hi, yourself."

"How long have you been standing there?"

She didn't expect his smile. But suddenly it was there, tugging at the corners of his mouth. The beauty of it made her heart race even faster.

"Not long," he said. "How long have you been awake?"

"A minute or two. Aren't you cold?"

He shook his head.

"You okay?" she persisted.

It had to be a trick of the light, because it was too dark in the room for her to see anything clearly. Still, she could swear that, for just a moment, his eyes had filled with tenderness.

"I'm fine. I've just been thinking."

She raised her hand to push her hair out of her eyes, and the sheet fell to her waist. A surge of heat shot through her when his gaze went immediately to her breasts.

"No, don't," he said quickly when she made a move to recover herself. She let the sheet lie.

"You always think standing naked in front of a window?" she asked, surprised that she felt so comfortable with him. There was no awkward awareness of what they'd done together. No regret. At least, not on her part.

"I do some of my best thinking this way," he said. "You should try it sometime. It's liberating."

What was liberating, she thought, was making love with him. Never had she felt so alive. Her senses seemed more acute, so that the brush of cotton against her skin felt like the smoothest silk, the whisper of her name on his lips like the soft flutter of butterfly wings in the rain forest.

"I think I'll pass. There's an ordinance in this town forbidding exhibitionism."

"That's why I only do it in the middle of the night," he said with a chuckle. "Fewer witnesses." He sobered. "Want to know what I've been thinking about?"

"If you'd like to tell me."

"I've been thinking about Anna. And about us." He paused. "I've been thinking about what happened here tonight."

She waited for the space of a heartbeat before asking, "Do you regret what happened?"

His eyes glittered in the moonlight, and he looked pointedly downward. She followed his gaze and saw that he was fully aroused.

"I think you have your answer. The question is, do you regret it?"

How could she regret something that had been so wonderful? Right now, as she stared at him, the blinding need to know his possession once more fought for control of her sanity.

She patted the empty space to her left. "Why don't you come back to bed, and I'll show you just how much I regret it."

"In a minute. First I want to talk to you about a couple of things. As you can see, I won't be able to think clearly if I get any closer."

Oh, no, she thought, *not the I-can't-get-involved speech. Please don't ruin everything by giving that speech.*

"I'm not expecting anything, Brady," she said quickly. "What happened here tonight doesn't change anything. You don't have to worry."

He shook his head. "That's not what I want to talk about. What I want to talk about is me. You see, up until this point in my life, I've been a completely self-centered bastard."

How could he think that after what he'd been through, after what he'd sacrificed? How could he even dare to believe it, when he'd rushed to be by his daughter's side the minute he'd learned of her existence? Was it self-centered of him to enter into a marriage he didn't want or need in order to ensure his daughter's happiness?

"That's not true—" she began hotly, but his quickly raised hand stemmed the flow of words.

"It is true, Haven. Until a week ago, everything I've done, every choice I've made, has been solely for me. I put myself first. Everyone else came second, if I bothered to think of anyone at all."

She felt compelled to defend his actions. "Anyone who'd lived through what you did would have behaved the same way. You were just trying to protect yourself from further hurt."

"Maybe. But now, everything's different. I have a daughter. It's time for me to stop thinking about myself. Time for me to put Anna first. And what she needs most is what I always wanted when I was a kid. What you wanted, too, I think. A full-time father. Don't you agree?''

Her heart gave a sickening lurch. From the very beginning, she'd been afraid of this. He'd finally realized how much Anna meant to him, and he was no longer willing to live on the periphery of her life. He was going to take her away.

That he'd bring it up now, after they'd just made love and when he stood there in front of her still aroused, was unspeakably cruel. Honest, but cruel. But then, he'd always been honest with her.

"Yes," she managed past the lump in her throat. "I agree."

She supposed she should put up a fight, remind him of the promises he'd made. Threaten, cajole, cry. But she didn't. Because she knew that, whatever she did, ultimately it wouldn't matter. Ultimately, all he'd have to do was go to court with proof of his paternity, and he'd win. And, in the process, if she antagonized him enough, she might lose Anna altogether.

"Good," he said. "I've been going over some alternatives. Want to hear them?"

No, she didn't, she thought at the same time that she nodded her assent.

"The first alternative is for me to petition for full custody of my daughter."

Fear sucked the breath from her lungs. Blinking back sudden, hot tears, Haven plucked restlessly at the sheet at her waist. She'd been so certain, after his revelations about his childhood, that he would be as good as his word. That he would leave Anna with her. What a fool she'd been. What a blind, stupid, optimistic fool.

"I don't like that alternative at all," she said in a wooden voice. She felt grateful for the darkness of the room. Not for the world would she betray to him how close she was to tears.

"I don't, either," he replied, surprising her. "You see, you're the only mother Anna's ever known. She needs you as much as she needs me. I can't take her away from you."

Haven sagged in relief against the pillows. Thank God.

There was a short silence. "Did you really think I'd take her from you?" he asked finally.

His admonishment was gentle, but her heightened senses heard the hurt he was trying to disguise.

"I hoped you wouldn't," she said softly. "I prayed you wouldn't. But no, I wasn't sure. After all, Anna is your daughter. I'm the one without any rights here." She drew a deep, shaky breath. "What about alternative number two?"

"We go ahead with what we've already planned. As soon as we get the Zieglars out of the picture, we divorce. Anna stays here with you, and I visit her as often as I can."

"You can't be a full-time father that way," she noted.

"My thoughts exactly. Not to mention the effect on Anna when we dissolve our marriage. I've already missed too much of her life as it is, Haven. I don't want to miss any more. So, that leaves us with alternative number three. Can you guess what it is?"

She had an idea, and the mere thought of it made her light-headed.

His gaze settled squarely on hers. "We make this marriage a real one. We give Anna what she needs most. A mother and a father, together, under one roof."

For the longest time Haven couldn't speak. She was so stunned she didn't know what to think, let alone how to feel.

"It would mean making a commitment, Brady," she finally said.

His gaze remained fixed on hers. "I'm aware of that."

"It would mean putting down roots and staying in one place."

"I'm aware of that, too."

"I thought you weren't into commitments. Or roots."

"I've changed my mind. For Anna, I'm willing to do most anything. What about you?"

How could he even ask? And what was she hesitating for? He was offering her everything she'd ever wanted: Anna and himself.

"Besides," he added, "we didn't use anything earlier. You could already be pregnant with my child."

She froze. "Do you want more children?"

"Surprisingly, I do. Now that I've come this far, why not do things up right?" His arm swept the room. "Let's fill this house with children, Haven. Let's be for them the parents we never had."

Now was the time to tell him that, though she'd give anything in the world to be able to, she couldn't give him those children. But the words refused to form in her throat. Doubts seethed in her tired brain.

If there had been any mention of caring, any hint that his decision wasn't just for Anna's sake, she might have been able to tell him. But there hadn't been. Besides, he'd said he would do anything for Anna. So her inability to give him children shouldn't matter one way or the other.

Which was the reason she should tell him. She opened her mouth, then closed it just as quickly. She was tired of being found wanting. She'd barely survived her parents' disappointment in her. Also devastating had been the abrupt ending of what she'd considered two promising relationships when she'd disclosed her infertility. It would kill her to have Brady look at her the same way those men had. Men whom she'd believed had loved her.

She bit her lip. "I don't know if I'm ready to think about children." It was the closest she could come to talking about the subject without telling an outright lie.

"Then why don't we get used to each other first," he said. "Later, when the time is right, we'll talk about it."

A heavy weight settled on her chest. Later, when the time was right, maybe she'd be able to tell him the truth.

"What about love?" she asked.

"What about it?" He sounded as if he was choosing his words with care.

She shrugged. "Usually, when two people marry and settle down, they do it for love."

"We are doing it for love, Haven. Love of Anna."

Impatience stabbed at her, but she tamped it down. The man was being deliberately obtuse.

"I'm talking about romantic love, Brady. Marriage is hard enough when the couple involved love each other. I can't help but think the odds are stacked against us."

"I disagree. There are dozens of cultures in this world that believe romantic love should never be the basis of a marriage. Arranged marriages are still doing a thriving business. Surprisingly, most of them do quite well. We like each other. We respect each other. We love Anna." His gaze ran hotly over her. "Sex isn't a problem. Seems to me a pretty good basis on which to build a marriage."

She stared at him for a minute before replying. "What if one of us meets someone and falls in love?"

His frown was swift, his reply immediate. "If we're concentrating on making a go of this marriage, that won't happen."

Not to her, but that wasn't who she was worried about.

"Look," he said, "I know this is a bit sudden. Take all the time you need to make up your mind. I won't rush you. Until then, maybe it would be better if I stayed in my own room." He took a step toward the door.

"No, Brady."

He stopped and turned toward her.

"I don't need any more time. I already know my answer." She saw his hands clench. "Yes?"

Pushing back a vague sense of unease, she said, "All right. Let's try to make a go of this."

Slowly, his hands unclenched. Without a word, he crossed the floor and climbed back into bed beside her. Once the covers were arranged around him, he smiled his devilish smile.

"Now, where were we, before all this talk sidetracked us?"

Heaven help her, just looking at him made her shiver. She held her arms out to him. "Come here and I'll show you."

When his arms closed around her and his lips captured hers,

Haven forgot about her doubts and inadequacies. She even forgot she was living a lie.

She was awakened, not by the sun streaming through her bedroom windows or by the jangling of her alarm, but by the soft mewing of kittens and a rocking motion that could only be made by a ship at sea. Or by a small body bouncing up and down on the foot of her bed.

Though sleep still held sway over the majority of her thought processes, she was fairly certain she wasn't on an ocean voyage. She hadn't taken a vacation in years. Which probably meant she was at home, in her bed, and, as usual, Anna was bouncing her awake. What wasn't usual was the warmth at her side that told her she wasn't alone in the bed.

Alarm signals went off in her brain, and Haven's eyes flew open. As she'd expected, Anna was perched at the foot of her bed, bouncing merrily, three protesting kittens clutched between chubby arms. Rolling her head toward the source of the warmth at her side, Haven saw that Brady was also awake. If the look in his eyes—half amusement, half panic—was any indication, he was as aware of their predicament as she. After a meaningful glance at each other, they carefully sat up in unison, sheet pulled high to hide their nudity, and propped their backs against the cool wood of the headboard.

"'Morning," Anna said brightly.

"'Morning," Haven said cautiously.

"Hey, squirt," Brady said.

"Is it my birfday yet?"

It was a question she'd greeted Haven with most mornings since the invitations to her party had gone out. "Not until Saturday. Today's Tuesday. Your birthday's four days away."

"Oh." The little girl turned her attention to Brady.

"Why are you in Binny's bed, Unca Bwady?"

Haven choked back unexpected laughter. Leave it to Anna to go straight to the heart of the matter.

"Binny and I are cuddling," Brady explained. "Married people do that a lot."

Anna tilted her head to one side and gazed at him curiously. "Don't you snore anymore?"

Haven reminded herself never to underestimate her ward's uncanny insight. In case Anna let slip that they weren't sharing a room, they'd told the little girl he slept in the guest bedroom because his snoring kept Haven awake. But here Anna was, questioning their invented story.

"I do, but Binny's decided it doesn't bother her. From now on, I'll be sleeping here."

The kittens squirmed their way out of Anna's arms and jumped off the bed. "Can I cwimb under the covers wif you and cuddle, too?"

"No!" they shouted simultaneously.

"Not this morning," Haven added in a calmer voice.

Never had she been more aware of her nakedness. Or of Brady's. If Anna let her impulsiveness get the best of her, as she was often wont to do, it wouldn't take her but a second to discover their state of undress. And Haven would have to rack her reluctant brain harder than she ever had before for a plausible explanation. She was all for answering whatever questions the little girl asked, whenever they arose. But trying to explain the birds and the bees to a three-year-old was just a little more than she was ready to handle at the moment. She'd been hoping to postpone that particular discussion until Anna was at least twelve—preferably until she was thirty.

"Why not?" The little girl pouted.

"Because it's a rule," Brady said. "Only married people can cuddle together in their bed."

Dismay was written plainly across Anna's face. "You mean we can't cuddle anymore?"

"Of course we can," Haven said quickly. "But in your bed, and right before you go to sleep."

"Another rule, Anna," Brady added, "is that children always knock on a closed door and wait to be invited in before entering. Can you remember that?''

The little girl nodded.

"Good." Brady beamed at her. "Now, why don't you gather up Glory Be, Praise Be and Hallelujah. We'll all get dressed and then we'll meet in the kitchen for breakfast. Okay?''

"Okay."

Kittens in arms, Anna raced out of the room. Haven sagged in relief against the headboard.

"That was close," Brady said.

"You're telling me," she murmured.

"Is there a lock on that door?"

"No."

"There will be, first thing after breakfast." He met her gaze, and she saw his lips curve. "You look a little shell-shocked."

"I feel a little shell-shocked." She knew by his expression that he understood she wasn't speaking just of Anna's unexpected appearance.

He reached out a finger to trace it over her lips, and the sheet fell to his waist. Haven was helpless to repress the shiver that shook her body at his touch, or the desire that flared hotly in her belly at the sight of his broad chest.

An answering desire burned in Brady's eyes. "It is pretty amazing, this chemistry between us, isn't it?" he murmured.

"I've never felt anything like it."

"I don't suppose Anna would be content to wait a little while for us to join her?"

Haven's breathing grew ragged as she stared into his smoky gray eyes. When had she ever thought them cold? "Anna's not very patient when she's hungry."

"Neither am I," he growled. His head lowered and his mouth claimed hers hotly. He kissed her just long enough to turn her knees to jelly. Then, with an audible sigh of regret, he drew back.

"She'd forget all about knocking, wouldn't she?"

Haven nodded. "Absolutely."

"That's what I thought." Throwing back the covers, he climbed out of bed and stood before her. "Mind if I take a shower first?"

As she stared at the magnificence of his naked body and replayed in her mind every minute of their lovemaking in delicious detail, Haven didn't think she'd have the strength to move even if the house were on fire.

"Be my guest," she said, her voice hoarse. "I want to go for a jog anyway." Hopefully, she'd get the strength to move once he was out of the room. She had a lot to think about, and jogging always helped her sort things out.

What was it about a man's backside that was so darned provocative? she wondered as she watched him stride toward the bathroom. She knew one thing for certain. If he didn't put the lock on the door, she would.

Brady paused outside the bathroom door and turned to face her. "No regrets?" he asked softly.

Only that she couldn't tell him the truth. Besides that, everything was hunky-dory. She shook her head and forced a smile. "No regrets."

It was nearing lunchtime when her assistant poked her head around Haven's office door. "Mail's here."

"Just lay it in the in box," Haven instructed absently, her attention focused on the grant request form spread across her desk.

Out of the corner of one eye, she watched while Violet deposited the pile of mail where she'd requested. Her pen stilled when she saw a large manila envelope. Her stomach lurched. The last manila envelope she'd received had not contained good news.

She waited until Violet left the room to reach for the mail. The manila envelope was on the bottom. It took a minute for her to recognize the name of the return addressee. Relief surged through her when she realized it was the report on

Brady she'd requested from the private detective. In all the upheaval and confusion of the past nine days, she'd somehow managed to forget about it.

Haven sat back in her chair and turned the envelope over in her hands, debating. A long moment later, she released a heavy sigh. It wouldn't be right for her to read it. After all, she had arranged for it at a time when she had known nothing about Brady or his character. She would do well to remember how she had felt when she'd found out he had commissioned a similar report on her. If it was an invasion of her privacy for him to read that report, then it was an equal invasion of his privacy for her to read this one.

Besides, what could the report contain that she didn't already know? She'd had to bully it out of him, but he'd already told her about his mother's abandonment and about bouncing from one foster home to another. He'd told her about his adoptive father and his inheritance. He'd told her about his nomadic life-style and his desire to live free from ties to any other human being. In a moment of sheer exhaustion, he'd even told her about his abortive meeting with his birth mother, a fact she was certain the private investigator had not uncovered. And he'd willingly volunteered the information about his time in captivity. What else could the report contain?

Nothing. Nothing that mattered, anyway. There was nothing vital about him that she didn't already know.

Without a second thought, Haven tossed the envelope into the wastebasket and went back to work.

Chapter 12

As she had every morning for the four mornings that had passed since she and Brady had decided to make their marriage a real one, the minute the sun climbed over the horizon, Haven disentangled herself from the warmth of his arms and went for a jog. Rain or shine, no matter how exhausted she was from making love the night before, she made it a point to run at least five miles. At a flat-out speed.

This morning, she pushed herself to the limit and ran ten. She'd discovered that if she ran hard enough, all she had time to concentrate on was the punishment she meted out to her body. There was no room for any thought but the source of her next torturous breath, and in that she found a measure of peace. The only thing she couldn't leave behind on her early-morning journeys was the realization that she was trying to outrun her problems.

When she stumbled through the front door, sweat plastered her hair to her head and her T-shirt to her skin. Her legs felt so weak it was a wonder they didn't collapse beneath her like the limbs of a newborn colt.

Thirst drove her to the kitchen, where the smell of frying bacon told her Brady was awake.

"Water's on the table," he said, his back to her as he worked over the stove.

"Thanks." Haven drained the glass he'd placed in the center of the kitchen table in one long gulp. After wiping the back of her hand across her mouth, she crossed to the sink and refilled it. This time, she drank slowly.

"Have a good run?"

She nodded. "It's a beautiful morning. Still cool, with just the hint of a breeze. The perfect day for a birthday party. Want to go for a jog before it heats up?"

"Thanks, but I'll wait till later." He removed the pan of sizzling bacon from the burner. "Since it's her birthday, I promised Anna I'd make her pancakes for breakfast."

Haven glanced toward the den, which was conspicuously silent. Normally at this time on a Saturday morning, the sounds of Anna's favorite cartoon would be blaring. "Where is she?"

Brady chuckled. "Believe it or not, still asleep."

"I'm not surprised. You know how excited she was last night. I thought she'd never fall asleep."

She set her glass in the sink. "Need me to help out around here?"

"Nope. Everything's under control. Why don't you go shower?"

Twenty minutes later, dressed in a pair of white shorts and a sleeveless black tank top, Haven went to wake Anna.

"Rise and shine, sleepyhead," she said as she opened the drapes to a stream of sunlight.

Stretching one hand above her head, Anna yawned and opened her eyes. "Is it my birfday yet?"

Haven turned from the window with a smile. "Sure is. And a beautiful day it is, too. Happy birthday, sweetheart."

All at once, Anna was wide-awake. "Yippee!"

She jumped from her bed and ran to give Haven a hug. "Can I open my pwesents now?"

Haven swept the little girl up into her embrace and thrilled to the feel of the chubby arms that wrapped around her neck. Anna's cast had been removed the day before, and her wrist was as good as new. "Not until your party."

"Aw, Binny!"

Haven kissed the soft cheek, then set Anna back down on the floor. "No pouting on your birthday, okay? Your party's just a few hours away. Now, in honor of this special day, I'll make your bed. Why don't you get dressed, so we can eat breakfast. Uncle Brady's making pancakes just for you."

Five minutes later, Anna raced toward the kitchen. "Unca Bwady, Unca Bwady!" she called.

"What is it, squirt?" Haven heard him ask as she followed a few steps behind.

"Do you 'member what today is?"

Haven paused in the doorway and watched Brady smile at his daughter. "Um, let me think." Leaning against the counter, he cupped an elbow in one hand and tapped his fingertips against his chin. "It's Friday—no, no, it's Saturday. Am I right?"

"Um-hmm," Anna said.

Brady spread his arms. "Well, if it's Saturday, then it must be mow-the-lawn day."

Anna giggled. "No, silly, that's not it."

"It's not?" He snapped his fingers. "I've got it. It's clean-out-the-garage day."

"Nooooh."

He scratched his head and squinted his eyes as if deep in thought. "Is it—now, let me think—could it be...your birthday?"

Anna clapped her hands with glee. "Yes. And I'm gonna haf a party wif a clown an' everthing."

"You are? That's great. How old are you?"

The little girl held up three fingers.

Brady looked impressed. "That old? I am impressed."

How he'd changed from the dour, unsmiling man who had marched into the center and baldly announced his paternity, Haven thought, not for the first time. Physically, he bore little resemblance to the wan, too-thin man he'd been then. Now he looked hale and hearty, and far too handsome for Haven's peace of mind.

But it was the internal changes that were, by far, the more profound. A smile seemed to constantly hover about his lips, and he'd totally relaxed—with Anna, at least. There were no walls between them. Gone was his awkwardness, his hesitation when he spoke to her. He'd submerged himself into fatherhood the way some actors submerged themselves in the role they'd been contracted to play, completely and unhesitatingly.

While Anna chatted about the doll she wanted for her birthday, Brady glanced over at Haven, the smile on his face loving and indulgent. Even though she knew the smile was for Anna, her heart thundered in response.

It amazed her that during the day they could act like platonic roommates who shared the same living space, while at night they couldn't keep their hands off each other. But then again, it amazed her that she'd grown into such an accomplished liar. She'd never expected she could keep secrets the way she had. From Josephine, as well as from Brady.

Why did children think that having a secret was such fun? She hated it. The weight of it never left her shoulders.

She'd have to tell Brady the truth. Soon. She'd have to tell Josephine the truth, too. She didn't know which chore she dreaded more.

"How many children did you say you invited?" Brady shouted to her over the din of squealing voices. They were in the den, playing Pin the Tail on the Donkey. After Haven placed a blindfold on a child, Brady would spin her around, hand her a tail and then aim her for the poster tacked to the wall.

"Ten," Haven shouted back. "Eleven, including Anna."

"Is that all? I could have sworn there were at least fifty."

She laughed. "It does sound like it, doesn't it?"

The phone rang, and she went to answer it. When she returned, Brady had arranged the eleven little girls in a circle and started a raucous game of hot potato.

He took one look at her face and crossed immediately to her side. "Bad news?"

"That was the clown. Actually, it was his mother. He can't make it. He has the chicken pox."

His eyebrows raised. "The chicken pox? How old is this clown?"

"Twelve. He's the brother of one of the kids at the center. What am I going to do, Brady? Anna's going to be so disappointed."

"How long can you hold the fort?" he asked.

"I don't know." She shrugged. "An hour, I suppose."

"Be right back."

He dashed out of the room. Haven heard the pounding of his feet as he raced up the stairs. When he raced back down, she thought she glimpsed something black hanging over one arm, but he was moving too fast for her to identify what it was. The slam of the front door was followed by the sound of his car engine roaring to life.

Exactly one hour later, the doorbell rang. When she opened the door, Haven saw Brady wearing his tuxedo jacket over his jeans. He had on a red bow tie and black gloves, and a huge plastic daisy rested in his lapel. A top hat sat on his head. At his feet lay a green duffel bag.

"What?" she said, laughing.

With a flourish, a deck of cards appeared in one hand. "Pick a card, any card."

Shaking her head, she drew the queen of hearts.

"Place it back in the deck, please. Anywhere."

She complied, and watched while he shuffled. After spreading the cards again, he riffled them with one gloved finger, then drew a card from the center of the deck. It was the queen of hearts.

"Is this your card?"

"Amazing," she said. "But can you pull a rabbit out of your hat? Something tells me those three-year-olds in there won't be thrilled with card tricks. They don't know a diamond from a spade, let alone how to read numbers."

"Don't worry about Brady the Magnificent." He picked up the duffel bag and brushed by her. "One of my army buddies was an amateur magician. He taught me a trick or two."

"Where'd the equipment come from?" she asked.

"I raided the five-and-dime. They have everything."

Bemused, she closed the door and followed him into the den. For his first trick, he pulled a bouquet of roses out of his hat and handed them, with a bow, to a delighted Anna. When she took them, he pointed to the daisy in his lapel. Anna gave it a squeeze, and water streamed onto Brady's face. He reeled back with a comic look of surprise, and eleven little girls erupted in laughter.

Forever after, Haven would remember that moment. Because, whether he knew it or not, Brady the Magnificent had just pulled the biggest trick of all. He made her do what she'd been fighting against from the moment she met him. He made her fall in love with him. Completely and irrevocably. It was crazy and irresponsible and beyond stupid. But she did it anyway.

She couldn't help herself.

Ten days later, Haven went to see Josephine in the day care center's kitchen. The day of reckoning had come. It was time to fess up. Time to tell the truth, or at least part of it. The hearing date was fast approaching. If the case went to trial, Josephine would be called as a character witness. She'd receive notice of that any day; she needed to be prepared.

Leaning against a stainless-steel table, Haven watched in silence for a minute while the older woman whipped up a batch of cookie dough. Bowl tucked in the crook of one arm, Josephine stirred the batter vigorously. Her entire body vibrated with the effort.

"Hey," Haven said.

Josephine looked up with a smile. "Hey, yourself."

"Haven't seen you much lately."

"Guess we've both been busy."

Haven smiled at the understatement. "Guess we have."

With one finger, she traced an idle pattern across the cool stainless steel. "I miss you, Josie. I miss our talks."

A tender light lit the older woman's eyes. "I do, too, child."

"Want to talk now?"

"I'd like that a lot." Josephine set the bowl down. After picking up a rolling pin and dusting it with flour, she plunked the dough on the table and began rolling it out.

Haven didn't want to baldly announce her news. She wanted to lead up to it slowly, to prepare Josephine for what was to come. But before she could ask the first in a list of several innocuous questions she'd prepared, Josephine beat her to the punch.

"So tell me…how's married life?"

Even though they'd agreed to make their marriage a real one, for Anna's safety they still couldn't disclose the reason for their union. Since she couldn't tell Josephine the truth, and she was tired of lying, talking about her marriage was the last thing Haven wanted to do. She couldn't tell Josephine that being married to Brady was torture. Sheer, unadulterated torture. For the past two weeks, she'd spent her days at the center, her evenings playing with Anna and her nights in the heaven of Brady's arms.

He'd noticed, as she'd known he inevitably would, the faint scarring on her abdomen. While she'd had to tell him about the car accident, she hadn't been able to bring herself to admit the extent of her injuries. Even worse, he'd bought condoms to protect her from the pregnancy she'd told him she wasn't ready for. Each time he used one, guilt stabbed at her.

Instead of his passion waning the more familiar they became with each other's bodies, with each passing night his love-making had grown more wild and intense. It was like riding on the winds of a hurricane. And every time the storm was over, and she lay in his arms, panting from exertion and beautifully satiated, she felt empty. The secret yawning between them only made the emptiness more vast.

To have Brady but not his love was like being a child who'd been let loose in a toy store and told she could have all the toys she could carry outside, except that the toys were bolted to the shelves. Try as she could, they wouldn't budge. While she could play with them in the store, they would never belong to her. Like that little girl, while Haven could have Brady in her bed and enjoy the pleasure his body gave her, she would never have his love.

Some of what she was thinking must have shown on her face, because Josephine's mouth tightened into a thin line. "What is it, child? Something's wrong, isn't it?"

Haven drew a deep breath. "There's something I have to tell you."

Josephine stabbed a cookie cutter into the dough. "I knew it, I just knew it. He up and left you, didn't he, child? I'm going to kill that man."

It amused Haven how, now that she thought the marriage was in trouble, Josephine conveniently forgot how excited she'd been about it at the time it took place.

"No, Josie, he didn't leave me. We're doing just fine. What I wanted to tell you is that Douglas and Pamela Zieglar are suing me for custody of Anna."

Lord, but it felt good to tell at least part of the truth, although Haven hated the lines of worry that now creased the older woman's eyes.

"Oh, child, no. When did this happen?"

"Not too long ago."

"Do they have a case?"

"We're hoping to put a stop to it before it goes to trial. But if we can't, I'm going to need you to stand up for me in court.''

"You know you can count on me for whatever you need."

Haven felt tears well up in her eyes. "I know, Josie. Thanks. I just wanted you to be prepared."

She drew a deep, steadying breath and let it out slowly. With an effort of will, she plastered a smile on her face. "So," she said brightly, pushing her problems to the back of her mind, "how are things working out with Jackson?"

Brady stretched himself out on the ground and watched while Pete planted a rosebush. Rivulets of sweat coursed down the middle of his back, plastering his shirt to his skin. Leaning back on his elbows, he tilted his face to the sun, and wondered if he would ever tire of the feel of it.

Three and a half weeks had passed since he'd talked Haven into making their marriage a real one. Three and a half weeks during which he'd made love to her endlessly almost every night, and still he couldn't get enough of her, any more than he could get enough of the sun. The need to touch her was like an addiction. It was a fever in his blood, hot and burning. A fever she seemed to share, because whenever he took her into his arms, she sought his touch as eagerly as he did hers.

Then why was he feeling so frustrated? he wondered. Why did he feel so hollow and empty inside? Why did he feel more alone now than he had when he'd been held captive in a solitary cell?

Because even though she gave her body freely to him at night, when they weren't in bed, he could feel a part of her pulling away from him. There was a distance between them, an invisible wall she'd erected. A wall that existed because she didn't love him. And he didn't have the faintest clue how to go about tearing it down.

"How do you court a woman?" he asked.

Pete sat back on his heels. Surveying his handiwork, he

wiped the perspiration from his forehead. "Haven's the woman you want to court, I take it?"

"Of course Haven's the woman I want to court." Brady didn't bother to hide his impatience. He'd been so careful with his emotions over the past three and a half weeks, it was a relief to give free rein to his feelings. "Who else would I be talking about?"

"Just checking."

"Well, now you know. So, what do I do?"

"Why do you want to court her? You're already married."

Ask Pete a question, Brady thought, and all you got was commentary. He should have known better. Unfortunately, he had no one else to go to.

"And I want to stay married. Now, are you going to tell me or not?"

"You really don't know how? The Casanova of Allegheny County, the man who's had women drooling over him since his voice changed, doesn't know how to court a woman?"

"I never needed to before."

A rueful smile curved Pete's mouth. "The sad thing is, I believe you. And I should hate you for it."

"I'm still waiting for an answer."

"Okay, okay. Don't get your pants in an uproar." Pete fingered his chin, leaving a smudge of dirt behind. "Let's see. How do you woo a woman? The possibilities are endless."

"Pete," Brady warned.

"Flowers are always good," Pete said. "Forget candy, though. Most women are so figure-conscious, they get highly insulted if you bring them chocolate. Unless it's PMS time, in which case you buy the five-pound box."

"Okay, I got you so far. Bring flowers. Forget chocolate. What else?"

"You could try an expensive restaurant. You know, candlelight, soft music, good wine. Follow that up with a romantic movie and she's yours. Of course, with your bucks you could really do it up big. Rent a yacht, the penthouse suite of the most expensive hotel... You get my drift.''

"Sounds easy enough.''

Pete reached out with his massive hands to pat down the dirt around the plant. "Nothing, where women are concerned, is easy.''

"I'm learning that.''

"Of course, what I really recommend doesn't cost a penny. But it's the hardest damn thing to do.''

"What's that?''

Pete's gaze was sober when it met his. "Be totally honest. Share your feelings. Tell her you love her. Tell her how she makes you feel.''

Much as he longed to, he couldn't do that. Not yet anyway. Not until he was certain his feelings would be reciprocated. He just wasn't that brave.

"I'll take it under advisement.''

After he left Pete, Brady spent the rest of the afternoon thinking about his future. His and Haven's and Anna's. When he heard Haven's car pull into the driveway shortly after six, he walked to the front door.

"Hi, Unca Bwady,'' Anna greeted him when he held the door open for her.

"Hi, squirt. *Sesame Street* is ready for you in the den. All you have to do is punch the play button.''

"Thanks!'' The little girl raced past him down the hall.

Chuckling, he turned his head and saw Haven framed in the doorway. The sound of his chuckle died, and his breath caught in his throat. For the briefest of seconds, it seemed that his heart stopped beating before jolting to a start again. The late-afternoon sun stroked the riot of curls that framed her face, making her hair shimmer like molten lava. She looked incredibly beautiful. And utterly unattainable.

"Hi,'' he said softly.

"Hi, back.''

It was probably a trick of the light, but her eyes looked warm and happy to see him. "How was your day?"

"Fine. How was yours?"

"Fine." He wanted to take her in his arms, to kiss her and hold her, the way he'd seen Pete kiss and hold Eileen at the end of a long day spent apart. Instead, he held his arms stiffly at his sides. He was not Pete, Haven was not Eileen and theirs certainly was not a "normal" marriage. Gestures of affection were reserved primarily for the bedroom.

"If you've got a moment," he said, "I'd like to talk to you."

She preceded him into the living room. When she'd taken a seat at the sofa, she looked up at him curiously. "Sounds serious."

"It is." He sat down next to her. "I've made a decision."

She stilled. "About what?" Her voice sounded subdued, cautious.

"About me. But in the long run, it will affect both you and Anna." He paused. "I've decided what I'm going to do with the rest of my life."

"You have?" She looked taken aback, as if this was the last thing she'd expected to hear.

He nodded, then smiled gently. "You don't expect me to hang around the house like a slug forever, do you?"

"No. And you're not a slug. You're taking a well-deserved vacation. There's no need to rush into anything, you know."

If only he could delude himself that her concern was more than what she would express for any man who'd been through his ordeal. "I'm not rushing, Haven. This is something I've been toying with for years now. I've finally decided to go ahead with it."

She wrapped her hands around her knees. "Tell me about it, then."

"I've decided to set up a foundation in Charles's name. I want to help kids like me, kids stuck in the foster care system." He heard the excitement in his voice as he got caught up in the idea. "The foundation will track these kids through school, and if they maintain a certain grade-point average and stay out of trouble, it will pay for their college education. Next week, I'm meeting with a man who established a similar foundation in New York. He's going to help me get started."

This time there was no mistaking the warmth and pleasure in her eyes. "Oh, Brady, that's a wonderful idea. If you need any help, you can count on me."

"I'll hold you to it. All my research tells me there will be a ton of paperwork to set this thing up."

The phone rang. While Haven moved to answer it, Brady solidified his plans in his mind. First, he'd go to New York and meet with Adam Bishop, learn everything he could. Then, when he got home, he'd get busy on all the paperwork. And he'd woo his wife. Good and proper.

His thoughts trailed off when he saw the look on Haven's face. Slowly, she lowered the phone.

"It's the lab," she said. "The DNA test results are in."

"I can't believe it," Haven said, staring unseeingly into her coffee cup. The full cup no longer felt warm to the fingers she'd wrapped around it—when? A minute ago? An hour? Two? She had no idea how long she'd been sitting at the kitchen table, staring at the unmoving liquid, only that it had been long enough for it to grow as cold as she felt on the inside.

"Neither can I," Brady replied in a low voice.

In the den, the grandfather clock chimed the time. Disbelief made Haven raise her head to stare at her surroundings. How could it be ten o'clock already? How could almost four hours have passed since learning the devastating news that had, once again, rocked her world?

"Maybe they made a mistake," she said.

Brady looked up from his undrunk coffee and gave a bitter laugh. "You heard the man as well as I did. He said there was a 99.97 percent probability that someone else is Anna's father. There was no mistake.''

Haven heard the underlying anguish in his voice and brought her thoughts up short. How selfish she was! Here she'd been, just thinking of herself and of how the news would impact her relationship with Brady. And there he sat, across from her, looking green in the face, as if he were going to be ill. He should be relieved, she thought. The pressure was off. He had no obligation where she and Anna were concerned.

But instead of looking relieved, he looked dazed and crushed. It didn't take a genius to understand why. He'd thought he had a daughter. He'd given his heart to Anna. For the first time in a long time, he'd thought he had a family. Now what did he have? Nothing.

"I'm so sorry," she said, her heart going out to him. "This must be very hard for you."

"I've been going over and over it in my mind, and I still don't understand it. Why did she do it? Why did she write that letter?" His voice sounded harsh and unnatural. He threaded an unsteady hand through his hair as his gaze sought and captured hers. "How could she lie like that?"

Haven didn't understand it any better than Brady did. All she knew was that she couldn't stand his pain. "I told you before, Melinda never lied. Deep in her heart, she must have believed you were Anna's father. She wouldn't have written you that letter otherwise. I guess, with everything she was going through once her illness was diagnosed, she got confused."

"It still doesn't change the fact that I'm not Anna's father," he said quietly.

"No, it doesn't," she agreed.

It was time. Time to broach the subject she'd been dreading. She swallowed as her heart faltered a beat.

"I guess this changes things. Between us, I mean."

A stillness came over him. "I guess it does."

She wished she could tell what he was thinking. But the

longer she gazed at him, the more he seemed to withdraw from her.

"So, what do we do now?" she asked.

"What do you want to do?"

What did she want to do? She wanted to crawl into his arms and stay there.

"Whatever you want to do." It cost her a lot to offer up those words.

He raised one eyebrow. "I have final say in this?"

"You certainly have one of the two votes."

He waited the space of a heartbeat before replying. "Then I vote we go on the way we have been. At least for now."

Stunned, Haven stared at him. "You want to stay married?" she blurted without thinking.

"Yes."

"Why?"

"The way I see it, Anna needs us more than ever. We're the only thing standing between her and the Zieglars."

In the stunned aftermath of the news, Haven had forgotten all about the Zieglars and the threat they posed. "Oh, Lord," she breathed, her hand flying to her mouth. "The Zieglars. I forgot."

"Well, I didn't."

"What about after?" she asked.

"After we make sure they can never touch Anna, you mean?"

She nodded.

Something flickered in his eyes. "I just can't walk away from her, Haven."

No, he couldn't, she realized. The last thing he would want Anna to feel was the abandonment he'd felt when he was her age. But was this feeling of obligation enough, in the long run, to keep him by her side?

As always, Haven's breath caught and her heartbeat speeded up just looking at him. "Will you still want more children?"

What a stupid question, she thought. Of course he would

still want children. Those children would be more important to him now than ever.

"When you're ready," he confirmed.

Here it was—time to tell him the truth. But she couldn't tell him now. With nothing standing between her and the Zieglars except a marriage that the court might look upon in her favor, Anna's future was too precarious for her to risk. No, she couldn't tell him. Not now. She'd have to wait until after the hearing.

"The lab report doesn't change my feelings for Anna," Brady said. "It doesn't change my desire to be her father." He rose from his seat and pulled her pliant body into his arms. "It doesn't change the way I still want you."

But would knowing that she couldn't give him children change that want?

Haven's heart hammered to a stop, then started again. Brady's eyes smoldered as he looked down at her, and she trembled with the prospect of a pleasure so keen it was almost unbearable. When his head lowered and he swept her mouth with his tongue, all her doubts and fears were driven from her mind. All that existed was the fire that roared to life inside her. All that mattered was Brady's kiss and the way his fingertips seemed to shoot more fire into the depths of her skin wherever he touched her.

Tonight, she decided, she would not allow herself to think of the future and all its frightening possibilities. Nor would she allow herself to think of the past, and its loneliness and pain. For tonight, she had this one moment, and she intended to cherish it.

Brady pulled his mouth from hers and laid his forehead against hers. "Tell me you want me to stay," he urged, breathing hard, his hands moving in restless motions up and down her arms.

Haven's throat worked, but no sound emerged. When she finally found the words, her voice was hoarse. "Yes, Brady, I want you to stay." Forever and ever.

"God, I want you," he said, his voice thick.

"I want you, too," she breathed, then eagerly searched out his mouth with her own.

Just when she thought she'd surely die from the yearning, he pulled away from her to collect the coffee cups and carry them to the sink. That chore disposed of, he turned off the light and gathered her up into his arms.

Haven expected him to carry her up the stairs to her bedroom, the way he had that first night they'd made love. Instead, he surprised her by gently placing her on the kitchen table. No sooner had he done that, than his mouth fastened on hers once more.

"Brady," she said between kisses.

"Hmm?" His hands were busy unfastening their clothing. She trembled as the cool night air flowing through the open window kissed her skin.

"Shouldn't we go upstairs?"

He paused in the process of unhooking her bra to gaze at her with fevered eyes. "I can't wait that long."

His head lowered and his mouth closed over one turgid nipple. In the blaze of desire that consumed her at his touch, Haven realized that, heaven help her, neither could she.

When Brady entered her a moment later with one long, hard, possessive thrust, she cried out with the glory of it. As she clutched her arms around his neck and met every movement of his hips with an answering movement of her own, she was totally unaware of the hardness of the table against her back. Her reality consisted of the feel of him, deep inside her, and the cries issuing from both their throats as, together, they reached the summit of their passion.

Much later, she lay in bed beside him, staring at the ceiling and listening to his deep, even breathing. Silent tears streamed down her cheeks as her heart ached with the secret longing for his love. Though their lovemaking had been more beautiful and satisfying than ever, she'd never felt lonelier in her life.

Chapter 13

"Turn around," Haven instructed. "I want to check how the jacket hangs again."

Brady grimaced at his reflection in the three-way mirror before turning as requested. It was the fifth suit he'd tried on in the space of an hour, and Haven had found all of them wanting in one way or another. Either the fabric was wrong, or the color was off, or the jacket or pants didn't hang just so.

His irritation mounted as the overeager salesman fussed at his lapels. It took all his willpower to resist the urge to slap the man's hands away. As far as he was concerned, the lightweight gray summer suit looked just fine. Why he had to keep pivoting this way and that to please both Haven and the salesman was beyond him.

"Is this really necessary?" he asked.

He knew his tone bordered on rudeness, but he couldn't help it. He hated shopping. All it took to make his hackles rise was the setting of one toe over the threshold of a store. To spend an hour there was sheer torture. Although, he admitted to himself, there was a small part of him—a very small part—that enjoyed Haven fussing over him like this.

Now, if he could only get the salesman to leave him alone.

"Yes, Brady," she said in a patient voice, "it is necessary. You're flying to New York this afternoon, remember? It would hardly be appropriate for you to show up at your meeting in a tuxedo."

"I know that. I meant all this—" He waved a hand at the people milling around the crowded store. "I feel like a peacock on exhibit at the zoo."

"Besides me, no one's paying any attention," she said dismissively. "Now, turn around and cross your arms over your chest, so I can see how the fabric pulls." Her tone was one that Brady was certain she reserved for her most stubborn and unreasonable students.

With a resigned sigh, he did as he was told. After all, he had no one but himself to blame for this particular predicament. Up until he'd started packing for his trip that morning, he'd forgotten all about the woeful limitations of his wardrobe.

"It's perfect," Haven said. "No alterations will be necessary."

Brady almost sagged in relief.

"Are you always this grumpy?" she asked, as the salesman, tape measure wrapped around his neck, helped Brady out of the jacket.

"I hate shopping for clothes. I avoid it at all costs."

Her eyes twinkled. "I know. I've seen your wardrobe."

Despite the harshness of the artificial lighting that bathed her face, it still managed to retain a soft, golden glow. He wondered how long he would have to stare at her features before he'd tire of them. He was fairly certain the earth would have stopped rotating on its axis long before that happened.

"Would the gentleman like anything else?" the salesman asked.

The gentleman would like to ravish his beautiful wife. "The gentleman would like to go home."

"The gentleman needs another suit, some shirts and ties and a pair of shoes," Haven corrected. At the pained look he sent her, she added, "If you're going to play the part of wealthy philanthropist, you have to dress for it."

At wit's end, he shot back, "If I was at all interested in playing the part of wealthy philanthropist, I'd be having my suits custom-made, instead of buying them off the rack."

"It was a joke, Brady," she said softly, her eyes gently reproachful.

That was the problem, he realized. Lately, everything with her was a joke. Whenever he tried to hold a serious conversation, all he got in return was light banter. Ask about the latest front-page crisis and they'd somehow wind up talking about the price of lettuce or some other such nonsense.

He knew she was terrified of the upcoming hearing, but she wouldn't talk to him about it. "Syd has everything under control" was the most she would say.

One evening, when he'd tried to share with her the pain he'd felt upon learning that he wasn't Anna's biological father, her body language had told him she didn't want to hear it. Next thing he knew, he'd been discussing the merits of slides versus photographs. He'd let the subject drop. He hadn't broached it, or anything remotely personal, since.

Her silence was driving him crazy. Which was the real reason behind his irritability. Funny, he reflected, how their roles had reversed. In the beginning, she'd been the one interested in talking and sharing. Now that he wanted to talk, all she wanted was to be left alone.

It was, he thought, almost as if they were hanging, suspended in time, with their future to be resolved only after the hearing was over and Anna's security assured. Brady knew what he wanted. He wanted to stay married to Haven. And even though she wasn't his biological child, he wanted to be a father to Anna. And it would give him great pleasure to see his child grow in Haven's belly. However, Haven's silence told him that she might not want the same things he did. He didn't try to fool himself that sex—even great sex—was enough to keep her by his side permanently.

An hour later, the back seat of his car filled with his purchases, he pulled to a stop in front of the day care center.

"Sure you don't want me to drive you to the airport?" Haven asked.

He shook his head. "You've been away from the center long enough as it is."

She seemed relieved. "When will you be back?"

"Friday evening. Don't wait dinner."

Will you miss me? he wondered. *Or will you even notice I'm gone?* After all, she was the most self-sufficient person he'd ever met. What did she need him for?

"You should have had lunch, instead of shopping with me," he said.

She shrugged. "I think the future of an untold number of children is a little more important than my stomach." She paused, and her blue eyes became meltingly soft. "I don't know whether I told you yet or not, but I think what you're planning to do is wonderful. I think it will give you a lot of satisfaction."

Though her admiration felt good, what he really wanted was her love. "Promise me you'll order a sandwich the minute you get back to your office, and that you'll eat every bite," he said, his voice gruff.

"I promise."

And promise that you'll miss me, just a little.

He reached out and pulled her as close as the confines of the compact car would allow. Finding the curve of her cheek with his palm, he let it rest there. As he gazed into her eyes, he wondered how many years it would take before such a simple touch didn't stop his heart.

They sat like that for a long moment without speaking. Then, when he could bear the distance no longer, he covered her mouth with his and kissed her fiercely. Her return kiss was equally fierce.

"Have a safe trip," she said when they came up for air.

"See you Friday." It was just two days, he told himself. Why did it seem like forever? Why did he get the feeling that nothing would be the same between them when he returned?

He pulled her close one more time and held her as if letting go would kill him, which was exactly how he felt. Reluctantly, when she pulled back, he allowed his arms to fall away. He heard the click of the latch, then she was out of the car and he was watching the gentle sway of her hips as she walked up the curved path leading to the center's front door. She turned and waved once before disappearing inside.

Brady put the car in gear and resolutely centered his thoughts on the tasks at hand. He'd had enough introspection for one day. Besides, it wasn't getting him anywhere.

First, he had to pack. Then he had an errand to run. It was, perhaps, the most important errand of his life. This afternoon, before he got on that plane to New York, he was determined to give Haven the one thing in the world she wanted above all else. He was going to give her Anna.

"Ready?" he asked.

"Ready," Pete replied.

"Let's go, then."

They climbed out of the car onto the circular driveway fronting an elegant stone mansion. To the untrained eye, the place exuded wealth and social standing. However, armed with the information from his sources, Brady could see the subtle signs of the beginning stages of neglect. The paint on the window frames had begun to flake just the slightest bit. The grounds, while not unkempt, were less than immaculately groomed. Another couple of months and the weeds would own the place.

And it was all because Douglas Zieglar was having money trouble. Big trouble. Brady couldn't be more delighted.

"Is this what it felt like when you left on one of your missions?" Pete asked when they reached the door.

Brady pressed the doorbell. "How do you mean?"

"Adrenaline surge, heart beating like a drum, blood pressure soaring, nerves stretched to the breaking point. Little things like that."

He nodded. "Pretty much." Although the stakes today were much higher than any he'd faced before.

"Now I know why you gave it up." Pete grimaced. "If my stomach was tied in knots like this every day, I'd be in ulcer city in no time. I'm amazed you lasted as long as you did."

So was he, but he didn't want to waste time thinking about it now. He needed to focus all his energies on the task at hand.

"Do you have the contract?" he asked Pete.

"In my pocket, along with a pen. And before you ask, it has plenty of ink." Pete lifted his hand so that the small black box he held cupped in his palm was in full view. "Camcorder's ready, battery newly charged, film in place. You have the check?"

Brady patted his jacket. "Signed and duly certified."

"Then I guess we have everything. I only have one question. You sure this is legal?"

"It's legal."

"Then why do you need me?"

"You're my insurance policy. If we get the whole thing on tape, there's no way Douglas Zieglar will be able to weasel out of the contract later. Or claim he signed it under duress."

The door was answered by a uniformed butler, and Brady wondered if the man knew how close he was to standing in an unemployment line. "We're here to see Mr. and Mrs. Zieglar."

"Who may I ask is calling, sir?"

"Tell them that Brady Ross is here."

Two minutes later, he and Pete were ushered into a living room that was easily the size of the entire first floor of Haven's house. The walls were painted a deep, oppressive green, the ceiling was nosebleedingly high and heavy brocaded curtains hung at the many floor-to-ceiling windows. Everything about the room was dark and brooding, including the intricately carved furniture, the Oriental carpets scattered across the floor, the oil paintings hung precisely at eye level and the expensive objets d'art that were strategically displayed.

Absently, Brady ran a finger over a Fabergé egg that sat atop a marble fireplace mantel. How soon, he wondered, before Douglas would be reduced to selling these pieces off, one by one? Had he already started?

Pete gave a low whistle as he did some exploring of his own. "Pretty fancy."

Brady eyed his surroundings with distaste. "If you like this sort of thing." His tone of voice left Pete in no doubt that he didn't. The good news was that the Zieglars did. They wouldn't take losing all this very gracefully. Especially, from what little he knew of her, Pamela.

He was well aware that he could be living like this, but the idea held little appeal. It never had, partly due to Charles's influence. His father had always insisted on living far below his means. But the real reason that Brady never could be comfortable in a place like this was that, after everything he'd been through, after all the suffering he'd witnessed, he would like to see his adoptive father's money used for something a little more important than the collection of "things." Besides, he much preferred the cozy intimacy of Haven's house. That was a home. This was just a showcase, with no personality. No warmth. Like its owners.

Their hosts kept them waiting for over twenty minutes. When they finally entered the room, Douglas and Pamela Zieglar looked cool and regal and condescending. Their patrician noses were pointed so high in the air, Brady thought it a miracle they could see in front of themselves. He wondered how cool and regal they'd look once he told them he knew, practically to the penny, the amount of the debt Douglas had run up.

Douglas's eyes flickered over Pete. "There was no need to bring a bodyguard, Mr. Ross," he said stiffly. "*You* are certainly in no danger here.'' His tone implied that he and Pamela might be.

''Mr. Loring isn't my bodyguard. He's my oldest and most trusted friend. I asked him to accompany me so that he could film our conversation.''

''Why would you want to film our conversation?'' Pamela inquired with a sniff.

''I want there to be no mistake about what was said... afterward.''

''I'm not accustomed to having my conversations taped,'' Douglas said haughtily, ''and I resent the implication that I can't be trusted.''

He raised a brass bell from a side table and rang it once. Immediately, the butler appeared in the doorway.

''Gordon, Mr. Ross and his...friend are leaving. Would you please show them the way out.''

The butler stood aside and waited for Brady and Pete to precede him into the hallway.

Brady shrugged. ''Have it your way. But before I go, there's something I'd like you to see.''

He pulled the check out of his pocket and waved it in front of Douglas's nose. The older man's eyes widened when he saw the amount written there, an amount large enough to cover his debt, plus leave him some money to play with afterward.

''It's made out to you, and it's certified. Of course, there are some conditions attached. However, if you're not interested...'' Brady let his voice trail off before saying, ''Let's go, Pete.''

They were two steps from the door when Douglas spoke. ''Perhaps I've been a bit hasty. Gordon, the gentlemen will be staying after all.''

Nodding, Gordon left the room.

Hiding a triumphant smile, Brady slowly turned to face the couple who had wreaked such havoc in his and Haven's lives. He stood silently in the doorway, refusing to be the first to speak. It was important they know who had the upper hand here. He could tell by the look on Douglas's face that it galled him no end, but Brady also knew the man was too desperate to let him go.

In the end, greed won out over pride. Squaring his shoulders, Douglas drew an audible breath and visibly schooled his features into an impassive mask. "Why have you come here, Mr. Ross?"

Brady nodded to Pete, who raised the camcorder and began filming.

"First, I'd like your permission to tape our discussion."

Douglas gave a grudging nod.

"Out loud, please," Brady said, moving to stand next to the man so that Pete could get them both in the frame. He nodded toward the camcorder. "For the record."

"You have my permission to film this conversation," Douglas said tightly.

"Thank you. For the record, then, let me state the date and time. I'm here today to make you an offer. In exchange for the withdrawal of your petition for custody of Anna Dolan, and for your sworn written statement that you will never again seek to remove her from Haven Adams's custody or try to gain control of any of her inheritance, I will give you this check."

Brady held the check up in front of him, and Pete duly zoomed the camera lens in on it.

"You're just afraid we'll win the court case," Pamela burst out. "If you think we can be bought off, you have another think coming."

"Shut up, Pamela," Douglas said softly.

Tossing a wounded look to her husband, Pamela shut up.

It wasn't that Brady didn't think Haven would prevail. He did. He was certain that any reasonable judge would choose her over the Zieglars. But, like Haven when she'd come to him and begged him to assert his parental rights, he couldn't take the chance that he might be wrong.

"You might win," he conceded, his gaze locked with

Douglas's. "And if you do, you'll undoubtedly be able to get your hands on a lot more money than the amount I've written on that check. But then again, you might not win. You see, Haven's lawyer plans on parading a whole slew of witnesses before the judge who will make her look more saintly than Mother Teresa."

"And we have witnesses who can prove she isn't," Douglas said.

"All you have is a vindictive ex-employee. All your charges can be rationally explained away. You know Haven. You know the impression she'll make on the judge. Your case is by no means a sure thing. But the check I'm offering you is. The question is, how much of a gambler are you? If my information is correct, and I have no reason to believe it isn't, your instincts haven't served you too well lately."

It took Douglas and Pamela all of two seconds to come to a decision. A phone call was made, and the petition for custody was withdrawn. Once that was accomplished, the butler and maid were summoned to witness the signing of the contract, and the check was placed in Douglas's hot little fist.

"Now, if you'll excuse me," Brady said, "I have a plane to catch." At the door, he paused and turned one last time. "A word of advice. I'd keep my investments in blue-chip stocks from now on. They're much safer."

"Why are you doing this?" Douglas asked, his face a mask of bewilderment. "She's not even your daughter. I'd think you'd be happy to get rid of her."

Brady felt nothing but pity for this sorry excuse for a human being. "Why am I doing this?" he said. "For a reason you will never understand. Love."

Too restless to sit, Haven crossed her office and stood at the window. Outside, the sun blazed, the birds sang and the flowers filled the air with their fragrance. But it could have been gray and rainy for all she noticed, so absorbed was she in her thoughts. At the moment, they centered on one person in particular: Brady.

He'd been gone only one night, and already she missed him dreadfully. The house seemed empty without him there, her bed unbearably lonely. Last night, she'd worn one of his shirts to bed, because it had comforted her just to have the scent of him near. Still, she'd tossed and turned all night, longing for the feel of his arms around her.

The phone rang, startling her to sudden awareness. Reaching behind her, she raised the receiver to her ear.

"Are you sitting down?" Syd asked without greeting.

"Should I be?"

"Sit down, Haven."

Her heart lurched at the seriousness of his voice, and her fingers tightened involuntarily around the receiver. Whatever it was, it had to be bad.

"All right," she said, willing herself to remain calm as she moved behind her desk. "I'm sitting. What is it?"

There was a long pause, during which her heartbeat accelerated. "You'll never believe it," he said finally. "The Zieglars have withdrawn their petition."

Relief left her light-headed. If she'd been standing, she knew her knees would have given out on her.

"But why? How? What happened?" She realized she was laughing and crying at the same time. She couldn't believe it. Anna was safe.

"I have no idea," Syd replied. "All I know is, I got a call from their lawyer not ten minutes ago, informing me the petition had been withdrawn."

When she hung up the phone several minutes later, Haven wished she could call Brady to give him the good news. Unfortunately, he hadn't left a number where he could be reached.

Brady. Some of the joy went out of her. The last week in particular, she'd noticed a strain in him, a peculiar tension. She knew she was the cause. Whenever he'd tried talking about something personal, she'd been so terrified he'd bring up the subject of children that she'd made a joke or deliberately steered the conversation to a safer topic. At odd moments, she'd caught him looking at her, his eyes questioning. She hadn't been able to keep from wondering if he'd regretted his decision to stay, once he learned the DNA test results.

He'd told her that Anna needed them more than ever now, because of the threat the Zieglars posed. Well, the Zieglars no longer posed a threat. Anna was safe. There was no reason for him to stay.

Except that he was an honorable man. Though he'd avoided them all his life, he'd made a commitment to Haven and their marriage. A commitment that had nothing to do with love, but a commitment nonetheless. She knew he would abide by it, unless she gave him an out.

From her hazy recollection of a law course she'd taken in college, she knew that when one party entered into a contract fraudulently, the entire contract was rendered null and void. It was time for her to tell Brady the truth, that she could never give him a child. Time for her to let him know she'd accepted his offer of making their marriage a real one under false pretenses. Time to give him an out.

And if he walked away?

Haven swallowed hard and blinked back tears. Deep down, she didn't know what would be worse: Brady walking out on her when he learned the truth, or spending the rest of her life with him without possessing his love.

It was pure impulse that led Brady to the phone booth when his plane landed Friday evening. Pure impulse that had him leafing through the dangling phone book until he located the address of one Asa Adams. Pure impulse that had him driving to the house where Haven's parents lived.

He was riding on a wave of euphoria. The threat to Anna had been removed, and his meeting had gone far better than he'd anticipated, leaving his mind churning with dozens of ideas he couldn't wait to implement. For the first time in more years than he could remember, he felt hopeful about the future. And it was all Haven's doing. Haven's and Anna's. They'd opened his eyes to all that was possible. They'd made him believe in goodness again.

He couldn't wait to get home to them, to tell them both that he loved them. But first, he needed to take a slight detour. Because it was time to start courting his wife, and he hoped Haven's parents could shed some light on the best way for him to go about it. And if, in the process, he brought about a reconciliation between them, so much the better. More than ever now, he realized the importance of family.

The woman who answered the door of the nondescript stucco house was Haven thirty years from now.

"Mrs. Adams?"

"I'm sorry," she said, her voice distant but polite. "We don't talk to salesmen."

"I'm not a salesman. My name is Brady Ross." Since there was no tactful way to break the news that their daughter had married without their knowledge, he simply forged ahead. "I'm Haven's husband."

She took the news without showing any emotion whatsoever. "So Haven's married."

"Yes."

He'd expected to be bombarded with questions about where they'd met, how long they had known each other and why hadn't she and her husband been invited to the wedding. At the very least, he'd expected to be asked about what he did for a living and how he planned to support their daughter. But the woman just stood there, staring at him politely. For all the interest she showed, they might have been discussing the weather.

"May I come in please?"

She led him into a room that was as impersonal as a hotel. It was neat and sparsely furnished, with just a sofa, coffee table and two armchairs. The sofa and armchairs were brown; the carpet beneath his feet, olive green. There were no family pictures scattered about. No knickknacks. The only personal touch was the books. Wall after wall of them. From where he was standing, they all looked scientific in nature.

Brady's gaze went to the middle-aged man sitting in one of the armchairs. He was smoking a pipe and reading the latest edition of the *Journal of Biological Chemistry*.

"Asa?" Doris Adams said. "This is Brady Ross. He says he's Haven's husband."

Asa Adams showed even less reaction than his wife had to the news. With obvious reluctance, he lowered his magazine. Standing, he extended his hand to Brady.

"Mr. Ross."

What was wrong with these people? Brady wondered as he shook the proffered hand. They acted more like robots than living, breathing beings. It struck him then that this was the state he'd been striving toward for so many years. If he'd reached it, he would have been just like them. The thought was chilling.

"I thought it was time we were introduced," Brady said. "And, while I was here, I was also wondering if you had any photo albums of Haven that I could look through."

Asa Adams shook his head. "None, I'm afraid. My wife and I aren't into photography. We're scientists, you see."

No, Brady didn't see. What did being a scientist have to do with taking pictures of your only child?

"Well," he said, struggling to remain calm against the anger surging through him, "perhaps you could tell me what she was like as a child. What was she interested in? What activities did she participate in?"

"I'm afraid I can't help you much there, either," Asa said. "That was her nanny's province."

"She did act in a play at school once," Doris volunteered. "Remember, Asa, when we traveled up to see her?"

"Oh, yes," the man said, nodding. "It snowed the whole way. Terrible trip. Terrible."

These people couldn't be real, Brady thought. Next to them, the Zieglars gave him the warm fuzzies. He was beginning to think that nothing short of a heart transplant would warm them up. He'd thought Haven had been exaggerating when she told him how they'd ignored her all her life. Now he knew she hadn't.

"Would you like to see her bedroom?" Doris Adams asked. "We've kept it the way it was when she lived here."

That didn't surprise him. It didn't look as if they'd changed a thing in the house since the mid 1970s.

As he followed the older woman out of the room, he glanced back over his shoulder. Asa Adams had resumed his seat and was once again lost in his journal. Brady knew the man had forgotten his presence.

"Here it is," Doris said when they reached the end of a narrow hallway.

The room was monastic, with just a single bed jutting out from one wall and a small desk and dresser. Where, he wondered, were the dolls? The toys? The posters? Anything to show that a young girl had once resided here?

His thoughts must have shown on his face, because Doris said, "We don't put much stock in playthings. Intellectual pursuits are much more stimulating to the growing mind."

Brady wondered if a two-year-old would see it that way. No wonder Haven surrounded herself with frills and bright colors. Her childhood must have been unbearably drab and lonely.

Had Doris Adams ever cuddled her only child in her arms and cooed to her? Or had she, instead, used flash cards with mathematical formulas as tools of bonding? And what about Asa Adams? Had he ever scooped Haven into his arms after she scraped a knee or fell off her bike, and kissed her hurt away? Brady found it impossible to picture. If ever there were two people in the world who had no business procreating, it was the two human icicles who called themselves Haven's parents.

Sudden rage filled him, and he had to clench his hands tightly by his sides to keep from putting a fist through the wall. How could they treat her that way? And who, ultimately, had been more cruel? His parents by walking out on him, or Haven's parents for sticking around and raising her?

"I've seen enough, thank you," he said abruptly. "I really have to be going now."

As he'd expected, Doris Adams didn't protest.

While he followed her through the house, Brady couldn't help marveling at the warm, loving woman who was his wife. Given her background, it was truly a miracle she could love at all.

"Is she still running that day care center of hers and taking care of that little girl?" Doris asked when they reached the front door.

That little girl had a name, Brady wanted to say. "Yes."

The older woman shook her head with disapproval. It was the first emotion Brady had seen from her.

"What a waste. She could have been the next Marie Curie, you know. She's that brilliant. Instead, she's throwing her life away on that child. I told her, after the accident, when the doctor said there'd be no children, that it was the best thing that could have happened to her. Why she couldn't be happy about it is beyond me."

Brady felt like his gut was being ripped out. "The accident?" he asked hoarsely.

"Didn't she tell you? When she was sixteen, she was in a car accident. There was internal damage."

Yes, she'd told him. She'd just left out a few, rather significant details. "And that was when she found out she couldn't have children?"

Doris nodded.

It wasn't that she'd lied to him, although that hurt like hell. It was what the lie meant that tore his heart to shreds. Her agreement to make their marriage a real one had only been for Anna's sake, nothing else. Feelings for him had never entered the picture.

Brady sat in the car for a long time, watching the sun go down. Then, with one sudden move, he pounded his fist against the steering wheel.

"Damn you, Haven!" he shouted. "Damn you for making me care."

Chapter 14

Haven was frantic by the time the grandfather clock chimed midnight. Where was Brady? He'd said his flight would arrive that evening. Although he hadn't given her a time, surely he should have been home by now.

Adrenaline surged through her veins, making her heart beat at roughly the speed of a hummingbird's wings. As she roamed from room to room, kittens scrambling to stay out of the path of her restless feet, her chest felt tight and her hands trembled when she ran her fingers through her hair. Every minute or so, she paused to peer out a window. No matter how many times she checked, her driveway remained resolutely empty.

She couldn't eat. She couldn't read. She couldn't sit still long enough to watch television or listen to the stereo. All she could do was pace and worry. She now knew exactly how many steps it took to get around her house. If she ever went blind, she'd have no problem finding her way.

Repeated calls to the airport had assured her that all flights from New York City had arrived on time, and that there were no air disasters to report. Likewise, the local hospitals had admitted no one named Brady Ross, nor did they have any John Does matching his description. Haven had stopped short of calling the morgue; her mind refused to entertain that possibility. She'd toyed with, then discarded, the idea of calling the Lorings to see if they had heard from him. Why worry them needlessly? As it was, she was already worrying enough for ten people.

The logical conclusion, she told herself, was that he'd decided to stay in New York another night. But surely, if that was the case, he would have picked up the telephone and let her know. Of course, he wouldn't be able to do that if he'd been beaten and mugged and his broken body was lying in some deserted alley.

When she heard the sound of his car pulling into the driveway shortly after one, relief left her limp and she had to sit down to collect herself. He was okay. All her worry had been for nothing.

The anger that flooded through her took her by surprise. He was okay. All her worry had been for nothing. She decided that when she saw him, he'd better at least have the decency to have a scratch on him, or to be suffering from temporary amnesia.

The front door swung inward, and her anger left her as quickly as it had come. Brady was home. She had a sudden need to feel his arms around her, and prepared to launch herself at him the minute he came into view. One look at his face, stony and expressionless, and she stopped cold in her tracks. She imagined she saw ice chips in his eyes. The old Brady was back. With a vengeance.

After drawing a deep breath and letting it out slowly, Haven spoke in a voice that gave no hint of her inner agitation. "How was your trip?"

"Fine." The word was clipped, emotionless.

He stood in the doorway, staring about him as if he'd never

seen the place before. Maybe he had received a bump on the head. He certainly didn't look himself.

"Are you okay?"

"Just tired." He thrust his fingers through hair that looked as if it had seen that motion a dozen times already. "It's been a long day."

"Can I get you something to eat?"

"I'm not hungry."

He made no move to come any farther inside. Feeling awkward and ill at ease, Haven searched for something to say.

"Syd called yesterday. The Zieglars have dropped their petition."

"That must make you happy."

Compared with Brady's, a robot's voice carried more emotion. The one thing Haven was certain of was his love for Anna. For him to show no reaction to her news meant that something was wrong. Very wrong. Her anxiety built.

"What aren't you telling me, Brady? Why are you acting this way? Did something happen on your trip?"

His eyes narrowed. Tension emanated from beneath his skin in a tangible wave. Haven felt a sharp, answering coil of uneasiness unfold in her stomach.

"I went to see your parents tonight."

Oh, no. No wonder he was behaving so strangely. Five minutes alone with her parents could suck the life out of anyone.

"You told them about us?"

He nodded.

"How'd they take it?"

The cynical smile she'd thought gone forever curved his mouth. "How do you think they took it?"

Her laugh was short and without humor. "Knowing them, they didn't blink."

"I've never met two more unfeeling people in my life," he said harshly. "And that includes the Zieglars."

"I'm sorry, Brady. If I'd known what you had in mind, I would have warned you about them."

The coldness left his eyes, and they blazed at her with accusation. "Your mother told me about your accident. Odd, how her account differed from yours."

A cold finger touched Haven's spine, and her breath caught in her throat. "So you know…"

"That you can't have children," he supplied. "Yes, I know." He gave a bitter laugh, and his face told her that what she'd dreaded most had come to pass. Their marriage was over.

"Were you ever going to tell me?"

She didn't try to evade his gaze. "Yes."

"When?"

"Tonight."

His jaw tightened. "Now that the Zieglars have dropped their petition, you mean."

She couldn't deny it. Simplistic though it was, it was still the truth. If she'd thought for a minute she'd have a chance of reaching him, she would have tried to explain. But the look in his eyes told her he wasn't interested in explanations.

"Yes."

His Adam's apple traveled the length of his throat and down again. His glance slid past her to a point at the end of the hallway. "That's what I thought."

Tentatively, she reached out a hand, then drew it back. "You're leaving, aren't you?"

His gaze came back to her. Once again his eyes were cold and remote. Lifeless. "Can you think of one reason I should stay?"

Only that she was hopelessly in love with him. A love he didn't return. Add to that the fact she couldn't give him the children he wanted and, no, she couldn't think of one good reason for him to stick around. Oh, she supposed she could use Anna to guilt him into staying. But it was no longer enough just to have him with her. Haven didn't want Brady to stay, unless his love was part of the bargain.

Her insides clenched painfully, and she wanted to cry out at the unfairness of it. Pride kept her chin thrust forward and her eyes dry.

"No," she said, "I can't."

"I can't, either."

For a brief second, she squeezed her eyes shut against the pain that knifed through her. When she opened them, she asked, "What about Anna?"

"What about her?"

She wished he wouldn't look at her as if he could see right through her. "Are you just going to walk out on her without so much as a goodbye?"

"Of course not." He paused. "I know I have no right, but I'd like to continue seeing her. I'd like to do things with her, take her places. That is, if you'll allow it."

Haven's throat tightened. "You know you don't have to ask."

"Thank you. I'll go gather my things now."

He brushed past her and began climbing the stairs. At the top, he stopped and turned. "About the kittens. I'd like Anna to keep them, if that's okay with you."

She couldn't speak past the lump in her throat, so she nodded.

"I won't be long," he said.

After he disappeared down the hallway, Haven moved into the living room. Glory Be rubbed against her ankle, and she absently reached down and scooped up the kitten. Holding the purring animal close, she parted a curtain and stared out into the darkness. Though the night was warm, she couldn't stop shivering.

When she heard Brady's footsteps on the stairs, she let the curtain fall back into place. Purposely, she kept her back to him, so he wouldn't be able to see her face. She didn't have the emotional energy to hide her feelings from him any longer.

"Thank you for all your help with Anna," she said. Her voice sounded brittle, instead of calm, as she'd intended. "I really do appreciate everything you've done."

"Haven…"

His hesitation made her wonder if he'd managed to pick up on her misery. So help her, if he offered her his pity, she would scream.

"Go," she said thickly, waving a hand. She was perilously close to losing all control. When he didn't move, her voice rose. "Just go, will you?"

There was a long, taut silence, and then she heard the quiet sound of the front door latching. A moment later his car engine roared to life. With a strangled sound of despair, Haven sank to the floor. Heedless of the kittens frolicking on her lap, she buried her head in her hands and wept.

Work became Haven's solace and salvation. Work and Anna. Though she did everything she could to immerse herself in the two, the thrumming pain inside her that pulsed in time with the beating of her heart never subsided. She wondered if it ever would.

On the morning marking the seventh day since the end of her marriage, someone opened her office door without knocking first. Looking up from her paperwork, Haven watched while Josephine carefully closed the door behind her before pressing her back to it. In one hand, the older woman held a hammer. Nails protruded from the closed fist of the other.

"What are you doing?"

"Child, I've had enough of your silences and your long faces. I've been waiting for you to come to me, but obviously I'll grow old before that happens. So, I've come to you. Either you tell me what's wrong, or I nail this door shut and throw the hammer out the window. Either way, we're not getting out of here until you talk. Understood?"

One glance at the determined look on Josephine's face told her the woman meant business. Haven felt her throat constrict.

The tears that never seemed far away since Brady's departure gathered in the corners of her eyes. Suddenly, she found herself wanting to talk. It was time anyway. She couldn't hide this from the world forever.

Slowly, haltingly, she began her story. From the beginning, when Brady had unexpectedly arrived at her office and rocked her world with his shocking announcement, to the end, when he'd discovered her infertility and decided their marriage was over, she held nothing back. Nothing, that is, except her true feelings for her soon-to-be former husband. Her love for Brady was too new, too precious, too painful to share with anyone.

When she finished, a long sighing breath left her throat. She felt like a huge weight had just been lifted from her chest. The dumbfounded look in Josephine's eyes, plus the woman's silence, told Haven her former nanny was still struggling to process everything she'd just heard.

"You know, child," Josephine finally said, "I ought to turn you over my knee and wail the living daylights out of you."

The mental image made Haven smile. "But you won't."

"I wouldn't be too sure of that."

"You won't," Haven repeated. "You never paddled me when I was little. I don't think you're about to start now."

"My mistake." Josephine shook her head in patent disbelief. "How could you pull such a stupid, irresponsible stunt?"

It was a question Haven had asked herself a thousand times since Brady left. "It was for Anna. We did it for Anna."

Hammer, nails and all, Josephine settled her hands on her hips. "I'm gonna kill that man."

Haven started in surprise. "Brady? Why? He hasn't done anything to you."

The light in Josephine's eyes turned fierce. "Oh, yes, he has, child. Whatever he does to you, he does to me. I warned him, but did he listen? No, he went ahead and made you love him. And he doesn't have the sense God gave a flea to love you back."

Haven should have known she couldn't hide her feelings from this woman. "I'm that transparent?"

"You forget, child. I changed your diapers. There's not much you can hide from me." Josephine paused, seemingly recalling that Haven had hidden something quite important from her. "Not for long, anyway," she amended.

"I'm sorry, Josie. But we had our reasons for not telling anyone. I still think they were good ones. Forgive me?"

Josephine laid the hammer and nails on a bookcase and sat down in the chair in front of Haven's desk. "Of course I do, child. How's Anna taking it?"

Haven bit her lip. "Amazingly well, considering we entered into this marriage without taking into account the impact our actions would have on her."

She still couldn't believe she'd been so shortsighted. "We were so convinced we were doing the right thing. And it couldn't have been more wrong. Anyway, as you might guess, Anna's disappointed that Brady's no longer living with us. Hopefully, this won't leave a permanent scar. Brady calls her every day. Three nights this week, he took her out for a treat."

And each time he'd picked Anna up, he'd treated Haven like a stranger. That was almost more painful than his leaving her.

"So you're going to let him continue seeing Anna?"

Haven nodded. "He's the closest thing to a father she'll ever have. She loves him, and he loves her." The ache in Haven's heart grew stronger.

"What about you, child? Are you okay?"

No, she was far from okay. But before she could answer, the phone rang.

"The divorce hearing is set for six weeks from next Tuesday," Syd said when she brought the receiver to her ear.

She drew a ragged breath and prayed her voice wouldn't crack. "What time?"

Pretending her heart wasn't breaking all over again, she wrote the information on her calendar.

"I found out why the Zieglars dropped their petition," Syd told her. "You'll never believe it. Brady paid them off."

Haven nearly dropped the receiver. "He *what?*"

"He paid them to drop the petition. *And* he made them sign an agreement stating they'd leave you and Anna alone from now until eternity. Which reminds me. Have you read today's paper?"

"No." What, she wondered, did the newspaper have to do with Brady's paying the Zieglars off?

"When you get the chance, turn to page four. There's an article there that might interest you."

A minute later, still in a daze, Haven hung up the phone. "I can't believe it."

"Believe what?" Josephine asked.

"Brady paid the Zieglars off. That's why they dropped the custody suit."

For a long minute, the older woman said nothing. Then she pierced Haven with her forthright gaze.

"A man who does that, child, has a lot of love to give." She spoke the words slowly, in a tone that hinted at an underlying message.

"You're trying to tell me something."

"Do I have to spell it out?"

Haven knew exactly what Josephine was not so subtly hinting. Because, Lord help her, she'd hoped the same thing, too. How seductive it would be to believe that if a man like Brady could love a child the way he did Anna, then maybe there might be a chance he could learn to love her, too. Yes, the fantasy was indeed seductive. Too seductive. She'd be a fool to fall for it.

Haven swallowed hard. "No, Josie, you don't have to spell it out. Brady has a lot of love to give to the right woman. I just don't happen to be that woman."

"Have you told him how you feel?"

"No."

"Then how can you be so sure?"

Would the pain ever become easier to bear? "Because he told me so."

The look of sadness in Josephine's eyes made her own mist over. "I'm sorry, child."

"Me, too."

After the older woman left, Haven dug out that morning's newspaper. When she turned to page four, she got the shock of her life.

"This is beyond pitiful," Pete said.

Brady looked up from the mountain of forms he'd spread across the kitchen table. He hadn't realized that setting up his foundation would entail so much paperwork, although he welcomed the distraction it offered. Lately, he welcomed anything that took his mind off his misery.

"I know there's a lot to fill out, but if we put our heads together, we'll manage."

Pete shook his head. "I wasn't talking about the paperwork. I was talking about you. You fill in a line, then you chew on your pen and gaze longingly out the window for a minute or two. Then you fill in another line, and start the whole process all over again. You're driving me nuts."

Brady hadn't realized his preoccupation was so obvious. Hard as he tried, and over the past week he'd tried harder than he'd ever tried anything, he couldn't stop the memories. Memories of Haven. Memories of shared laughter. Memories of a passion so deep, he'd thought it might consume him. Memories of a brief moment in time when he hadn't been alone. The last week had felt longer than his three years, seven months and seven days of imprisonment.

Each time he'd gone to pick Anna up and Haven had greeted him at the door, it had taken all his willpower not to haul her into his arms. His need to hold her was a physical ache.

Nothing had changed, he told himself, although for a time he'd tried to pretend it had. Life was the way it had always been. He didn't have anybody, or anything, to call his own. He was alone. It was better that way.

"If I've seemed…distracted," he said, "it's because this paperwork is overwhelming."

Pete snorted in derision. "Paperwork, schmaperwork. This is me you're talking to, remember? And I don't buy a word of it."

"What is it you want me to say?" Brady asked carefully.

"For starters, you could begin with why we're sitting here in this ratty apartment."

He hadn't told Pete about the demise of his marriage. There was no reason, really, except he'd been hoping to avoid the subject as long as possible. Until, at least, the pain of thinking about Haven wasn't as sharp as a butcher's knife.

It was on the tip of his tongue to lie, to say they were using this apartment because they could spread their papers out and leave them there, undisturbed, until they were finished. But before he could utter the first word, he changed his mind. He couldn't evade the truth forever. Besides, Pete already suspected something was wrong. Now was as good a time as any to tell him what had happened. He might as well get it over with.

"We're sitting here in this ratty apartment because this is where I live. Haven and I have separated."

Pete looked stunned. "When?"

A lifetime ago. "A week ago."

"I…don't know what to say. This is rather sudden, isn't it?"

"Not really. It was inevitable from the start."

Pete frowned, his brows knitting together. "I don't understand."

"It's a long story."

"I've got all afternoon."

It took Brady less than ten minutes to outline the whole sorry tale from beginning to end. He worded it in such a way that the breakup of their marriage was the natural outcome of discovering that he wasn't Anna's father, coupled with his paying off the Zieglars, thus ensuring the little girl's safety. That way, he didn't have to admit his love for Haven. Or her rejection of that love. He could salvage that much of his pride, at least.

"What a hell of a mess," Pete said.

Brady knew his friend wasn't talking about the papers spread out before them. He raked his fingers through his hair. "Tell me about it."

"Whatever made you two cook up such an idiotic scheme?"

Brady heaved a heavy sigh. "We did it for Anna."

"Guess you never expected it to blow up in your face, huh?"

"I suppose neither one of us was thinking too clearly at the time."

Pete peered at him closely. "So, it was all an act?"

"All of it."

"*All* of it?"

Brady thought of the kisses he and Haven had shared, of their lovemaking. The passion between them had been real, at least. "Most of it," he conceded.

"You love her, don't you?"

So much for his pride. "It's that obvious?"

"Only because I remember a certain conversation where you asked me how to go about courting her."

Brady nodded. "I'd forgotten."

"What I don't understand is, if you love her, why did you leave? Why aren't you at home, courting her, the way you planned?"

Too restless to sit still any longer, Brady pushed back his chair and walked to the open window. Six stories below, a group of preschoolers drew chalk pictures on the sidewalk while their mothers stood off to one side, chatting. A street cleaner made its slow way down the block, the swish of its brushes mingling with the excited cries of the children. It was just an ordinary day. An ordinary day without Haven in his life. Damn, it hurt.

"Could you stay with Eileen, knowing she doesn't love you back?" he asked.

Pete's reply was swift. "I'd rather go into the ring against a lion that hasn't eaten in a month."

"Then you know why I'm here."

"What about the kiss at your wedding?"

Brady turned to regard his friend. "What about it?"

"*That* was no act. It was the steamiest thing I've seen this side of a movie screen. And it wasn't one-sided."

After all that had happened to him, it amazed Brady that Pete could still be such a romantic at heart. "I won't deny there's a spark between us. But it's not enough to sustain a marriage."

"Have you told her how you feel?"

He'd wanted to; had planned on doing just that when he returned home from his trip to New York. And then he'd gone to see her parents. Even after that, when he knew she didn't love him, if she'd given him some sign there was a chance his love might be returned in the future, he still would have bared his soul to her.

His thoughts returned to that night. For just a minute, when he'd stood on her stairs, bags packed, he'd thought, hoped, prayed, she would ask him to stay. But she hadn't. On the contrary, she hadn't been able to get him out of her home—and her life—fast enough.

At this point, the only thing baring his soul to Haven would accomplish would be to make her feel sorry for him. And that, he couldn't abide. He had to face reality. And his reality was that his future did not include Haven Adams.

He returned to the table, pulled a form in front of him and picked up his pen. "There's no point. Haven has made it more than clear how she feels about me. Now, if you don't mind, I'm going to get back to work."

* * *

Promptly at seven, the time Brady always picked up Anna, the doorbell rang. Haven's heart jolted at first sight of him, so big and strong and handsome in a pair of black jeans and a short-sleeved shirt.

"Is Anna ready?" His gaze was centered at a point over her right shoulder, his voice distant, carefully polite.

It hurt to have him treat her like a stranger. She hoped the news she had to relate would at least make him look at her like a person again, instead of someone whose presence he had to tolerate in order to see Anna.

"She's watching the end of *Sesame Street*. Would you mind stepping into the living room for a minute? There's something I'd like to discuss with you. It's important."

He looked at her then, and she saw the worry that flashed in his eyes. "Is something wrong? Is Anna okay?"

"Anna's fine," she reassured him. "Please, Brady, come in."

When they reached the living room, she indicated he should take a seat on the sofa. Smoothing her skirt down the back of her legs, she sat a safe distance away at the opposite end.

"What is it you wanted to discuss?" he asked.

She drew a deep breath. "Syd told me what you did for Anna. I...I can't thank you enough."

"You're welcome. Was there anything else?"

He wasn't making this easy for her. "Yes."

She reached over to the coffee table and picked up the article she'd clipped from the newspaper. "I wanted to show you this."

He raised his eyebrows. "A newspaper article?"

"Just read it."

"'Lab errors investigated,'" he read aloud. After a glance her way, he lapsed into silence.

"It's the lab we used to do the DNA testing," she explained while he continued reading. "Looks like one of their technicians got sloppy and made a lot of mistakes." She paused. "I called. The technician in question did your test."

When he finished the article, Brady didn't say a word. Throat working, he stared off into space.

"You know what this means, don't you?" she said. "It means Melinda might not have been mistaken after all. It means there's still a chance you're Anna's father."

Brady exploded off the sofa. Balling the article between his palms, he threw it across the room with a violence that shocked her. He rounded on her, eyes blazing.

"Is there no end to your self-sacrifice?" he shouted.

She hadn't been sure how he'd react when he heard the news. While cautious optimism, even disbelief, had seemed possible, she'd never expected the fury she saw blazing in his eyes.

Standing, she faced him. "What's the matter, Brady? What did I do?"

He threw out an arm. "What did you do? You took in your dying friend and quit your job to nurse her during her last days. You took her place as mother to her child. You married a man you didn't love to keep that child safe. Then, even though you might be giving me all the ammunition I need to take Anna away from you, you showed me that article. That's what you did, Haven."

"You wouldn't take Anna from me," she said quietly, while she tried to figure out what was going on. Why was he so angry?

"Wouldn't I? Maybe you don't know me as well as you think you do." The look he aimed at her was full of scorn. "So, tell me. Is there no end to the things you'll do for Anna?"

Haven was growing angry herself. "You act like it's a crime," she said stiffly.

"It is, if you sacrifice any semblance of a life to do so. You're not awarded sainthood until after you're dead, Haven. What good does it do you then?"

She balled her hands into fists at her sides. Tears of anger and frustration burned behind her eyes. "I'm not bucking for sainthood," she said through clenched teeth.

He rolled his eyes. "Really? Tell me, when's the last time you did something that was just for you? And I don't want to hear about the bubble bath you took last week."

Mutinously, she stared at him in silence.

"You can't remember, can you?" he taunted.

"I thought you'd be happy about this," she burst out.

"Well, I'm not."

"Why not?"

He turned his back to her, and his shoulders slumped as all the fight seemed to go out of him. "There's a limit to what a man can take, Haven," he said in a low voice. "I've just about reached mine."

She had no idea what he was talking about. "I don't understand."

"That's the problem," he said wearily. "You've never understood."

When he turned to her again, his face was impassive, his emotions under control. He drew an audible breath. "I'm sorry. That was uncalled for. My only excuse is that this has been a difficult time for me."

She nodded her acceptance of his apology. "It's been difficult for all of us. So, are you going to have the test redone?"

His answer was immediate. "No."

Once again, he'd thrown her a curve. "No?"

"No," he confirmed.

She didn't bother to hide her confusion. "But...why? Don't you want to know the truth?"

"What would be the point? Whether or not Anna is my biological daughter doesn't matter. She's the daughter of my heart, Haven. I don't need any test to confirm that for me."

If he felt that way, Haven wondered, why had he been so upset when he'd discovered she'd lied about being able to bear children? An impossible answer formed in her brain. Her heart swelled as hope bloomed. Could she have been wrong all along? Could it be possible that Brady did have feelings for her?

She'd thought her love for him had been more than apparent. But had it? Yes, she'd responded with everything in her heart whenever he'd taken her into his arms. But even then, he'd always made the first move. She'd never done the reaching. Maybe it was time for her to do some reaching. Maybe it was time to stretch out her neck and take a risk. The way Brady had all his life.

She'd never demanded that her parents love her. Instead, she'd sat back, waiting and hoping they'd notice she was alive. Was she going to make that a lifelong pattern?

Josephine was right. Brady had a lot of love in him to give. It was time for her to demand her share.

She looked at him, and her courage faltered. What if she was wrong? What if he didn't love her, and she was about to make herself look like the biggest fool of all time?

So what? her inner voice niggled. *So you make a fool of yourself. Big deal. Will you be any worse off than you are now? At least you'll know.*

For too many years, she'd played by the rules and patiently waited like a good little girl for everything she deserved to be handed to her. And what had it gotten her? Nothing but loneliness.

It was time to listen to her heart, time to follow it where it led. Time to take a risk. Cowardice was not an option.

"You asked me the last time I did something that was solely for me," she said softly. "Since I married you, every time I've touched you, kissed you, made love to you was for me. Just for me, Brady."

He went still. She tried to read the expression on his face, but it was as blank as ever. Determined to see this thing through to the bitter end, she forged ahead.

"In case you haven't already guessed, I'm in love with you. And I'm hoping—" She bit her lip. "I'm hoping there might be a chance you could love me a little, too."

For endless seconds, he just stood there. Haven's heart quailed. She'd been wrong after all.

"I'm sorry," she muttered, turning away. "I didn't mean to put you on the spot like that."

In a movement as unexpected as it was swift, Brady closed the distance separating them. The next instant his arms—his big, strong, wonderful arms—were around her. Miraculously, he held her as if he'd never let her go.

"Tell me I'm not dreaming," he said thickly into her hair.

"You're not dreaming," she said, wrapping her arms around his neck and tilting her head back to gaze adoringly at him.

"I'm warning you now," he said. "I'm not letting you go ever again."

Her heart felt as if it would burst with happiness. "Don't worry. I don't plan on moving out of your arms for the next seventy years or so."

"That's not going to be nearly long enough." He settled his mouth on hers with a passion that took her breath away. When he raised his head a few minutes later, his eyes were warmer than a summer day. "I love you, Haven."

How precious those three little words sounded. She wondered if she would ever tire of hearing them.

"Say it again," she commanded.

"I love you, Haven Adams Ross. More than life itself."

The question would not be denied. "If you love me, why did you leave?"

He squeezed his eyes shut. "It damn near killed me. But when you didn't tell me about the aftermath of your accident, I was convinced it was because you didn't love me. I couldn't stay around then. It hurt too much."

She knew the feeling. Intimately. "I thought it was because I couldn't give you children. Especially after you found out Anna wasn't your daughter. That's why I didn't tell you when I should have. I was afraid of how you'd react."

His eyes filled with gentle reproach. "I'm an adoptee, remember? I'm not one of those people who get hung up on biology. We'll have our children, Haven. We'll adopt them. Older kids, who need us as much as we need them.''

The tears spilled over then, and she buried her head in his chest.

Cupping her face between his hands, Brady kissed the tears from her cheeks. When he settled his mouth on hers, he kissed them out of her heart forever.

''Unca Bwady,'' Anna said from the doorway. ''You're kissin' Binny.''

Brady lifted his mouth from Haven's and smiled at the little girl. ''I sure am, squirt.''

Anna raced across the room and pulled on Brady's pant leg. ''Kiss me, too,'' she demanded.

Laughing, Brady dropped his arms from around Haven to sweep the child up into the air. ''I'd be honored.'' He placed a kiss on her forehead.

Anna shook her head forcefully. ''No, not that way. Kiss me wike you kiss Binny.''

Brady shot Haven a look of amusement. ''Sorry, squirt. Only married people get to kiss like that.''

Anna's eyes went round. ''Are you and Binny mawwied again?''

''We sure are.''

''You're comin' home?''

As he reached out an arm to include Haven in his embrace, the loving light in his eyes told her that her lonely days were gone.

''You bet I am,'' he said. ''And I'm not leaving ever again.''

*   *   *   *   *

Take 2 bestselling love stories FREE

Plus get a FREE surprise gift!

INTIMATE MOMENTS®

™ *Silhouette*®

Coming in October from
Silhouette Intimate Moments...

BRIDES OF THE NIGHT

Silhouette Intimate Moments fulfills your wildest
wishes in this compelling new in-line collection
featuring two very memorable men...tantalizing,
irresistible men who exist only in the darkness
but who hunger for the light of true love.

TWILIGHT VOWS
by Maggie Shayne

The unforgettable WINGS IN THE NIGHT miniseries
continues with a vampire hero to die for and the
lovely mortal woman who will go to any lengths to
save their unexpected love.

MARRIED BY DAWN
by Marilyn Tracy

Twelve hours was all the time this rogue vampire
had to protect an innocent woman. But was
marriage his only choice to keep her safe—if not
from the night...then from himself?

*Look for **BRIDES OF THE NIGHT** this October,
wherever Silhouette books are sold.*

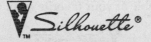

™ *Silhouette*®

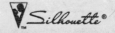

MATERNITY LEAVE

Coming September 1998

Three delightful stories about the blessings
and surprises of "Labor" Day.

TABLOID BABY by Candace Camp

She was whisked to the hospital in the nick of time....

THE NINE-MONTH KNIGHT
by Cait London

A down-on-her-luck secretary is experiencing
odd little midnight cravings....

THE PATERNITY TEST by Sherryl Woods

The stick turned blue before her
biological clock struck twelve....

*These three special women are very pregnant...and very
single, although they won't be either for too much longer,
because baby—and Daddy—are on their way!*

Available at your favorite retail outlet.

INTIMATE MOMENTS®
™ Silhouette®

COMING NEXT MONTH

#877 LONE WOLF'S LADY—Beverly Barton
Way Out West
The last person dark and dangerous Luke McClendon ever wanted to see again was his former lover Deanna Atchley. With just a few careless words she had stolen five precious years of his life—and now she was at his doorstep, looking for salvation. Was this Luke's golden opportunity to seek revenge...or rediscover love?

#878 IF A MAN ANSWERS—Merline Lovelace
Molly Duncan was being hunted for what she'd heard! The love-shy lady had *intended* to call her supremely obnoxious, superbly masculine neighbor Sam Henderson to insist he quiet down, but instead of Sam's deep, sexy "hello," she heard gunshots. Could this spirited woman who'd accidentally dialed *M* for murder, redial *L* for love?

#879 A STRANGER IS WATCHING—Linda Randall Wisdom
Years ago, Jenna Wells had gotten too close to federal marshal Riley Cooper, and it had cost her everything—true love, career, even her identity. Now a dangerous stranger had pieced together her past... and was determined to destroy her future. Impenetrable Riley was once again her protector, but who was keeping watch over this loner's heart?

#880 GIRLS' NIGHT OUT—Elizabeth August
Men in Blue
Detective Adam Riley's investigation uncovered the rocky terrain of Susan Hallston's secret past. In fact, proving her innocence to this cynical cop would be about as effortless as climbing Mount Everest. But unearthing the truth could cause a monumental landslide of emotion...in granite-hearted Adam!

#881 MARY'S CHILD—Terese Ramin
Whose Child?
Gorgeous Hallie Thompson had agreed to be a surrogate mother for her best friend, Joe Martinez, and his wife. But that was before Joe's wife was killed, and before Hallie discovered that she was pregnant...with Joe's child. Now Hallie wanted to adopt the beautiful baby girl —but was she willing to take on a husband, as well?

#882 UNDERCOVER LOVER—Kylie Brant
John Sullivan was the one man Ellie Bennett trusted. He was her dearest friend—and now he was her lover. But what she *didn't* know about him was immense. Like his troubled past, his top-secret profession...and whether he could love her forever....